Books by J. C. S. Smith

NIGHTCAP (1984)
JACOBY'S FIRST CASE (1980)

Nightcap

Nightcap

A Quentin Jacoby Mystery

J. C. S. SMITH

New York 1984 *ATHENEUM*

*The persons and events depicted in this book are, of course, entirely
fictitious. Any resemblance to actual persons or events is completely
coincidental. J. C. S. SMITH*

Library of Congress Cataloging in Publication Data

Smith, J. C. S.
  Nightcap: a Quentin Jacoby mystery.

  I. Title.
PS3569.M5374N5   1984   813'.54   83-45085
ISBN 0-689-11411-7

Published simultaneously in Canada by McClelland and Stewart Ltd.
Composition by Westchester Book Composition Inc.,
Yorktown Heights, New York
Printed and bound by Haddon Craftsmen, Scranton, Pennsylvania
Designed by Harry Ford
First Printing April 1984
Second Printing August 1984

To Lucia and the guys

Nightcap

Chapter 1

The middle of August is a slow, steamy time of year in New York. Muggers, con artists, and second-story men work overtime to fill some kind of seasonal quota, but everyone else takes things easy, just trying to make it through the grit and the thermal inversions until September arrives and the city starts to come alive again. People who can afford to leave town. Ordinary types haul a deck chair up on the roof and work on turning their sunburn into tan. Singles give up on finding a summer romance and start thinking about whether they should look for a new apartment instead. Kids hang around the playgrounds, too hot to play ball, too bored to think of anything else to do. Even the tourists begin to look a little brown around the edges.

I'm no tourist, but the heat was getting to me, too. I had visited all the parks and beaches I could stand, seen every movie in town, and worked out at the pistol range at Pelham Bay Park until they were starting to joke about how I had retired from the Transit Police to go into business as a hit man. Nights I would go out to the track with Sam Fuentes, my neighbor from downstairs who shares my commitment to the fine art of harness racing. When it rained, I would stay home and watch the steam come up off the asphalt.

Which is what I was doing when Gloria Gold called on Sunday

night. Five foot two, eyes of brown, mind like that famous steel trap you always hear about. Gloria went to Morris High School with me right here in the Bronx, more years ago than she likes to be reminded, and we never quite lost sight of each other. After her divorce she became a travel agent, and for ten years she phoned religiously every six months to try to interest me in a package tour of Mexico. Gloria can be the biggest, brassiest pain in the ass you've ever met, but she would also be my candidate for person best qualified to run the universe, should that office ever get on the ballot.

We went out together a few times after my wife, Bea, died, but Gloria was interested in something a lot more permanent than I was ready for, and we hadn't parted on the best of terms. Therefore, the conversation was more than a little stiff at first. She asked about my health, and what had I heard from my sister Rowena, out in Denver. I asked about her daughters, and how was the travel business doing. That gave her the break she was looking for.

"Tell you the truth, Quentin, that's why I called." I braced myself for a hard sell on the joys of Tijuana, but I needn't have worried. Gloria had something much worse than that in mind.

"I'm not booking tours anymore," she explained. "After some creep broke into the office last winter and stole all the typewriters, I got real nervous and did some checking around on how to protect myself. That's when I found out the real future is in security systems and personnel."

Her voice got more excited as she made her pitch. "Fear is big business right now," she announced, making it sound like great news. "Did you know there are more than twice as many private security guards as there are police officers in the entire country? Forty thousand right here in New York! A real growth industry!"

Like I said, Gloria always was a lady with her eye on the ball.

"So anyway," she continued, "I sold my share of the travel

agency and bought into a security service in Manhattan. Very small, very customized. We're located near Wall Street, and business is real promising, what with all the banks and brokerage houses and the new buildings going up along the Hudson River. Then, in June, my partner decided to relocate in Houston, where you're practically nobody if you don't have a personal bodyguard and a solid-state alarm system for your Mercedes. So for the last six weeks I've been the boss."

"That's great," I said. And I meant it. Some guys might beef about a woman getting into that line of activity, but Gloria always was a hard worker and a tough cookie besides, and she deserved to have things fall her way. "I'm very glad to hear everything's going so well."

"Almost everything," she said glumly. Then she started talking real fast, like she was afraid I'd hang up. "You've got to help me out, Quentin. Otherwise I don't know what I'll do."

I could imagine her on the other end of the line, frowning and pulling nervously on her short blond hair. Gloria was the first girl I knew to take up smoking and the first woman I ever saw with bleached hair who wasn't either a movie star or a tramp. The last time I'd seen her she was letting the gray show through, with just the highlights coming from a bottle, and the styles had changed enough to make it seem businesslike instead of brassy. But she didn't sound very businesslike right now. She sounded like someone in trouble.

I reminded myself that you shouldn't believe everything you hear. One of the first things I learned about being retired is that everybody right away assumes you are available for any kind of time-wasting chore that happens to come along. Neighbors want you to take in their packages. Relatives ask you to show up at the kid's class play. And people like Gloria Gold call out of the blue, acting like she was some kind of damsel in distress when probably all she really needed was someone to help out at the office.

5

"What's the problem?" I asked cautiously.

Sure enough, Gloria's big crisis was too much success, too little manpower. All her people were booked into overtime through the end of the month, and all of a sudden she had a new customer who wanted a security guard on the double.

"Ordinarily," she said, "I'd just let the contract go. But John Lombardo is no ordinary client. He manages the Pinnacle Room, that new restaurant on top of the Interdine Tower. Plus he's the chief consultant on restaurant operations for the entire Interdine Corporation, which is no small potatoes, as well as being the most innovative person in the food industry today and widely acknowledged to be an absolute genius. It's a big piece of luck that he should even want to do business with me; it seems my ex-partner did some work for a friend of Lombardo's, long before my day. The friend referred him to Global."

Before I could congratulate her, Gloria was off again.

"If you're wondering how I know all this," she said, "it's because Lombardo told me himself, including the part about being a genius. That came right after the bit about how he came to me because he knows you can get personal service only from a small, exclusive firm. And for *personal*, read *picky*. He called up out of the blue, last night, insisted I open the office Sunday morning to see him, and then started laying down conditions like you wouldn't believe. He wants a guard, and he wants him tomorrow, but he insists on having someone *intelligent*. Someone with a sense of *style*." Gloria stressed the words like they were in a foreign language, which I guess they were for her usual trade. "So naturally," she finished breathlessly, "right away I thought of you.

"All right," she said after a second, "laugh away." Which is just what I was doing. "I admit you're no Einstein, and the best-dressed list is going to keep right on passing you by. But you should see some of the losers who come to me for jobs. 'Custom service for the discriminating customer.' That's what I say in my ads, but it's a hard slogan to live up to. At least you've read a book or two in your life. I've been to your place. I've seen them. And as for style..." She hesitated, then started laughing herself. "You don't blow your nose on your fingers, and that'll have to do."

"Thanks a lot," I muttered. "I'm glad to see I made such an impression on you."

"You had your chance a year ago, sweetie, and you threw it away."

"I'm sorry." It seemed inadequate, but what could I say? I'm sorry the city is rough on single women. I'm sorry my wife died. I'm sorry I'm not in love with you. I know all about lonely, I felt like telling her. But being lonely together is not enough. "I'm sorry," I said again.

"Forget it," she answered briskly. "That was last year, and this is now. If I were still mad at you, I wouldn't have called."

So much for sentiment. If it was efficiency Gloria wanted, that was fine with me, and the first item on the agenda was to get out of this particular assignment. She could call it a security agent or even a surveillance analyst, but what Gloria was looking for was a plain old-fashioned night watchman, and it was a crummy job under any name. The work is boring, the pay is mediocre, and the hours are guaranteed not to improve your social life. Even without this character Lombardo and his special requirements, I wasn't surprised Gloria was having trouble finding top personnel. When I hinted as much, though, she got very huffy.

"You act like I was asking you to watch the cash register at Burger King," she said angrily. "Haven't you ever heard of the Interdine Corporation?"

"Nope."

"Well, you just haven't been listening, because it's the biggest thing to hit the restaurant business since the expense account. Ten years ago it was nothing, and now Interdine operates the top four restaurants in the city, to say nothing of their resort

7

holdings overseas. Plus with this new headquarters, they're moving into commercial real estate. Right now Lombardo just wants a single guard for the Pinnacle Room, but if we handle it right, it could grow into a contract for their entire metropolitan operation. Office buildings! Condominiums! Don't you see what this could mean?"

I could see, all right, and I didn't like the picture one bit. I tried another approach.

"If this joint is so classy," I said, "you should get someone who knows all about manners and like that. The only place I've ever worked was on the Transit Police, and you don't get a whole lot of experience with the jet set when you patrol the subways for a living. I'm too old. I'll screw up. I'll fall asleep. I'll use the wrong fork. Do yourself a favor and get someone else for the job."

"Quentin Jacoby," she said, just like my mother used to when she was getting ready to bawl me out. "Don't give me this modesty nonsense. You are a healthy, active man in the prime of life. You have over thirty years' experience as a police officer, two citations for valor, and a cleft chin that used to drive me wild in high school. This is a classy restaurant. Appearances count. They take one look at you in that uniform that shows off your big blue eyes, and believe me, you'll knock their socks off."

"Oh, God," I groaned. "A uniform?"

"Not necessarily," she said quickly. "Not if you mind. A jacket and tie would be fine." Her tone changed, and I could tell that getting this contract meant even more to her than she was letting on.

"Just do it for a week," she pleaded. "Until I can find someone else. Please. For me. And for you, too, Quentin. You're a young man still. Stop being retired and come back to life. You won't regret it." Then she gave me the address of her office and hung up before I had a chance to say no.

I spent the rest of the evening drinking beer and looking out at the rain. Co-op City is not what you would call an impressive address, but as middle-income housing projects go, I guess it's not too bad. It just doesn't seem to have much to do with my life. It had been three years since we moved here, right after I left the mole force on the early retirement option. Two since Bea died. I looked back over the record of my time. One year of running around from doctor to doctor, acting like a crazy and learning to cook and keep house on the side. One year of walking around in a fog, writing notes to myself to remember to get dressed in the morning. One year of just hanging around, like I was waiting for heaven to send me a telegram about what I should do next. Was this the secret message? That I should become a night watchman for Gloria Gold? I guess I had been expecting more from that big Western Union in the sky. But it would be only temporary, and it would be a change. And I felt somehow like I owed Gloria a favor.

If I had known then that the Pinnacle Room was about to be booked for a murder, I would have sent her some flowers and left it at that.

Chapter 2

The city of New York is made up of five boroughs, only two of which touch each other with anything more intimate than a bridge. From Co-op City at the north end of the Bronx to Gloria's office on the southern tip of Manhattan isn't the longest trip you can make within the city limits, but I allowed myself over an hour to get there. On a good day it might take less, but I had worked the subways too long to think that a Monday morning in August had any chance of being a good day, as far as public transportation was concerned. The citizens of New York had been idle all week-end, with nothing better to do than dump dead animals on the tracks, rip off the brake signals in the tunnels, and paint over the motorman's windows so he can't see where he's going. Even if the train worked, it was five to one that the air conditioning didn't, and Monday is the day when everyone puts off going to work as long as possible and then crowds into the last set of cars.

By 8:00 A.M. it was already turning into a hot, muggy monster of a day. I stood on the platform at Baychester Avenue, my shirt going clammy under my jacket, but I had to admit I was excited to have someplace real to be going in the morning. When I got on the train, I was nervous as a kid, all dressed up for a new job like I hadn't been since I joined the force.

The thrill of it all wore off before we got to Grand Concourse, when the car had already reached 120 percent of capacity. By the time we crossed into Manhattan and made our way down to Fourteenth Street, I was ready to swear that half the population of New York had had salami and wine for breakfast. The half that was riding in my car. I had been planning to switch at Nassau Street for the Canarsie line going west, but instead I got off at the Brooklyn Bridge stop. It meant walking a few extra blocks, but that was all right. It wasn't like I had told Gloria I'd be there at nine o'clock sharp. I hadn't told her I'd be there at all.

But there I was, and only fifteen minutes late. Gloria's office was on one of those little side streets west of Broadway, in an old four-story brick building that hadn't heard about the twentieth century. The place next door had been gutted to put in a hamburger joint, but the rest of the block looked pretty much the way it must have when this area was full of wharves and warehouses and everything else that catered to the shipping trades. Looking up, I spotted a set of arched windows on the second floor where the bottom half of the glass was covered over with sky blue signboards. GLOBAL SECURITY, each window said in big red letters, with a little round map of the world between the words. On the top half of the windows I could see traces of gold paint, where another company had written its message seven or eight decades before. The name had flaked away, but I could still make out the faded promise of "Insured."

How, I wondered, had a dump like this attracted a customer interested in style? I walked up a flight of stairs to a dark, stifling hall that couldn't be doing anything to encourage business. Outside room 205 there was another of the signs, but when I turned the knob, nothing happened.

"Global Security. May I help you?"

It was one of those snobbish Manhattan accents that try to sound like they're halfway to England, and it was coming from an intercom over the door. At least the equipment was more up-to-date than the décor.

"I'm here to see Mrs. Gold." I felt like an idiot, talking to a plastic box, but I didn't seem to have a choice.

"Is this in regard to your personal security needs, or are you representing a firm?"

"Neither," I answered, getting impatient. "Just tell your boss that Quentin Jacoby is here, but I won't be for long if she doesn't open the door." Maybe it impresses the clients when they can't even get into the office without a security check, but I for one did not like being grilled while I stood out in the hall.

A buzzer went off, and the door opened in front of me.

"I'm terribly sorry, Mr. Jacoby," gushed the secretary who went with the voice. "Ms. Gold is expecting you. Won't you come in?"

She had red hair, and the file cabinets were painted white to match the wall, which was all I had time to take in before I was shoved across the room and through the doorway of a tiny inner office. And there was Gloria, coming around her desk to meet me.

She looked great. Her hair was longer and curlier than I remembered, and she'd put on a few pounds since I'd seen her last. Not fat, you understand, but just enough to give her some comfortable padding. I don't mind if a woman wears a suit, like Gloria was doing, and I can see how it maybe gives a more executive look than a dress. But I like it a lot better if the wearer has enough substance to show you there are a few curves underneath the tailoring.

"Quentin!" she exclaimed, greeting me with the kind of joy most people save for rich, old relatives. "I'm really glad you came. I was afraid you wouldn't, you know."

"I almost didn't," I answered. "Now tell me again about this big man of yours and why he's so important."

"In a minute," she said, smiling nervously. "In a minute. Just fill out this questionnaire first. The customers love them, and the government gets very edgy if I don't keep feeding it paper."

She handed me a printed form and a clipboard with a pen tied to a string and motioned to a chair against the wall. "It'll only take a second," she added apologetically.

It took ten minutes, and when I handed it back, Gloria leaned back in her chair to look over what I had written.

"Quentin D. Jacoby," she read out loud. "Fifty-six years old. Six feet tall, one hundred and ninety-five pounds. Health excellent. No corrective lenses. No disabilities. No dependents. Honorable discharge, United States Army. Thirty-one years with the New York City Transit Police, final rank of sergeant. Willing to work days or nights, experience in night work. Current gun license. No firearms violations. Training in crowd control and first aid. Two units of criminal psychology, John Jay College of Criminal Justice. Reads, writes, and speaks English like a native." She frowned over that last item. "Very funny," she said, glaring at me over the top of the clipboard.

"Come on, Gloria. You know all about me. Now either invite me over for dinner or tell me what's really going on. Unless inviting me over for dinner is what's going on."

"Sure, come for dinner," she agreed absently. "We'll get takeout from the Chinese place on the corner. But that's not why I asked you to come down." She put down the clipboard, lit a cigarette, and reached with her other hand for a file folder that was lying on her desk. "It's like I told you on the phone. All of a sudden, out of the blue, I've got a chance to get a foothold in the Interdine Corporation, which is not a contract that I can afford to miss. So let me fill you in on what I know."

She took a drag on her cigarette and skimmed through her notes, running her finger across the page the way they teach you to in those speed-reading courses.

"You'll be working in the Pinnacle Room," she said after a minute, "and the first thing you have to understand is that the Pinnacle Room *is* John Lombardo. He's the hottest thing there is in the fancy eating trade. Features on him in *New York*,

Food & Wine, and *Business Week*. His puss on the cover of last month's in-flight magazine for TWA. They may have a computer over at the Pinnacle to do the billing, but everything else is decided by the creative genius of John Lombardo, just like it has been at all the other Interdine restaurants. Lombardo planned the menus, hired the cooks, built the wine cellar, picked out the dishes and the rugs. He even designed the cover for the matchbooks. Now that they've opened and the design end of things is settled, he's down at the markets every morning, nabbing the best of the brook trout and the broccoli at an hour when sane people are still at home in bed. Told me all about it when he was in here yesterday. Whatever is good about that restaurant is due to John Lombardo, and he's not shy about saying so either."

Gloria looked up from her notes. "Reading it off like that, it sounds like he's got an ego as big as the Ritz, but when you talk to him in person, Lombardo is a very charming man." She put down her papers and tried to explain. "There's something about him, like he's just been to some wonderful place and is about to go to another, and nothing would make him happier than if you came along. I can't describe it exactly, but I think he's telling the truth when he says he's the most popular restaurateur there ever was.

"Anyway, the record seems to bear him out. Thirty-five years ago, when he was barely twenty, Lombardo opened his first restaurant way out in some broken-down storefront near the Chicago stockyards, and suddenly you weren't anybody in the Middle West if you weren't eating there. The place still exists, I think, but Lombardo sold out long ago. After that he was off to Havana, back before Castro. Then Houston, Boston, and San Francisco. Every place he went, he opened a restaurant that was the newest, most elegant, sexiest place in town. Also the most expensive. For the last ten years he's been here in New York, and everything he touches turns to gold. Every restaurant he designs is different, but he always operates the same way. First he spends a year or

14

two in planning, all very secret and mysterious. Then he opens to instant mobs and rave reviews. The food is great. The service is perfect. The atmosphere is exquisite. The setting is inspired. Even the salt shakers get a special mention in the design columns. People are killing each other to get in, making reservations six months in advance. At which point, instead of basking in his triumph, Lombardo starts getting ready to hand over the management and move on to the next project."

A regular shrinking violet. Before I could say so, Gloria lit up another cigarette and went back to singing the praises of her new hero.

"Aside from all this," she noted, "one of the things Lombardo prides himself on is always taking some run-down part of town and practically turning its economy around. He was the one who did the Venetian restaurant under the Triborough Bridge and that roof-garden place that was so popular they ended up renovating half of Hell's Kitchen to accommodate the overflow crowds. Then he did that restaurant in the bowling alley on First Avenue, north of Yorkville. Lanes, they called it. Maybe you read about how he kept the wooden floors and filled in the gutters with black marble to get an Art Deco effect? No? Well, I hear it's pretty spectacular. And then—"

"Okay, Gloria," I interrupted finally. "So the man's a genius. I mostly eat at home. Get to the problem already. If you want me to be the big hero on the white horse, you still have to tell me where to gallop. This guy Lombardo need a bodyguard or what?"

"Sorry," she said brightly. "I thought you liked the human interest angle. Besides, this is background on the client. Right now Mr. Lombardo is working his magic at the Pinnacle Room, on the sixty-eighth floor of the Interdine Tower. And it's not his body that needs guarding. It's his baby."

I was dumfounded.

"You're joking," I said. "I don't know anything about kids. Get some nanny with karate training if that's what you're after." It was bad enough having to sit through the biography of this joker, just my age and eighty-five times as successful, without having to hear about his gorgeous young wife and lovable little brats, too.

"Not that kind of baby," Gloria assured me. "The man's not even married. It's the new restaurant. Open only two months, and already he's having a lot of trouble with theft. Strange disappearances, like it's ten minutes to opening and all of a sudden they discover somebody's filched the pans for their special crêpes suzette. Or Lombardo's buddy the mayor is throwing a banquet for the Prince of Wales, and nobody can find the sacred bottle of hundred-year-old port they were planning to serve. Lombardo thinks it may be sabotage, and he wants someone who can sit up all night and guard the specials, make sure they don't run away."

"Seems more like a job for a private investigator," I observed. "Not to insult your service," I added quickly.

Gloria shrugged. "Never argue with a customer. Besides, he was very insistent. He wants a guard. An intelligent guard. Someone who can watch the premises and also maybe sniff around a little for signs of enemies. But mainly a guard. He doesn't want anybody disturbing his staff with a lot of questions, he says, upsetting the delicate equilibrium of their operations. Those were his very words. Delicate equilibrium."

"Do I get an hourly bonus for sniffing?" I joked.

"Sure do," Gloria answered quickly. "Mr. Lombardo suggested it himself." Before I could change my mind, she hauled a bunch of forms out of a drawer. "Now here's your contract, and these are the liability and indemnity agreements. This is the duty manual, which you probably know by heart except for the number of the local station house—I copied most of it from the training orders for police. Just sign here, and here, and here, and you'll be all set."

I had the clear sense I was being railroaded, but I signed

anyway. "Is that it?" I asked when I was done. "Where's my gun? My can of Mace? My fancy two-way transistorized walkie-talkie with built-in bomb defuser?"

"Weapons?" Gloria recoiled in horror. "Have you looked at the price of insurance lately? I never arm a guard unless the customer absolutely insists, and luckily Mr. Lombardo didn't mention it. As for the fancy electronics, get me a two-year contract with Interdine and you can buy all the toys you want. Until then you'll have to use an ordinary telephone to keep in touch. Be thankful I'm not making you shell out for a uniform."

I tried to mutter something that sounded grateful. In answer Gloria leaned back, glanced at her watch, and changed the subject completely. "Remember when we were kids, how we were all nuts about Ronald Colman?"

Remember? How could I forget? For me, he was the biggest movie star there ever was. Even after other guys started trying to imitate Bogart, smiling out of the side of their mouths and smoking too much, Ronald Colman was still my idol. I must have spent all of my fifteenth year trying to grow a mustache, checking in the mirror every hour to see if any bristles had appeared.

"All you guys were trying to look like him," Gloria continued. "Remember Danny Russo, how proud he was of that trench coat of his? He wore it all winter, freezing to death to look like his hero. God, we were young!" she exclaimed, smiling.

I nodded, thinking back on those days. A bunch of the guys would always sit together at lunchtime, chewing away on our egg salad sandwiches while we argued about the important issues. Politics. Idealism. Which girls would go all the way. Then I realized that Gloria was still talking.

"You know," she was saying, "forty years later, I'll make a confession. I always thought you were the only one who pulled it off, the Ronald Colman bit. You always had that nobility thing, like you were ready to step in and save Ruritania, or Shangri-la, or anyplace else that needed help, with nothing in it for yourself.

17

When you decided to join the police, I thought it was so romantic. You were going to be a real-life hero."

"I was also planning to get married," I reminded her before she got too carried away. Bea was earning fifteen dollars a week as a secretary, and a cop's pay seemed like a fortune. We were going to live it up, have an apartment on Pelham Parkway with a sunken living room and everything. Except they wouldn't take me until I was twenty-one, so instead I got a bunk at Fort Dix and a satin jacket with a picture of Okinawa embroidered on the back. But at least I came through alive, and after that police work seemed easy. "As for saving the world, I don't know. Maybe I thought so at the time."

"Well, I hope you think so now," Gloria said bluntly. "Because my little world of Global Security is going right down the tubes if I don't find someone who can satisfy this character Lombardo. It cost me a lot of money to buy out my partner. I need a big contract soon, or I'm through."

Great. At least now I knew why Gloria was acting so nervous. Not only did I have to cover for the holes in her staff, but I also had to perform a miracle for her finances. By Saturday, too, because I had no intention of working beyond the week it would take her to find a replacement. I said that very loud and clear, before she started getting any funny ideas about keeping me around forever, and than asked when I was supposed to show up at the Pinnacle Room.

Gloria looked at her watch. "Right now," she answered. "Mr. Lombardo is waiting. You'd better get moving. When I talked to him last night, he was very firm about your getting there at exactly ten forty-five, so he would have time to interview you before lunch. Two blocks south, turn right at the corner. You can't miss it—it's the big shiny thing between the World Trade Center and the Statue of Liberty."

Waving good-bye with one hand, she handed me my ques-

18

tionnaire with the other and was on the phone before I even got through the outer office. Gloria was no fool. She pretended like she wasn't sure I'd show, but she'd already made an appointment for me with Lombardo. All that stuff about Ronald Colman was just a stall, keeping me around until it was the right time to go see him so I wouldn't have a spare second to back out. Not that I minded. I hadn't thought about Danny Russo for years.

Chapter 3

It was a five-minute walk from Global Security to the Interdine Tower, but the two places were so different I could have been in another country, if not another planet. After Gloria had started gabbing about the wonders of the Interdine Corporation, I remembered reading somewhere that its new headquarters was supposed to be one of the most expensive buildings in the world. What I hadn't realized was that it was also one of the most beautiful.

They called it a tower, but what it really looked like was some kind of giant crystal, different heights of mirrored glass and steel climbing to jagged peaks five, ten, even twenty-five stories around the base, and then a narrow central column seventy stories high. By current standards that made it something of a midget, but rising above the grimy streets and warehouses of the southwestern tip of Manhattan, it looked like a vision of the future breaking out of the dirt. Next to it the twin towers of the World Trade Center, off to the north, were a couple of clumsy, oversize shoe boxes set on end.

I had to walk practically around the entire building before I found the way in. The north façade was a blank wall, broken only by a downward-sloping driveway that led to the freight entrance. I went around to the west side, facing the river, and began to see what Gloria meant when she said Lombardo and his buddies made a big deal about doing things with style. While everyone else was still arguing about whether the West Side Highway should be fixed up and reopened for traffic or torn down so the money could go to public transit, the Interdine people had bought the air rights to build over their stretch of the road. The street was still there, shadowed by the rotten stretches of condemned highway where people jogged, walked their dogs, and carried out less reputable transactions. But above that, level with the second floor of the tower, was a glittering, glass-enclosed causeway that led over the wreckage and down to a helicopter pad and a private marina, for those tenants and visitors who preferred to arrive by yacht.

Not having brought my water wings, I moved on, past the solid glass and steel wall on the south side of the building and back to Washington Street on the east, where I finally found a door. Not the usual revolving job, of course. This one was a huge slab of stainless steel, twenty feet high but counterweighted so that a small push was all you needed to get it open. I probably wouldn't have found that either, if it hadn't been for a hundred-pound cream puff who clicked past me on her three-inch heels and showed me the way into the magic kingdom. At which point I realized I'd been passing entrances all around the building, except I hadn't recognized them for what they were.

Inside I found a high, bare lobby with marble floors and big modern tapestries mounted on the walls. This hour of the morning there weren't many people passing through, and the space was dominated by a massive mahogany reception desk in the center of the floor. INTERDINE was spelled out in eight-inch steel letters, sunk into the wood. On top of the desk was an enormous electronic console with three TV screens, the kind that hooks you up to forty circuits at once and lets you know the second anyone blows his nose on the forty-seventh floor.

Behind the console was a heavyset guy in a beige and silver

uniform, and behind him was a gray marble wall, two stories high and absolutely blank. I suppose the wall was to hide the elevator shaft, but the effect was a combination of luxury and authority like I hadn't seen since the newsreels of those amphitheaters Mussolini liked to build.

Otherwise the place was empty. No newsstand. No phony flower cart. No coffee shop. They might have offices in the Interdine Tower, and condominiums, and a very fancy restaurant, but they sure weren't looking for any drop-in trade. Everyone who came here knew exactly where he was going and how to get there.

Everyone, that is, except me. I had put on a sports jacket for the occasion, tan gabardine and new last May, but that didn't stop the guy at the desk from sneering when I asked for directions to the Pinnacle Room.

"It's not open yet," he said discouragingly. "And you need a reservation."

I wondered if he knew that I was the competition, all set to take over his job. I tried to imagine myself staring at three televisions at once, then gave it up and asked again how to get to the restaurant. Grudgingly he steered me to the other side of the marble wall. When I got there, I took some satisfaction in noting that half the spaces in the building directory were blank.

Not that they weren't ready for total occupancy. There were three different banks of elevators, all set to accommodate the crowds. The first ones were locals for floors one through forty, which were offices. The second set was for floors forty through sixty, which were condominium apartments—though who would want to live there was beyond me. Nice views and fancy architecture are all very fine, but it would be faster to have your groceries flown in than to try to get to a supermarket from the Interdine Tower. Maybe that was the reason for the helicopter pad.

The last set of elevators was for the Interdine headquarters and the Pinnacle Room. I rode up all by myself, and had plenty of time to study the buttons. Floors sixty through sixty-seven were all offices, with names like Research, Accounting, and Overseas Operations printed on brass cards, next to the buttons. Sixty-eight was the Pinnacle Room, with its own separate button on the other side of the wall, but it turned out it wasn't even at the top of the building. Above it were two floors marked "Executive" and then a Garden Health Club on the roof. Each of the last three buttons had a little brass slot next to it, which meant you couldn't even get up there unless you had a key. I understand this kind of thing is considered very swank in some circles.

When the doors opened on the sixty-eighth floor, I stepped out and sank up to my ankles in pale beige carpeting. Instead of the dining room I'd been expecting, I was facing a windowed alcove with a velvet sofa, same color as the rug, and a spectacular view of Upper New York Bay. Right in front of me was the Statue of Liberty, with Ellis Island off to the right and Staten Island stretching out in the distance. I stared out at the water, trying to imagine how my folks had felt when they first got this view from the other direction, arriving in the promised land. Then I turned to find Lombardo.

To my right was a short corridor that featured several blank doors before it ended in a mirrored wall reflecting the biggest bunch of cut flowers I'd ever seen. The prospect to the left was more promising in terms of finding the boss, but it still wasn't much like anyplace I'd ever gone for a meal. Most of the joints I eat in limit their decorating to flocked wallpaper with maybe a framed poster of the Acropolis or the Bay of Naples behind the cash register. But most of the restaurants I eat in don't take reservations either, so it made sense that the Pinnacle Room would be a notch or two higher up on the decorating scale. Therefore, I wasn't surprised to find the entryway walls covered in alternating panels of mirrors and brass, separated by thin strips of dark blue stone. Impressed, yes. But not surprised.

23

The only real surprise was that there weren't any people. I walked past the coat checkroom, the rest rooms, and the telephone booths all by my lonesome. Finally, I came to a kind of landing that looked out over the restaurant proper, a few steps below. On the other side of the landing, built into a balcony that looked over the dining room, was the bar, but that was as deserted as everyplace else. Down below, though, at the bottom of a short flight of stairs, I finally found signs of life. The dining room was full of people setting up tables, stocking serving carts, and doing all the other things that have to get done before any kind of beanery opens its doors. I watched the action for a minute until my watch said exactly 10:44, then walked down and asked a young fellow with a short red beard where I could find Mr. Lombardo.

"I'm sorry, sir," he said, putting down the flowers he was arranging in little vases on the tables. "Luncheon service doesn't begin for over an hour."

"I'm not here to eat," I answered. When that didn't seem to reassure him, I added, "He's expecting me."

The florist shrugged and moved on to the next table. "He's in the Coronation Room, I think. Follow the windows to the left until you get there." He turned to a kid in a gray apron who was working at the next aisle. "Hey, Vinnie," he called. "I need more chrysanthemums."

Following directions, I made my way past a gray-aproned napkin folder and past a girl arranging fancy cakes on a big glass cart. Through the window I could see the rest of the harbor and then the skyscrapers of Wall Street up close. The Brooklyn Bridge had already come into view when I finally spotted my goal, a small dining room set off from the rest of the place by an arched doorway and a whole different style of decoration. Instead of brass and marble and lots of light from the big picture windows, everything here was dark wood and peach-colored satin upholstery, with candles on the tables and dim little lamps mounted on the walls.

There were maybe ten tables, each fitted into its own little alcove and backed on three sides by satin curtains looped up in big old-fashioned swags. I wasn't too sure what a Coronation Room should look like, but a hunch told me I was in the right place. A hunch, and the fact that three executive types were standing in the middle of the room.

It wasn't hard to guess which one was John Lombardo. He was a short man and even a little stocky, but he had the kind of physical presence you associate with top entertainers and popular politicians. If he had been a little taller and not so tanned, he could have been a TV evangelist, too. He already had the head of wavy white hair that usually goes with the job. The white suit matched the hair, the beige and white striped shirt set off the tan, the pink silk handkerchief in his jacket pocket doubtless matched the tie he would put on later to greet the customers, and the whole outfit, which would have seemed ridiculous on someone like me, made him look healthy, prosperous, and happy with life. Just the kind of guy, in fact, you'd love to have invite you to a party.

The other two were less impressive. One was a dark fellow in a black waiter's tux, his shoulders bent with the stoop that comes from years of hovering over tables. The other was younger and taller, wearing a plaid summer suit that couldn't hide the broad shoulders and narrow hips of a man who had been a real athlete not too long ago. Somewhere along the way, though, he'd traded in his team jersey for a briefcase and a deferential air.

They all looked up when I came in. "Global?" asked the one I had picked out as Lombardo. When I nodded, he waved me toward a chair at the side of the room and went back to his conversation. The three of them were bending over a stiff red folder, and the young one seemed to be taking notes. Every few seconds he would scribble something on one of the papers inside the folder. In between times he clasped his pencil between his palms and pushed like he was trying to flatten it out. Very good for the pectorals, though not so hot for the pencil. After awhile I realized they were planning what to have for dinner.

"We start off with the duckling à l'orange mousse," Lombardo said. "With that the Walter & Wisdom fino sherry 1908. Then let's scratch the cucumber vichyssoise and do a zucchini blossom consommé instead—the flowers just came in this morning, and they're so beautiful you could cry. No new wine there," he added brusquely. "We want them to have a good dinner, not get soused. We've got forty-six covers coming tonight for the tasters' dinner, and if we give them a good time, we'll have the Coronation booked every Monday for the rest of the year. A good time, let me remind you, does not mean indigestion at midnight or a hangover the next morning. Got that, Pierre?"

Before Pierre could answer, Lombardo turned to the note taker.

"Not such big portions on the appetizers, Robert," he ordered. "The Pinnacle Room is not some dive where we fill the people up on rolls so they won't notice that we're skimping on the meat. This is a seven-course dinner with five fantastic wines, and I want the people to be able to go the distance without having a stroke. Got that?"

The young assistant nodded impatiently while Pierre, the dark one, fiddled with a little silver cup he kept putting in and taking out of his vest pocket. I wondered if Lombardo gave them the same pep talk every day. Seemed to me the troops would have caught on by now.

"Then we go on to the Pacific salmon with sorrel dressing," he said, consulting his folder again. "Grilled over mesquite, of course. And the Château Montelano chardonnay '79. Just a simple rack of lamb next, and sautéed zucchini with walnuts, but with that we've got the Château Pétrus '71, our featured vintage. Beautiful bouquet! And rare—they'll die for it!" Lombardo beamed happily out into space, and I pictured the room full of ecstatic corpses, their bellies full of high-class chow.

"Don't forget to get it breathing in plenty of time, Pierre," he added. "Pierre? Pierre! Will you put away that damn cup and listen? Or is there something the matter with this menu we agreed on three days ago? After all," he said, with heavy irony, "we have eight, maybe nine hours before we start serving, and all we have to do in between is take care of a few hundred customers at lunch. I can always whip out to the market and start over again."

The wineman put the cup back in his pocket, this time for good. "It's the Pétrus," he said sadly. "Last night we had five cases. Today we have two."

Lombardo closed his eyes and let his hands drop to his sides. He looked like a person who was consciously cultivating a coma. When he opened his eyes again, he was staring straight at me. I gave the smallest possible nod, to let him know I'd been listening without making it seem like I was butting in. Most of what they'd been saying was gibberish to me, but at least I gathered that something was wrong. Something was missing, and it wasn't just a six-pack of Bud.

Lombardo sighed deeply. "That's it," he said, talking to no one in particular. Then he started waving his hands and giving orders.

"Pierre, you know where all the good wine is hidden in this city. Get on the phone and round up some more Bordeaux. I put that Pétrus down five years ago, before they even broke ground for this building, back when it went for under a hundred dollars a bottle. Now you'll have to go for a Latour or a Lafite, I guess. Maybe even a Mouton. If you can't get something spectacular, we'll spotlight a Château d'Yquem with dessert instead. I was saving the Sauternes for another menu, but if we have to use it, we can. Unless, of course, you have bad news about those bottles, too."

27

Pierre shook his head and started to hurry away, but Lombardo held him back, at the same time motioning for me to come over.

"Thank you so much for waiting," he said, beaming at me like I was the one true friend he'd always hoped to find. "I knew that marvelous Mrs. Gold would find me just the person I wanted."

He poured on the charm for a while longer, while the other two stood there and tried not to look too curious about who I was. When Lombardo decided I had soaked up enough of his personality to be thoroughly pickled, he turned to his assistants.

"I thought about your concerns with security, Robert," he said to the younger one, "and I decided you were absolutely right. Then Pierre and I were talking last Saturday about future plans for the Pinnacle Room, and I realized we couldn't possibly move ahead until our current problems were cleared up. This stealing has got to stop, and stop now. I'm only sorry we couldn't act before we had to deal with this latest outrage. Latest but also last."

He turned to the wineman for confirmation, and Pierre quickly nodded his agreement.

"Saturday night," Lombardo continued, "I contacted the director of the Global Security Agency with a request for an after-hours guard. It's a small company, very discreet. Just right for our needs. The director personally vouches for this fellow as experienced, intelligent, sophisticated, and nosy as hell." Lombardo beamed at me, then reached up and patted his assistant on the shoulder.

"Show the man around, Robert," he said. "If everything seems to be in order, as I'm sure it will, he can start tomorrow night. As for you, Pierre, get moving on that wine. We open for lunch in half an hour."

Chapter 4

I don't like being pigeonholed under any circumstances, and especially not in a secondhand bio from Gloria Gold, but it looked like all the introduction I was going to get. After all the time he'd spent with Gloria, insisting on his special requirements for the job, Lombardo had hardly even looked at me before he passed me over to the number two man. Pierre had vanished at the first hint, and the boss himself was also out of sight by now. The next minute I could hear him up at the bar, screaming at the girl doing the setups that her lemon peels were all twisted the wrong way. At least he hadn't said anything about my famous sense of style. I held out my hand to my new guide.

"Quentin Jacoby," I said.

"Robert Lyder," he answered, absent-mindedly breaking my fingers with a muscle man's handshake while he stared off in the direction Lombardo had gone. "I'm the assistant manager here, and everybody reports to me."

That wasn't the impression I'd been getting, but I let it pass and handed him the personnel questionnaire Gloria had given me to bring along. I waited while he looked over my credentials.

"Transit Police," he murmured. "What's that?"

"We're the officers you see patrolling the subways and buses," I answered, trying not to sound like I'd heard the question a thousand times before. Most people see a cop underground and they think he's been sent downstairs for bad behavior. They can't believe that any of us actually like the work or that we'd rather be fighting crime on the subways than harassing the sidewalk vendors overhead. "It's a whole separate force from the New York Police Department," I added. "Has been since the 1930s."

"I see," said Lyder, sneaking a peak inside his folder while he talked. "Lots of robberies, I guess."

"Mostly fare evasions," I answered evenly. "Some robberies, though. Also muggings, rapes, murder." Lyder looked up, blinking fast. "Also a lot of people asking for directions," I added soothingly. "Or complaining about the service."

"Right," he said, smiling uncertainly. "Well, you won't get much of that here. Except the robberies, of course. You heard about the wine. Three cases of top Bordeaux at about fourteen hundred dollars a case. Keep that up every week or two, and before you know it you're losing thirty thousand dollars a year. It costs enough to run a restaurant of this caliber without getting into that kind of red ink."

Just thinking about the losses made Lyder angry. "All this month I've been telling him someone is stealing from the kitchen, stealing from the wine cellar," he exclaimed, "but he just brushed it off. 'The help has to eat, too,' he told me. I asked him why the things that vanished were always what we needed most, right away, and he just laughed. A joke, he called it. Somebody trying to tease him. As long as everything was perfect out front, he said, he didn't care about the costs. Well, I'm glad he's finally taken steps before I had to. I didn't want to call in the police because police mean publicity and restaurants do not thrive under that kind of attention. But this mismanagement has got to stop!"

He glared at me like I was already shirking on the job, then glanced back at his folder and muttered, "What else?"

"Is it always wine that's missing?" I asked.

"No," answered Lyder. "Sometimes it's wine, but often it's

food. We lost forty pounds of imported goat cheese last month, shaped by hand and flown over from Greece before the grape leaves in the wrapping even had a chance to wilt. They've even gone after the fixtures. When we opened, we had a wonderful silver duck press. Not sterling, of course, but enormous, with Corinthian columns around the base and a lion and a unicorn as handles. It was made for the coronation of Edward the Seventh, 1902, and we planned this whole room around it. Mr. Lombardo adored it. Then one day it was gone—I had to run out and buy an onyx urn and two sphinxes to fill the space."

He pointed dramatically at a big wooden pedestal against the far wall, where a hidden spotlight was shining on a black jug and a couple of squatting cats.

"Of course, it was the day all the people from *Gourmet* were coming to take pictures," he said. "But leaving that aside, who would want to steal a duck press? The thing cost a fortune, but it would be worthless melted down, and so far it hasn't turned up at any of the dealers."

He looked at me questioningly, but I was still puzzling over who would want to iron a duck. "Any cash gone?" I asked.

Lyder shook his head. "The waiters pool their tips and divide them up before they go home. The cash goes downstairs with me and straight into the bank. There's a night deposit in the lobby. Most of our business is credit cards, of course, and so far nobody's thought to make off with the receipts. Not that I don't look for that to happen next."

"You know who's doing it?"

Lyder looked up in surprise. "What do you mean?" he asked.

"Well, it certainly sounds like your thief is someone who knows the restaurant. A delicatessen holdup, that could be anyone, but to lift the most expensive wines and the fancy doodads takes a certain amount of inside knowledge. I thought you might have some ideas about who it could be."

"I've thought of that," he conceded. "But I can't believe it.

We pay our people well, and I can vouch for the fact that they're all unusually dedicated. Some of them have been with Mr. Lombardo for years. Pierre started out washing glasses behind the bar twenty years ago, and look at him now. They care about food, they care about service, and they also care about their own careers."

All this time Lyder had been sneaking little glances at the papers in his folder. Now he snapped it shut and squared his shoulders in a way that told me I was about to hear a speech.

"Let me explain to you about the Interdine system," he said. "Everyone who works here is considered an apprentice, moving up in the corporation, and everyone is made to feel that he or she has a stake in the company's success. Here at the Pinnacle Room, as at every branch of Interdine operations, we have staff council meetings once a month, where everyone attends, and shared bonuses for particularly profitable periods. That's the way they do it in Japan, you know—terrific sense of company loyalty—and that's the way we're doing it here, too. Mr. Harwell, the founder of Interdine, has made a long study of Japanese management techniques, and he has been very successful in applying them to American conditions. Why ruin a great career with a company like Interdine for a few hundred dollars' worth of stolen goods?"

Lyder himself had said it was more like a few hundred dollars a week, which I suspected was more than enough to make some people give up a future of scraping dishes at three-fifty an hour. Looking at the way the Japanese had destroyed Detroit, though, I could see why management types like Lyder were getting all fired up about things like company T-shirts and group calisthenics in the morning. Who was I to say it wouldn't work? I've never been able to prove there isn't a tooth fairy either.

Lyder took my silence for agreement and started peeking back at his folder. "What else?" he asked again. "There are two guards on duty in the lobby all night, so I think our thief must be coming through the freight entrance. If you stay in the kitchen by the freight elevator, you should nab him pretty soon. Yes, that's it," he said more firmly, turning to go. "Make the kitchen your station. Follow me, and I'll show you around. Might as well keep a low profile, though. If anybody asks what you're doing here, say you're from upstairs, checking management accounting."

Lyder turned around and grinned. "Nobody knows what the hell that means," he confided. "Just keep repeating the phrase."

Then he was off, peering at his watch and muttering, "What else?" It seemed to be his personal theme song. I had to look sharp just to keep up as he scurried through the dining room and behind a mirror-covered screen that shielded the entrance to the kitchen.

"There's the freight elevator," he said, pointing with his folder. "There's the walk-in refrigerator and the freezer, and there's the telephone in case you have to call out. There's another line at the reservation desk, top of the stairs before the dining room. There's a floor plan and a guide to the circuits mounted on the wall over there, along with an emergency set of keys. I'll have them leave you a dinner and a full pot of coffee. You'll need an employee identification card to get back in here tonight. I'll get you one from the office in a minute."

Back in the fifties, there used to be a lot of talk about the wonders of automation. It was the first thing I thought of when I saw the Pinnacle kitchen. Out in the dining room everything was brass and candles, linen napkins and beautiful views. In here it was all white tiles and stainless steel machinery, and the only thing to look at besides the food was a set of framed photographs of fat guys in white chefs' hats, high on the wall where the glass wouldn't get spattered. There must have been twenty people in there, working away to get ready for lunch, but no one was talking, or singing, or even yelping when they sliced their thumbs, which some of them must have done from time to time. All you could hear was the buzz of mixers, the clank of knives, and the whir of a giant dishwasher that was already sloshing away in the corner.

While I watched, Lombardo came darting through to check on the cooking. For sixty seconds he was everywhere, lifting lids, sticking his finger into the sauces, giving last-minute tips to the cook at the grill. Everyone puffed up when the boss came by, flushed and eager and fired with some of Lombardo's own energy, but as soon as he was gone, they went back to work and let the machines take over. Personally I associate good cooking with a lot of shouting, tasting, and rummaging in the cupboards to see what else might go into the pot, but I could see that the efficiency of the Pinnacle operation appealed more to Lyder. He stared approvingly as a good-looking kid in a white apron chopped the hell out of a mound of parsley, mechanically changing the big green bunches on one side of his board into little green snowflakes on the other. He was so pleased with the picture he even stopped using his pencil as an exercise mat.

Then the moment passed. "What else?" he asked himself. "Hours." He turned to me. "Come in at eleven, when the kitchen closes. Stay until seven in the morning, when the bakers get here; that way we'll have the plant covered around the clock. And unless you object, you might as well start tonight. That's the best way to do it," he assured me. "Stay up all night, and you'll be tired enough to sleep through the next day. Then you're in the rhythm before you know it."

"Whatever you say, Mr. Lyder." I'd been staying up all night when he was in diapers, but if he wanted to give me advice, I wasn't going to argue. His plan for my duties wasn't exactly what Lombardo had outlined to Gloria, but I figured that wasn't any of my business either. Let the two of them hash out the question of who was really in charge.

"I guess we're set then," Lyder said. "I wanted to show you some other things, but I've really . . . well, finally!" he exclaimed,

34

catching sight of a new arrival in the kitchen. "You're late, Janine. As usual. But you're also just the person I was looking for."

Janine was just the person a lot of guys were looking for, especially if their taste ran to strikingly beautiful women. I'd been feeling a little cooped-up, trapped back there in the kitchen, but seeing her opened up a whole new vista on the job. She was a tall, thin lady, built like a model, with a perfect face and a body that managed to be both slender and ripe at once. She was also very black, her dark skin set off by a white linen suit and a white straw fedora with a blood-red hatband. She had that elegant, expensive look you see on the covers of the fashion magazines, but more than that, she had a kind of knockout gorgeousness that made you forget everything you ever thought about how you liked redheads, or dames with big breasts, or cute kids with freckles. When you saw this lady, you didn't think, Nice, but not my type. To tell the truth, you didn't think at all. Just sort of panted softly.

I guess she was used to being stared at. She looked me right in the eye while I took my time going over her assets, and there was a tiny flutter around the mouth that could have been a smile. The smile faded, though, when she turned to Lyder, and I could tell there was no love lost between them. He introduced her as Miss DuPage, mumbled something snide about how she was in charge of seating and reservations "when she wasn't too busy," then told her to show me the wine cellar and get back on the double for the menu briefing.

"He's from upstairs," Lyder added mysteriously, then dashed off to check his folder with one of the chefs.

Janine smiled, the best hostess in the world, and I could see right off that a lot of the local bankers and lawyers found it easier to wait for a table when it was this doll who assured them she would be seating them as soon as she could. She led me back through the pantry, behind the screen and into the dining room, but we weren't ten feet on our way before the smile was gone.

"Who are you?" she demanded. Not mad. Not mean. Just very curious and not about to be ignored.

"Quentin Jacoby," I answered. That seemed safe.

"My word. And I thought Janine DuPage was a silly name. But that's not what I meant. Why are you getting the grand tour?"

At that point I wasn't sure. According to Gloria, I was guarding the empire of a genius against unknown evil saboteurs. But the genius himself could hardly be bothered saying hello and had fobbed me off on his fussbudget assistant. According to the assistant, I was supposed to sit outside the meat locker, ready to grab the first slob who tried to lay a finger on the fricassee. The top management didn't even know I'd been hired, and the staff wasn't supposed to catch on.

"Management accounting," I said stiffly, trying not to sound as stupid as I felt. "From upstairs."

Janine snorted. "Did Lyder tell you to say that? It sounds like him, but he doesn't fool me for a minute. The people upstairs have enough smarts to know they should leave Johnny alone and be happy just to count their profits at the end of the month." She stopped and gave me a speculative look. "If you're here, it's because Johnny wants you to be, and I guess I'll find out why soon enough." Then the smile went back on, and she gestured to an open door on the side of the dining room, away from the windows.

"The wine cellar," she announced simply. "The finest in New York."

I was in no position to judge, having never seen a wine cellar before, but I could tell right off that the place looked nothing like the aisles of Joe Johnson's Liquors over on Gun Hill Road in the Bronx. It also looked nothing like a cellar, which was all right since we were quite a distance above the ground. The wine was there all right, though, piled up along three sides of the long, narrow room in thin silver racks that looked like the work of a very rich spider. Every few feet there was a slot in the racks for an inventory card, and the place had enough dials and thermostats to let you know that some fancy kind of air conditioning was making it so cold.

But whoever heard of a cellar where the floors and walls were all covered with pink marble and the light fixtures looked like bunches of grapes? At the far end of the room, about two feet from the back wall, was a bronze statue of some guy prancing around in the altogether, holding up a cluster of grapes like he was waiting for them to fall right into his mouth. The base of the statue was big enough to double as a kind of cocktail table, and there were a couple of broad stools with beige leather cushions pulled up alongside.

"Like it?" Janine asked.

As a matter of fact, I didn't. Pink is not my favorite color and wine is not my favorite drink. It crossed my mind that Lombardo's glitter was the kind that I myself would get tired of pretty fast. I grunted something noncommittal.

"A marble grotto," Janine chanted, in the singsong tone of a guided tour conductor, "dedicated to Bacchus and maintained with the most sophisticated climate control devices known to modern engineers. Also," she added in her natural voice, "the best selection of wines in the city, put down by a man who knew ten years ago what was going to be the finest drinking today, and tomorrow, and ten years from now. From time to time, once every other blue moon, somebody may come through with a palate as good as Johnny's, and then he'll set up a private tasting. Monday nights we're starting a series of special dinners in the Coronation Room that may draw a few people interested in wine. Mostly, though, the wine is wasted. We get a lot of business dinners, people so full of scotch by the time they sit down, they could be drinking grape Kool-Aid for all they'd care.

"Johnny cares, though," she continued, "and that's what matters. To be successful in the food racket, you've got to have a

37

head for business, but if that's all you've got, you'll never make it the way Johnny has. You've got to have taste, and style, and a sixth sense about what the public is going to want tomorrow. The man is a genius," she said reverently. If I heard that one more time, I might start believing it myself.

"And I," she added, "am late for the menu briefing. Note the doors on your way out. Triple padlocks hinged to the left on door number one. Triple locks hinged to the right on door number two. Both open during business hours. Pierre is the wine steward, and he can tell you anything you want to know about the vintages on hand. Tom, the floor captain, can answer any other questions. I must fly."

And fly she did, or at least as close to it as you could come when the longest legs I'd ever seen were wrapped in a tight white linen skirt. She was one of the few young women I'd met who managed to look both efficient and attractive. She was also, I noticed, the only person around who called Lombardo by his first name.

Chapter 5

After I got through admiring Janine's exit, I walked back through the dining room and up the stairs. Pierre was still on the telephone, the receiver wedged under his chin and a black leather address book open in his hands. While I watched, a bald-headed gent with a handlebar mustache darted into the wine cellar and popped out again with a couple of bottles tucked under his arm. Pierre glanced at them and nodded without taking the receiver from his ear. "Yes, yes!" he shouted into the phone, suddenly animated. "I have need of three cases. You can deliver them here?"

I looked around me, wondering if I had already seen the thief without knowing it. Was it the kid at the bar, arranging little round pieces of toast on tiny metal plates? Or the girl at the coatroom, furtively pulling down the jacket of her uniform every time she finished getting something down from the shelf? The place was swarming with prospects now, but how was I to know? Lyder trotted by, still clutching his red folder full of menus. "Eleven tonight," he repeated hurriedly. "Here's your ID card, with Mr. Lombardo's signature. What else? Nothing."

I took the hint and turned to the elevator, just as the door opened with the first customers of the day. Four men in banker's pin stripes, looking like a blue-chip version of a barbershop quartet. I watched them charge off toward the bar, then stepped into their empty elevator. Two flights down I was joined by a herd of key punch operators from the Interdine office, arguing about which park to eat their yogurt in today. We got to the ground before they had settled it, and I left them debating the superior shade of Trinity Churchyard versus the higher caliber of young executives at the plaza at Bankers Trust. Personally, I had already decided where I was going. High noon on a fine summer's day, and probably the last for a while when I'd be awake. If I was going to be spending my nights standing watch in the Interdine Tower, I figured I might as well get a fix on my new surroundings.

The obvious place to start was with the competition to the north, but I hadn't really braced myself for the shock of the transition. Going from the Interdine Tower to the World Trade Center was like going from a private parlor car to the Times Square shuttle. Interdine was sheltered and exclusive, the kind of place you rent in when you're so rich you'll pay anything for privacy. The World Trade Center, by contrast, was so big and busy that if it were in Nebraska, it would most likely be the largest city in the state. The place was immense in several directions, with offices shooting up a thousand feet in the air, a whole shopping center laid out underground, a major subway station where four different lines come together, and a full-size hotel tucked in by the side. All of which would make for a busy enough scene at lunch without the added fact that the joint had become one of the biggest tourist attractions in the city.

When I got to the plaza at the center of the buildings, I just stood there for a minute and gawked at the crowds. I'd been through there on the subway lots of times, but I'd never bothered to get out. The project was financed by the Port Authority of New York on funds they took from transit revenue, and it burned me up that at the same time they were raising subway fares, cutting services and reducing patrols by thirty percent, they also went and put up this set of monster office buildings in a run-down part of Manhattan whose main virtue was being close to the Hudson Tubes, in case you wanted to make a quick getaway to Jersey. They said it was going to transform the area into a new commercial hub, but that wasn't how it looked to me. The way I see it, a skyscraper is nothing but a street standing on end, and the Port Authority had no business going vertical until it had cleared up the problems with the horizontal traffic.

As usual, though, nobody had asked me, so there was the World Trade Center, bigger than life and twice as busy, and after all my years of grouching I had to admit that it had become a commercial hub after all. Without the Trade Center there probably wouldn't have been an Interdine Tower, just for starters. But beyond that, there would have been none of the mobs of office people and tourists who were pushing their way across the plaza, going into one building or another, ducking underground for the trains and the stores, or heading into a restaurant to grab a bite to eat.

Weighing the pros and cons of it all, I joined the crowd. In January it would be a killer here, with the wind whipping right off the river and nothing but a circle of concrete benches for shelter. This time of year, though, it was a regular seaside resort, with the air off the water taking the mercury down a few blessed degrees. Rows of folding chairs had been set up for some kind of noontime concert, and people were sitting patiently, eating lunch out of paper bags and waiting for the music to begin. Three little kids were leaning over the edge of the big marble fountain in the middle of the plaza, teetering on their stomachs while they splashed in the water. A bag lady had set up her station next to a concrete planter full of red flowers. Passing her by, I headed for the first of the towers. If I was going to be a tourist, I might as well start at the top.

Inside the building, half the lobby was filled with banners advertising a troupe of Balinese dancers performing there that afternoon. The other half was divided into lanes with brass stanchions and velvet ropes for the lines of people waiting to get up to the observation deck. It was amazing how many people were willing to pay for a chance to see the world's highest, clearest view of Hoboken.

Not being big on lines myself, I decided to settle for lunch in one of the joints in the subway arcade. I was turning to go when I heard someone call my name.

"Hey, Jacoby! Baby! Over here!"

At first all I could see was a bunch of women with cymbals on their fingers, setting up for their dance just like it said on the banners. When I saw who was really calling, the ladies with the cymbals seemed more likely.

It was Sam Fuentes. Sam put in close to thirty years pushing a wagon through Central Park, peddling sno-cones and anything else he thought the season called for and the market would bear, but since he'd saved up enough to retire to Co-op City, his main occupation had been avoiding exercise and fresh air. Except for when he was out at the track, he spent most of his time playing pinochle with the super in our building, hanging around Maybelle's Donut Shop, or mooching beers and color TV from me. I would have bet good money that he hadn't been downtown during daylight hours in years. So what was he doing in the World Trade Center, lined up for the observation deck right behind a busload of people whose shoulder bags said they had come all the way from Pasadena?

While I was trying to figure this out, Sam kept right on shouting. "Over here, baby," he yelled, ignoring all the tourists in pastel double knits who were giving him dirty looks. "Come on. I save you a place." He sounded overjoyed to see me, but I knew better than to be flattered. Sam would embrace the devil himself and be boasting about how they were cousins by his second day in hell.

"Hello, Sam," I said when I got up to him. "I didn't know you liked views."

"Views?" he repeated scornfully. "You gotta be kidding, baby. Sam Fuentes don't pay *dinero* to see no views."

Grabbing my lapel, he pulled me down to where he could whisper in my ear. "You really lucky to be here," he said, "because I am on to a *very* big tip. But I gotta go to the sky to check it out."

Sam plays the trotters, just like me, but this was the first I'd heard of any rooftop bookies. The last time I looked, the Off-Track Betting office was down on the subway concourse. The line moved forward with Sam still holding onto my lapel, and I decided to duck under the rope and join him. It was either that or tear the only jacket I owned.

"I buy you a ticket," Sam said, darting off to the booth by the elevator. "You pay me back," he added over his shoulder. Then we were at the front of the line, piling into the car with the last of the group from California. I still didn't have any idea what was going on, but I figured Sam would tell me eventually. He likes to boast too much to hold on to a secret for long.

What you're supposed to do in an elevator is keep quiet and stare straight ahead. Nobody had ever gotten that message to Sam, though. As soon as the doors closed, he started jabbering.

"Some ride, eh?" he asked, poking me with his elbow. Sam is considerably shorter than I am, and his nudges can be quite painful. I tried to move away before he could land a second jab, but in a crowded elevator there's no place much to go.

"Some ride!" he said again. "All the way down on the subway to go all the way up on the elevator!" Sam pronounced *elevator* like it was four different words, and he practically smacked his lips on each of them, he was having such a good time.

All the way up he kept on yakking, right over the canned announcements about heights and speed that were coming from the loudspeaker, but I noticed he still wasn't saying anything about what he was doing down there. I also noticed he hadn't introduced me to the three other guys he was with. I hadn't seen

43

them before, being too surprised with just meeting Sam, but now I recognized his cousin Hector, who makes a good living selling cameras and sometimes comes with us to the track, and also his buddy Ysidore, who looks a lot like Sam even though they're not related. The last fellow I couldn't place, though, no matter how I figured, and yet I was pretty sure he was part of the group. He stood between Hector and Ysidore, whistling a little through his teeth and holding his cowboy hat in his hands like a well-bred country boy in church.

The hat was the first thing that was strange about him, but it certainly wasn't the last. He was a real beanpole of a man, about my height but at least forty pounds lighter, dressed in faded, pressed blue jeans and a brown checked shirt that couldn't have been bought within five hundred miles of Madison Avenue. The quality of the clothes went with his coloring, which had the same faded, washed-out look, but none of it matched Sam.

It took us a couple of minutes to reach the observation deck on the 107th floor. By that time Sam had switched into Spanish and was giving Hector his ratings on the women in the car, which I hope to God none of them understood. Sam is partial to women with big chests and high, little asses, while most of our fellow passengers seemed to have the opposite arrangement. He wasn't quite finished when the doors opened, so he just stepped out and moved to the side of the room without missing a word. Sure enough, the cowboy came along, and as soon as we stopped, he turned to introduce himself.

"Good day to you," he said, looking me briefly in the face and then staring over my shoulder at a map of the New York skyline mounted on the wall. "My name is Ezra Faerbrother."

"Quentin Jacoby," I offered in return, but he shook off the name like it was an interruption.

"Seeing that you are a friend of Mr. Fuentes," he said solemnly, "I will reveal to you that I have been blessed with a psychic knowledge of horses. It is a sacred gift, and I must use

44

it wisely, but if you have the faith to join our group, I can promise that an investment of one thousand dollars will multiply twentyfold by three o'clock next Sunday afternoon."

Just like that. Twenty thousand dollars. Buddies who worked the rackets squad had told me about operators like this one, downhome boys with prayer books in their pockets and hayseed behind their ears who could steal your socks without taking off your shoes, but I'd never seen one in action before.

"What happens on Sunday?" I asked. It was the least of my questions, but you have to start somewhere.

Ezra looked at me slowly, like he was waking from a trance. "You ask Mr. Fuentes for the details," he said, with more of a twang than I'd noticed before. "I have some work to perform." And with that he eased off around the corner, toward the north side of the deck.

Sam was standing a few feet in front of me, pretending to fool with a telescope but really waiting for my reaction. I walked over and planted myself between him and the view.

"Okay, Sam," I said. "What's going on?"

In answer he looked slowly right and then left, checking that no one was listening. I thought for a second he was going to complete the act by putting a finger across his lips and tiptoeing away, but instead he broke out in a huge grin that let me admire all five of his gold teeth.

"Is beautiful, Jacoby," he chortled. "Is a miracle. A dream. A gift from Our Lady to a poor sucker like me for all those years I push that damn sno-cone wagon and earn not enough to buy myself a pinkie ring. This man, this Meester Faerbrother..." Sam stopped to look over his shoulder again, but there was still nobody there but his cousin and his friend Ysidore, both of them nodding agreement to everything Sam said. "This man," he continued, "can talk to horses."

Sam waited for it to sink in. I waited, too. Nothing happened. "So what?" I asked finally. "I can talk to horses, too. 'Here, horsie.

45

Nice horsie.' Nothing to it. I've never tried politics, but we get along fine on the weather."

"*Muy cómico*," Sam said scornfully. "You a big comedian, I send you off to Johnny Carson. But you dumb. You don't get it. This man talks to horses, and they *listen*. They do what he says. They run fast, they run slow, just the way he wants. You find a man can do that, baby, you make a lot of money at the races. Lucky thing you come by while there still time to invest. We be rich, baby! I show you how to live for real!"

"Sam," I protested, moving aside before his elbow could connect with my kidneys, "this is crazy. Who ever heard of someone who can fix a race by talking to the horses? You can drug a horse, or beat it, or get to the jockey. It happens all the time, something you've got to figure in along with the rest of the odds. But talking? You are being conned, and no doubt about it."

"No, no," said Ysidore. "It's true." It was the first time he had spoken, the first time he had given any real sign of going along, and it amazed me to think that this Faerbrother character had bamboozled not just one person but three. Sam, I knew, would fall for anyone who promised easy money, but I thought the other two had more sense. Looking around, I saw that the psychic beanpole had finished his mission on the other side of the building and was working on a hot dog at the snack bar.

"Ysidore is right," agreed Hector. "I saw it, too. We all did. Saturday afternoon, when they had the trials out at Meadowlands, we saw him tell a pacer to stop dead after the second turn. Yesterday there were no races, so we all went up to Central Park. You know those carriage nags, pull the tourists around the park? We saw him tell one to turn down Sixth Avenue. And, man, he did it! That horse acted like he was going for lunch at Rockefeller Center, with the driver cursing and pulling on the reins all the time. And fast! I saw it, I tell you!" They all nodded at once, like the Three Stooges.

"Well, when he tells a broken-down gluepot at Belmont to outrun the winner of the Triple Crown, then you can give me a call."

"Won't work," said Sam shortly.

"Why not?" I asked. "I thought this guy could boss around anything on four legs."

"Only works on harness horses," Hector explained. "A horse with a rider, it interferes with the message. That's why we wait for Sunday."

These guys were even more gullible than I had thought. But at the same time, I was getting interested in the crazy logic of it all.

"Okay," I said. "So it has to be harness racing. This time of year they've got men in sulkies getting pulled around the track at Meadowlands every night of the week. Today is Monday. You make a bundle tonight, and then maybe I'll be more impressed with your friend the psychic talker."

Again Sam shook his head, like he couldn't believe how ignorant I was. "Has to be daytime," he said. "He needs the light beams to pick up the message."

Sam and I have had some good times together, so I tried my best not to laugh in his face. "Let's see if I've got this right," I said slowly. "This guy stands at the rail and beams messages to the horses?"

"Nah," said Sam, shaking his head at my stupidity. "He stands far away, high up. The messages have to travel down. They are heavier than air, man. What you think we doing up here anyway?"

"That was my next question."

"Listen," he said impatiently. "I tell you once, you get it, okay? Has to be daytime. Has to be a horse in harness. Mr. Faerbrother, he has to be outside and high up. Saturday morning he go to the top of the clubhouse. Yesterday we way up on the Empire State Building. Today we do the final test, see if he can reach Meadowlands from here. Work on his distances, you know? So he be all ready for Sunday."

Ah, yes. The big day. "What happens Sunday?" I asked again.

Sam looked so pleased he was practically choking. "Sunday," he purred, "we get very, very rich, backing the long shot at the Hampton Stake. That's what happen Sunday."

Harness racing is a workingman's sport. The horses run at night, after quitting time, and the purses are usually about half what they are for thoroughbreds. The Hampton Stake is something else, though, the trotting equivalent of the Kentucky Derby. It's the final card of the summer season, always on a Sunday afternoon with a whole weekend of preliminary races and other hoopla to warm up the crowds. It has the best horses, the biggest purse, the most bets, and also the tightest security. The idea of fixing the race was as juicy as it was nuts, and I began to see how Sam had gotten hooked. Not that that made him any less of a fool.

"Tell me, Sam," I asked. "You guys give this Faerbrother any money?"

"Not to worry," he answered evasively.

"Well, just in case you have," I said, "let me remind you that there is a special department at the police station where they take care of rackets like this. You call up, and they will have an experienced officer come and get your money back from Skinny over there. If you've been fool enough to give it to him, which I sincerely hope you have not. Then you can put the dough in something sensible, with a nice guaranteed return. Like lottery tickets. Or shares of the Brooklyn Bridge. Or maybe a passenger seat on the space shuttle, which you can sell at scalpers' prices in about twenty-five years."

Sam looked wounded, like I should have known he would. "We gonna be on easy street," he said. "And because you my good friend, I offer you this chance to come along. We gonna be on easy street for sure."

The last time Sam was going to be on easy street was when he got the bright idea of staging cockfights on the midnight flight from New York to San Juan, which worked for exactly one-half of one trip before they had a mug shot of him posted at the Eastern terminal at La Guardia. He lost about fifty dollars after expenses, and his apartment smelled like a poultry yard for months. But like many deeply cynical people, Sam's a great optimist about his own affairs. If he wanted to throw away his money on some backwoods psychic con man, that was his business. Between Lombardo and Faerbrother, I'd had my fill of genius for the day.

By this time Faerbrother had gotten bored looking through postcards at the snack bar and was coming back our way. "Remember what I told you," I called to Sam, but he and his buddies were already gathered around their new savior, and a more fervent bunch of true believers I never did see.

"Very fine line to East Rutherford from here," Faerbrother said. "I had no trouble with my communications." Then he turned to me. "I can tell that you do not believe in my gifts, and I am sorry." And with that he made me a strange, stiff little bow, put on a pair of sunglasses he'd just bought at the souvenir stand, and marched into the waiting elevator.

We all crowded in behind him and rode down in silence. As we got off at the ground, he announced, "Sutpen's Hundred will scratch tonight," and strode off to the revolving doors that led to the concourse, the trains, and wherever Faerbrother went to gloat over the large supply of suckers the world had been good enough to provide.

The rest of us moved more slowly, making allowances for Sam's bunions and all. When we passed the building directory, I stopped to point out something that caught my eye.

"See that?" I asked. "The New York State Racing and Wagering Board. Seventy-fourth floor. There's a law against what you guys are planning, and I'd be a lot more concerned if I thought you had a chance in the world of pulling it off."

It was good advice, but Sam just shook his head, and sure enough that night Sutpen's Hundred scratched. I learned that by listening to the late-night "Racing Roundup" on a radio I found in the Pinnacle kitchen.

Chapter 6

By the time I got rid of Sam and had some lunch, it was going on to three o'clock. I called Gloria to let her know I got the job. That took about two minutes, which still left me with eight hours to kill before I was supposed to show up for work. For a while I just wandered around, turning corners at random until I found myself at the New York Stock Exchange, facing the spot where George Washington was sworn in as president before anybody thought of building a city with his name. From there I walked down Wall Street, which is lined with tall, boring buildings where people in dark suits push around little pieces of paper worth billions of dollars. When the heat and the money got to be too much for me, I headed over to Battery Park, as far south as you can go in Manhattan without falling off the edge of the island.

Bea and I used to go down there a lot, way back before we got married. We'd visit the old aquarium, then ride back and forth on the Staten Island ferry until we ran out of nickels. Now the fish have moved to Brooklyn and the ferry is up to a quarter, but it's still a good place to catch a breeze on a summer's night. When I got there, the park was full of commuters hurrying to get home to Staten Island, but after six the crowds thinned out, and by eight o'clock there was nobody there but the derelicts and me. At nine-fifteen three kids arrived with the biggest, loudest portable tape machine on earth and gave us a free disco concert while they practiced a precision dance routine, We watched politely, me and the winos, and two guys even clapped at the end. The rest of us went back to sleeping and studying the stars.

At ten o'clock I shook myself awake and started walking back to the Interdine Tower. I could have ridden up in five minutes on the Broadway local, but I felt like a stroll. I went up State Street, past the spot where Peter Stuyvesant stole Manhattan Island from the Indians for a handful of beads, and past the Custom House with its ring of statues around the roof. Then north on Trinity Place, where the church spires look like they've been squeezed into points by the office buildings crowded in on all sides. A left-hand jog got me to the Interdine Tower. At night it looked less like a crystal and more like a piece of the Alps that had somehow broken loose and landed in lower Manhattan, which wasn't a bad effect either.

In the lobby there was a new goon stationed at the console and another man in uniform by the elevator. I wondered again why Lombardo had gone to Gloria for a guard, when there seemed to be so many people already on the Interdine payroll. These guys had as much style as I ever would, plus nice little touches like company uniforms, closed-circuit televisions, and knowing the building's tenants by name.

After he finished saying good-night to a couple of regulars and sending them up to beddy-bye, the elevator starter turned to me. "Pinnacle Room," I told him, then added, "Staff," when I realized he was checking my name against a reservations list. Security here was pretty good. While I was fishing for the card Lyder had given me, the elevator door opened and a half-dozen people got out, flushed with good eating and the heady energy that sometimes grabs you in the city on a hot summer night. A woman in a clingy red dress did a dance twirl out into the lobby.

"That was marvelous, darling!" she exclaimed. "Tomorrow I

want you to take me to dinner in a hot-air balloon. Or on the moon. Let's never descend again!"

Darling caught up with his dance partner and put his arm around her waist. He whispered something in her ear that made her laugh a very promising, throaty kind of laugh, and I could bet she was agreeing to more earthbound adventures. Like everybody said, Lombardo was a genius.

When I got upstairs, the genius was standing by the landing above the dining room, saying good-bye to the last of his guests. Lyder was hovering right behind him, like he was trying to pick up the technique, and I could see Janine chatting it up with the stragglers down below. Pierre was stationed by the bar a few feet away, standing at attention in case anybody needed a nightcap before he could face the elevator ride down. All the crude details of bills and charges had already been taken care of, and there was nothing to get in the way of the compliments, the hand kissing, and the very discreet palming of tips.

I stood there watching for a while until Lyder spotted me and hurried over. "Follow me," he said briefly, and before I knew it, we had gone through one of the doors on the other side of the elevator, down a ramp, and into the back of the kitchen.

Everybody here had already gone home. The chopping blocks had been scoured, the big pots left upside down on the counters to drain. Next to the freight elevator were two huge canvas bins full of dirty laundry. "The chefs just throw in their aprons and hats when they leave," Lyder explained, "and the laundry service picks it up in the morning, when they drop off the clean linens." He showed me a few more things around the kitchen, including a covered tray with my dinner, then led me out the pantry and back into the main dining room.

In the few minutes it had taken us to tour the kitchen, the rest of the place had emptied. The coatroom was dark and the wine cellar locked. Even Lombardo had disappeared. Lyder closed up the reservation desk, locking the credit slips in a drawer and tucking the cash in an envelope to take down to the night deposit, just like he had told me. As we left each room, he turned out the lights. When we got to the elevators, he jabbed the button, eager to get home himself, then turned back to me. "These robberies have got to stop," he said firmly. "Somebody is trying to ruin the Pinnacle Room, but I don't intend to let it happen." The elevator arrived, and I nodded solemnly as he stepped inside.

After he was gone, I came back to reality, which was that I was all alone in an empty restaurant. My first move was to turn the lights back on. I knew Lyder was a bug about expenses, but I doubted he'd notice the extra buck or two on the bills. Thrift has its limits when you're also interested in security. Next I went back to the kitchen and moved the laundry bins so they were blocking the freight elevator. They were real heavy, and the wheels squeaked a lot, just like I'd been hoping. Then I turned on the radio to catch the racing results, which is how I learned about Sutpen's Hundred.

All this took a few minutes. By that time it was after midnight, and I decided to check out the tray of food in the pantry. A hunk of cold salmon with cucumber sauce. Another plate with some cold beef and carrots and tiny little pink potatoes all frilled up with parsley. Salad on the side, and a huge slab of chocolate cake for dessert. Not bad at all. I settled myself at the table in the kitchen and was just starting to work on the fish when all of a sudden I lost my appetite. From somewhere outside the kitchen, where no one was supposed to be, had come a very loud crash.

I was on my feet and up the ramp to the elevator level in less time than it took to swallow. From there I edged forward more slowly, checking every hiding place I passed. Nobody behind the bar. Nobody crouching under the reservation desk or inside the telephone booths. Nobody in the bathrooms. I was beginning to think I had imagined the noise, but as soon as I walked down to the dining room I saw that the door to the wine cellar was open.

I didn't even have to go inside to recognize John Lombardo. He was the most dead-looking person I had ever seen.

It looked like a grotesque valentine: the pale man in the white suit; the pink marble floor of the wine cellar; the dark red puddle of blood that was spreading across the front of his shirt. He was sprawled over backwards, propped up on his elbows with his head twisted around as though he were trying to look at the statue at the back of the room. His eyes were open, and there was a thin cord of blood coming from his mouth. There was also six inches of pointed metal sticking out of the front of his chest. After a second I realized that the strange position of the body came from the handle of whatever it was Lombardo had been stabbed with. It was holding him up, keeping his back from resting on the floor. When I went closer I could see that his head had been smashed against the marble pedestal. I felt for a pulse, but only out of reflex.

I stood there another second, making my mind take in what I was seeing. Then I looked around. There was no one behind me. I backed up against a wall to make sure it stayed that way. A quick glance was enough to show that no one else was hiding in the room. Then I noticed the canvas sack by the door, lying on its side with the neck of a wine bottle sticking out. Above it, one of the silver shelves had been stripped of its contents. Was that the crash I had heard? The sound of a robbery suddenly abandoned? The noise of a thief turned assailant?

I made myself look back at Lombardo. I'd seen dead bodies before. Every cop has, and thirty years on the Transit Police had given me my share. I'd seen people who died from stab wounds and gunshots and from being pushed under the wheels of a moving train. I'd seen people who died of too much drink, too many drugs, or just because it was time for them to die and when the time came they happened to be on the subway. This was the first time I'd found a body that had been murdered under my nose, though, and I didn't like the experience at all. My job had been to stand guard in the kitchen, and I hadn't even known that Lombardo was still around, but I couldn't help feeling that I was somehow responsible for his death. It wasn't a great record for my first night on the job.

Lombardo had been holding a bottle of champagne when he went down, and the thin, fizzy noise of the wine dripping out of the broken bottle was a background to the slower, heavier sound of blood hitting the marble floor. It was cold in there, and it echoed, and I couldn't get over the conviction that the whole room was slimy with blood. What I wanted more than anything right then was to be someplace else. Next to that I wanted one of the fancy walkie-talkies that should have been standard issue for this kind of job. Lombardo had been so concerned with his crazy ideas about style he hadn't even shopped around for a company with decent equipment.

Then I realized I was getting angry at a dead man, as though he had meant for me to be trapped with a killer on the loose and no communication with the outside. Much as I wanted to be someplace else, Lombardo must have wanted it even more. But only for a second. The tiny moment of recognition, when his usual confidence gave way to the look of surprise that was still on his face. It was the last expression he'd ever had, and now it was there forever. No more than a minute had passed since I'd first come into the wine cellar. I turned around and started thinking about getting out.

Chapter 7

When a detective on television finds a body, he usually pokes his handsome puss out the door, looks briskly right and left, then casually sashays over to the phone to call the police station. He always knows the number and the first name of the sergeant at the desk, and he usually has time to grapple with the killer and knock him out before the squad car even arrives. But on television they have to wrap things up in an hour, including commercials, which means they can't waste precious air time being careful. I didn't have a contract guaranteeing I'd live to the end of the season, plus reruns, so I spent a few long seconds listening by the door before I decided to go out. It was no more than thirty feet from the wine cellar to the telephone on the landing, but I felt like I had made it across a minefield by the time I got there. And I don't mind admitting that I looked behind me and under the table before I picked up the phone.

First I tried 911, the police emergency number. It was busy. Next I dialed the four digits that would ring up the desk in the lobby. The guard answered on the first ring, and I blessed his fancy console and all its screens.

"Jacoby here," I whispered. "Security guard at the Pinnacle Room. John Lombardo's just been killed. Get the police, fast. Close the elevators. Call the garage, and tell them to block the freight exits. I don't know who's up here with me, but he must be trying to get out."

"Oh, my God," he gasped. Then he pulled himself together. "Lombardo. Police. Garage. Elevator," he repeated. "Stay cool. I'll have help up right away."

Easy advice. I wondered how many murders he dealt with, as a usual thing. Not that I cared, as long as I didn't end up boosting the numbers.

Common sense told me to stand still and wait for help, but my nerves told me to keep moving. The nerves won. I started in the kitchen. One look at the laundry piled in front of the doors convinced me that no one had gone out that way. Not unless he had some magic system for putting things back behind him after the door was closed. I checked all the storage areas, including the dishwasher and the dumbwaiter shaft to the executive dining room on the sixty-ninth floor. The first was empty, and the second was locked in place. The chefs glared down at me from their frames on the wall, and I kept on looking.

Through the pantry. Through the dining room. Through the Coronation Room, where I practically had heart failure when it seemed like one of the satin draperies was moving. Back past the wine cellar and up the stairs to all the places I had checked before. Still no police. Finally I moved past the elevator, away from the dining room down the hall to the little office where Lombardo kept the books. My hand was sweating when I tried to turn the knob. I stopped to get a better grip, then froze when a voice came from inside.

"Where you been, Johnny love?"

I flung open the door, and there was Janine DuPage, stretched out on a sofa in front of the window. Behind her were all the lights of Manhattan, but it was hard to concentrate on the view. She had traded in her white suit for a pale pink satin undershirt and a very skimpy pair of lace panties. It only took a second for her to start screaming and crouch up into a ball, but that was long enough to reconfirm that Miss DuPage was a very beautiful lady.

Also a very surprised one, which made for two people in a state of near shock when the police finally showed up. They came off the elevator and right into the office. It was easy to find us, of course, with Janine still screaming. As for me, I just stood there, waving my flashlight at my feet and trying to make like I was used to hanging around with naked ladies. The wall was covered with autographed pictures of famous people, but my eyes kept on going back to the live number on the sofa.

Two patrolmen arrived first, a young lummox who looked like Prince Valiant, only even dumber, and an older officer, a black man in his middle thirties who seemed to know his way around. He looked around the room, took in Janine cowering by the window, and decided to take charge.

"You the guard?" he demanded.

I nodded silently.

"This your assailant?"

"No," I answered automatically. "Maybe," I added a second later. "I don't know," I finally confessed. His partner was standing there dumbstruck, his hand on his holster, his mouth hanging open like a landing field for flies.

"All right, sister," said the senior officer. "No call for you to be parading around like that. Find your clothes right now."

He turned to his partner. "Out of here," he ordered. "Check the victim. Search the rest of the premises. Take him with you." We both hesitated. "Move it!" he barked. We both hurried back into the hall. Janine had finally stopped screaming, though it looked like she might start up again at any time.

The lummox went ahead of me. By now he had pulled his gun. I was still holding the flashlight, and the two of us must have looked like the Keystone Kops, rushing through the empty rooms and finding nothing. The officer's knees buckled a little when he saw Lombardo, but then he got his bearings and we kept on making our tour. We were just coming out of the men's room when his pocket began to crackle. Quickly he pulled out a radio and jerked up the antenna.

"You hear me, Tony?" cracked the voice of the dispatcher. "Captain Powers is on his way up. Manhattan One. Homicide." As the radio stopped, the passenger elevator door opened on two plainclothes detectives.

The first man out was a short, solid guy in his late forties with curly brown hair and a bald spot on top like Friar Tuck. He was built like a roly-poly clown, but he had the quick eyes of a detective, glancing around and taking everything in. He stopped when he came to me.

"I'm Captain Powers. Homicide. You the one who found the body?"

"Yes, sir. Quentin Jacoby. I work for Global Security."

He turned to the lummox. "Your name?" he asked.

"Kelly, sir. Carter and me were on patrol on West Street when the call came over the radio."

The other detective came forward and stood next to Powers. He was a younger man, as bony as the captain was round, with wispy white-blond hair and a nose like a cheese knife, long and narrow with a sharp turn up at the end. There was something dank about him, like he had just been underwater. It didn't help any that he was wearing a jacket the color of seaweed.

"Where's Carter?" he asked.

"Down the hall with a suspect," Kelly answered. He blushed at the memory, and I wondered if the young detective would warm up any when he saw Janine.

"Check it out," Powers ordered. "I'll go see the victim."

Before he left, though, he turned around to take another fix on the entryway, settling the layout in his mind. The doors of the elevator he had come up on had just closed when the car next to it, as if in answer, slid open. Out stumbled Robert Lyder, lurching forward as though he had been pushed.

"Where is he?" gasped Lyder.

"Who are you?" Powers asked at the same second. They stared at each other; then Lyder started to talk.

"Robert Lyder," he said, struggling to catch his breath. "The assistant manager. The garageman told me. I came right back up." He was clutching a small black rubber ball, squeezing it nervously while he talked. I don't think he even knew he was doing it. The man looked terrified, which was perfectly reasonable, seeing as how there was a killer wandering around. I wasn't exactly relaxed myself. Then it turned out his fears had to do with the business, not himself.

"You can't let this get in the papers," he said to Powers. "Publicity like this, front page in the morning editions, will shut us right down, and we can't afford to lose a single day."

Powers looked at him curiously. "Let's at least look at the body before we start putting up the barricades, okay? I'm Captain Powers, from homicide. My men and I will do everything we can to help your company. But I understand we've got a dead man here, and that has to take precedence over lunch."

Lyder didn't have any answer to that, and the captain didn't wait for one anyway. "Let's go," he said to me. When he realized that Lyder was tagging along, he slowed his steps.

"Come along if you like," he said. "But if you feel faint, please leave. Whatever you do, don't get sick on the evidence."

Lyder turned green at the suggestion, and I made a mental note to stay near him and push him toward the door if need be.

The wine cellar was just as I had left it: pink marble; white body; red blood. I think I half expected it all to have vanished, a bad dream from hanging around too much rich food late at night, but it was still there. Powers took two steps inside the door and stood still, looking. He turned to me.

"You can make a positive ID of the victim?"

"I can," Lyder volunteered shakily. He stepped forward and would have gone right down on the floor if Powers hadn't grabbed

61

his arm. Lyder didn't even notice the sudden restraint. He stood and stared in front of him, his head twisted in an unconscious imitation of his boss.

"That's Mr. Lombardo," he said finally. "He's dead, isn't he?"

It was a crazy question. He'd been dead when I found him half an hour before. I remembered the clammy feel of his neck when I'd checked for a pulse. You can't do chest massage on someone who has a skewer through his heart. Lombardo was very dead.

Powers didn't bother to answer. "You have any idea what that thing is in his chest?" he asked. "It doesn't look like any kind of stiletto I've ever seen."

Lyder peered at the red stain on Lombardo's suit. He started to weave a little, like he was going to pitch forward, but Powers had him by the arm.

"Steady," he said, the way I've heard trainers talk to skittish horses. "Steady now."

Lyder nodded and took a couple of deep breaths through the mouth.

"I'm not sure," he said finally. "I'd have to see the handle. But it looks like one of the brass brochettes we use. Mr. Lombardo had them specially made at Tiffany's for the Pinnacle Room. They're solid brass, with a twisted wire handle that's really a beautiful little modern sculpture. There's a vase full of them on display right by the stairs—people usually mistake them for artificial flowers. If you turn it right, the handle looks like the logo of the restaurant—a hollow globe with a mountain peak inside. I can't believe it," he added flatly.

"Thank you," said Powers. "You don't have to stay anymore. I'll get the photographers up here as soon as possible."

Lyder turned awkwardly and stumbled against the canvas sack by the door, sending a bottle rolling across the marble floor.

"All those bottles," he said slowly, like he hadn't noticed them before. He looked around, then stared at the empty rack. "A whole shelf of Dom Pérignon. There must be four hundred dollars' worth of wine right here on the floor. Well, there you have it," he said abruptly. "Killed by his favorite wine."

"What do you mean?" Powers asked.

"It seems pretty obvious," Lyder answered. "The empty shelf. The sack of bottles dumped by the door. We've had several robberies lately—that's why we hired the guard. Mr. Lombardo must have stayed after closing, without telling anybody, and then surprised the burglars at their work." His voice trailed off as he looked down at Lombardo's body. "They killed him," he said at last.

"And then panicked and dropped the wine as they fled?" Powers asked, filling in the rest of Lyder's story.

The manager blinked. "Right," he agreed.

"Maybe," said Powers, looking back across the room. "Maybe not."

Chapter 8

As if Lombardo had called to us, we all turned to stare at the
body on the floor. But Lombardo's days of giving orders were
over. Lyder started to shiver, and I knew it wasn't just the air
conditioning that was getting to him. Then suddenly he began
to laugh, an uncontrollable giggle that was as scary as anything
I'd heard that night.

"I just thought of something," he gasped, still laughing. "I'm
in charge now. I'm the new manager! It says so right in the
protocol book. A regular line of succession, just like the government. Call out the Secret Service! I want my bodyguards!"

He was laughing so hard now the words were shrieks, but it
wasn't a bit funny. Captain Powers moved us out of the wine
cellar and sat Lyder down in one of the dining room chairs. Then
he stood at the foot of the stairs and yelled, with a surprisingly
large voice for a not very tall man.

"Thorson!" he bellowed. After a few seconds the wet-looking
detective appeared on the landing.

"Find anything?" Powers called, not waiting for him to come
down the stairs.

"A half-naked woman having hysterics down the hall," Thorson
answered. "We're trying to calm her down before we start questioning. All I can tell you is, if she's got a concealed weapon on
her, it must hurt like hell."

Thorson swallowed his smirk when he saw Powers's expression. "Nothing much else," he added in a more serious voice. "It looks like somebody was eating in the kitchen and left suddenly. We have all the exits covered, and the patrolmen are searching the stairs. We'll begin a total canvass as soon as the people from the lab arrive. I called the morgue and also asked Sergeant Hong to come up. I thought we'd be needing an extra man if we were going to do any questioning."

"The dinner's mine," I said. "I don't feel like finishing," I added.

Powers nodded, then looked back up at his lieutenant. "Good work," he said. "Keep the uniforms around as long as you need them. Start the photographer in the room with the bottles, but call me before anyone touches the body. I'll start taking statements from the people here."

"Start with him," said Lyder suddenly. He had his face buried in his hands, but now he raised his head and glared at me.

"Start with him," he repeated. "He was supposed to be guarding the place. Telling me all about his great experience as a transit policeman. Where were you when Mr. Lombardo was killed? Out in the kitchen making choo-choo noises?"

"Where were *you?*" I shot back. The words came out on impulse, but as soon as I said them, I realized how surprised I'd been by Lyder's reappearance. Had it really taken him half an hour to get from the restaurant to the garage? He looked shocked that a lowly watchman would ask such a question. Then he flushed when he realized the detectives were waiting for his answer.

"I was down in the lobby," he said defensively. "After I deposited the receipts in the bank vault, I stayed awhile to talk to Frank, the night guard. About sleeping bags, if you want to know. He's going on vacation next week, plans to go camping. Then I went outside for a few minutes. I should have known something was wrong when those two cops nearly ran me over, pulling up to the curb, but it never occurred to me they were coming up here. So I stayed out a bit longer before I went down to the garage. That's when I heard. Of course, I came right up."

Lyder stared at the wine cellar for a moment, lost in the memory of what he'd seen. Then he turned on me again. "That's where I was," he said. "Now let's get back to you. You must have known this was happening. How much did they pay you to close your eyes?"

"What do you mean?" I demanded, but before I got an answer, Powers interrupted.

"Have Mr. Lyder wait in the kitchen with one of the patrolmen, Thorson. Then come back here. I will indeed talk to this gentleman first."

Thorson came down the stairs and ushered Lyder through the dining room and behind the mirrored screen that led to the kitchen. When they were gone, Powers acted like Lyder had never accused me of anything. Like the man hadn't been there at all. He looked around for a second, then thumped his hand across a row of brass buttons mounted on the wall. The ceiling fixtures had been on before. Now they were joined by the pink shaded lamps on the tables, and the hidden bulbs that framed each of the giant picture windows in a pale white glow.

"Nice," Powers remarked to himself. Then in a louder voice: "Let's use that table on the end, where we'll be out of the way."

After crossing the room, he slid onto the leather seat in front of the window and pointed to a chair on the other side of the table for me. Thorson came back, pulled up a chair from another table, and took a notebook from his pocket.

"Lieutenant Thorson will be taking down your statement," Powers said. "Then we'll read it back to you, and you sign it for the record. Don't leave anything out, even if it seems unimportant."

Powers had placed us so he could see everything that happened in the dining room and I could see nothing, but he'd also given me the view. While the detectives got their papers in order,

I watched the lights of the moving cars make red and white stripes across the night. Down on the street, people were peddling dope and sex and anything else they could get a price for, and at this hour most of them were the kind of creeps you don't even like to let into your nightmares. From way up here, though, the city looked like a beautiful toy, wound up and mounted in a picture window for my enjoyment. The people who came to the Pinnacle Room were the kind who always told everybody how much they loved New York, but the way they loved it was usually from behind some kind of wall. How affectionate would they be, I wondered, if they had to do without their limousines, their doormen, their helicopter shuttles, and their restaurants with double-pane windows between them and reality? From here they could admire the show in safety, knowing their money had raised them above the dangers that were always jumping out and attacking the poor jerks down below. Except tonight someone had broken through the glass wall and penetrated the sanctuary to get John Lombardo. I started to talk.

Not that there was so much to tell. Things were vanishing from the Pinnacle Room, had been since they had opened in June. I had been hired as a night watchman, starting that night. I had heard a noise, gone to investigate, and found what was left of John Lombardo. Then I had called the police, and then I had found Janine, all dolled up for a private party that wasn't ever going to happen.

Powers interrupted from time to time, asking me details about what instructions Lombardo had given, how other people had shown me around, exactly how Janine had been lying when I found her. Mostly he let me tell the story my way. Thorson took down everything in shorthand. Behind me I could hear a lot of talking and movement, but I didn't even turn around to see who had arrived. Lombardo had been a big man on the local scene, a friend of the mayor's. Already a captain was running the investigation, and I knew without looking that they'd brought in

67

vestigation, and I knew without looking that they'd brought in extra crews of fingerprint dusters and the like. I didn't care. I just wanted to finish.

I was going back over some of the details, describing again the route I had taken when I first went to investigate the noise, when Officer Kelly, the lummox, came bursting in from the kitchen.

"Captain Powers," he called in an excited voice, "we were going through the freight elevator, and we found a man hiding behind the garbage bins. He started talking right away, except we can't figure out what he's trying to say. When we brought the stiff into the kitchen to take him down to the morgue..."

Before he could finish talking, the stowaway himself came rushing into the room. At first all I could make out was waving hands, crazy yells, and tight black clothes like a dancer's. Then I recognized him as the parsley chopper I had seen in the kitchen that morning.

He was the kind of person you remembered, once he caught your eye. A young man, slim like a kid, with dark, wavy hair and those long black eyelashes women always complain are wasted on a boy. But it was more than a good build and striking hair and eyes that made him so noticeable; he had a kind of polished beauty that made him look more like a work of art than a real person. He should have been hanging in a museum, dressed in velvet with a falcon or something on his wrist. I remember thinking when I first saw him that if this were one of those Walter Scott books my father had been so crazy about, he would have turned out to be a nobleman in disguise, hiding his identity among the common people until he could regain his rightful lands. But this was the real world and not the Waverly Novels, which nobody even reads anymore, and so the Young Pretender was chopping up vegetables and lucky to have the job. And then Janine had come in, and I had wondered if it was part of the Interdine system that everybody who worked there had to be gorgeous.

68

Not that the kid looked so attractive right now. What he looked was hysterical.

"No robbery! No robbery!" he was yelling, over and over. Powerd had already hinted at something like that, but what made this kid so sure of it? While he was yelling, he was also running across the room, and poor Kelly was no match for the slinky speed he used to weave around the tables. Before anyone could collar him, the kid was kneeling by Powers's chair, holding onto the captain's knees and blubbering like a baby. "I didn't do it," he was wailing now. "I love Johnny. I love him. I didn't do it."

Powers held up his hand for Kelly to stay away. Thorson had got up from his chair, but now he sat back, watching. They had no more idea than I did of what was going on, and probably less of who this person was, but it wasn't hard to grasp the outline of the situation. Someone had hauled the kid out of wherever he was hiding and right away accused him of murder. Faced with the corpse, he had panicked and bolted. The trick now was to find out if he was in shock because Lombardo was dead or because he had been collared so fast.

Powers let him cry for a while more; then he started talking. "You didn't kill him," he said gently. The kid looked up and shook his head from side to side. Tears were still streaming down his cheeks, but at least he wasn't screaming.

"And there wasn't any robbery." Again the kid nodded his agreement. He looked like he had forgotten how to talk.

All of a sudden Powers seized him by the shoulders and yanked him upright.

"Well, if there was no robbery," he bellowed, "and you didn't kill Lombardo, who did?"

The kid stumbled up to his feet and twirled around, still crouching.

"He did," he yelled wildly.

He was pointing at me.

Chapter 9

He stood there for a good long time, frozen in position like a statue of the avenging angel. I stared back, too dumfounded to argue. This was the second time in not so many minutes that somebody had accused me of killing Lombardo. What about the mysterious sneak thief they hired me to catch in the first place? What about Janine? Or this kid? He sure looked like a suspicious customer to me. Why was everybody jumping on poor old Quentin Jacoby?

It was a good question, but I knew better than to expect any answers. Powers shifted wearily in his chair.

"All right, Kelly," he said. "Is Sergeant Hong here yet? Good. Take our friend here back to the kitchen and tell Hong to talk to him some more." The two of them headed back the way they had come. Just before they turned behind the screen, Powers called out, "Find out what he means by 'no robbery,' okay?" Kelly nodded and disappeared.

"Now, Mr. Jacoby," Powers said to me, "let's take it from the top. Would you happen to know who that fellow was who just came in here?"

"Yes and no," I answered carefully. It had dawned on me that anybody alone in a locked building with a murder victim would have to be considered a suspect, even without crazy people popping out of the closet to point an accusing finger. But Powers was waiting for an answer, and playing dumb was no way to get out of there without a police escort.

"I don't know who he is or what he's doing here," I explained. "But I saw him once before. In the kitchen this morning. Yesterday morning, I mean."

"The kitchen?" Powers repeated.

"Yeah, the kitchen. But if you think I knew he was waiting in there all the time, you're wrong. And he's wrong, too," I added.

"Wrong?" echoed Powers. He looked like everybody's idea of a jolly old soul, but he had a way of repeating things that could make a person feel very guilty.

"Wrong," I said again, maybe a little too loud. "I did not kill John Lombardo."

"Then why would he say you did?"

"You ask him."

Powers nodded, like he had heard it all before but wasn't surprised to be hearing it again. Before we could get any further into the interesting subject of all the reasons why I hadn't killed John Lombardo, Officer Kelly stuck his head out from behind the screen that shielded the pantry from the dining room.

"Captain Powers," he called, "I think we've got something. We found a pile of hot stuff in the garbage, including a set of bloody clothes. And I think the girl is ready to talk."

Powers hesitated, then got up. "What kind of clothes?" he asked, then went on without waiting for an answer. "Keep her in the office. I'll question her myself. Thorson, you finish up here. I'll talk to you when you're done."

He turned to me. "You know your rights, Jacoby. Right now your only accuser is that young man in black who came flying through here a few minutes ago, but if you want to obtain counsel before making any further statements, that's your privilege."

I didn't answer, and he turned to leave the room. From behind, Powers had that faint start of a waddle that separates heavyset from fat. Somewhere off to my left I could hear Thorson droning through the formal statement of my right to remain silent, my right to obtain counsel, and a lot of other stuff I knew by heart. Technically it's the speech you make after an arrest, and hearing it now would have made me very nervous if I had been more awake. As it was, I took the words at face value and considered their message. I didn't have a lawyer, and I couldn't imagine finding one at that hour. As for remaining silent, I'd already told them all I had to say. I'd seen enough of the criminal justice system in action to know that innocence is not enough to clear a person of a crime, but I just couldn't connect myself with someone who was suspected of homicide.

The evidence crew was still messing around behind me, trying to act hopeful about finding something significant in a place several hundred people had passed through in the course of the day. I stared out the window at the statue of Civic Fame on top of the Municipal Building, trying to figure out why the parsley chopper had pointed at me. And what had Lyder been talking about, suggesting I was on the take? The whole scene was screwy, starting right from when Lombardo had gone out to hire a guard, and things were getting stranger by the minute. But now at least it was somebody else's job to straighten it out.

"No," I said to Powers's back. "No, I don't want a lawyer." I turned to the lieutenant, ready to finish up.

I hadn't paid much attention to Thorson until now, but I realized as soon as I looked at him that he had become a different character in the few seconds his boss had been out of the room. While Powers was around, he had been the right-hand man, dutiful, obedient, always watching and ready to take orders. Now he had taken control. Instead of sitting forward in his chair he was leaning back, and the notebook he had been clutching on his knee was spread open on the table. His whole figure seemed to have expanded, and his first words confirmed my sense that the change wasn't for the good. Some people are not meant to be large.

"Sit down, friend," he drawled, even though I was already sitting. "Make yourself comfortable. It's going to be a long night, and I think we're going to spend it together. You'd probably rather be with someone else, but that's the way it goes. I'm Lieutenant Plato Thorson, and I'll be questioning you from here on."

We'd already been introduced, but I guess he liked to say his name as much as he liked to hear his own voice. Maybe if I stalled for a while, Powers would come back and get this jerk off my back.

"Interesting name," I said, trying to sound like I thought it fitted his intelligence. If there's one thing a fool likes to talk about, it's himself. Sure enough, Thorson smiled and leaned back even farther in his chair.

"My mother named all her children for the authors of the Great Books," he announced with a smirk. "The one hundred greatest volumes ever written. Four boys. Plato, Voltaire, Dante, Herman. For Melville. *Moby Dick* is a Great Book."

I myself am named after Quentin Durward, my sisters are Rebecca and Rowena, and the baby brother got saddled with Rob Roy, so I was more than a little familiar with the kind of parental nuttiness that Thorson was talking about. I don't make a habit of gabbing about it to total strangers, though, and especially not on working time. The whole conversation was about the least professional display I'd ever seen, which was saying something. If Thorson's vanity was backed up by ambition, which I could bet it was, he'd better tighten up his methods before his next evaluation.

Some of that opinion must have showed on my face, because the lieutenant all of a sudden snapped back to business. I'd already been through all my vital statistics with Powers, and the description of everything that had happened since I showed up for work, but Thorson had me do it all over again anyway. Then he read my statement back to me and I signed it, which should have been the end of the official business, except that Thorson showed no signs of being ready to let me go. Still no sign of Powers coming back. I was in for it. Sure enough, Thorson flipped to a new page in his notebook and started asking some questions of his own.

"When and where did you first meet John Lombardo?" he asked.

"Right here. This morning. I told you already."

"And before that?"

"Before that never. Never even heard of him. Or this restaurant."

"Was he with anyone when you saw him? Did he seem nervous? Apprehensive?"

I thought back to the first time I had seen Lombardo, going over the dinner menu in the Coronation Room. He had hardly even spoken to me. How was I supposed to judge the mood of a man I didn't even know? I looked back on the scene one more time, searching my mind for that special gesture that would make sense now that Lombardo was dead. Nothing came up. The man had struck me as one of the most self-assured people I'd ever met, and even death had done nothing to change my opinion. I tried to explain to Thorson.

"When he found out the wine was stolen," I said, "it was more like he was resigned than upset. Like he had been expecting it. When he saw I was there, he seemed glad that I had showed up but not relieved. None of that 'thank-God-I'm-safe' business I used to see all the time when I was on the force.

"Of course, I was only here for one day," I added, "but it all looked pretty routine to me. Checking the menus. Greeting the customers. Making sure the right stuff got onto each plate. For sure I didn't see anything that looked like the man was about to be murdered. No arguments. No sideways conversations. No worried looks. Not that I was looking for anything like that, mind you. Personal protection was not part of my contract, you understand."

"Ah, yes," said Thorson, like we had finally gotten to what he really wanted to talk about. "Your contract. Let's see now," he said, rifling back through his notes with the kind of exaggerated gestures designed to show me he didn't really need to look at them at all.

"Here we are," he said at last. "You are an employee of the Global Security Agency, on Thames Street. You retired from the Transit Police three years ago." He looked up from his notes. "I assume you've been spending your nights since then guarding empty offices and making sure undesirables don't loiter in the lobbies of the better apartment buildings."

"You assume wrong."

"Oh? Excuse me. You retired from the Transit Police to seek greater adventure and excitement and have been spending your time as a private guard foiling international jewel thieves and protecting the persons of starlets and tycoons."

Like I should have expected, Thorson shared the stupid opinion that being a subway cop was somehow easier than other kinds of patrol and that anybody who worked on the Transit Police was automatically of a lower-grade intelligence. If he expected me to be impressed with his vocabulary, though, he was out of luck.

"I retired to take care of my sick wife."

"I'm sorry to hear that," Thorson said, not making any effort to sound like he meant it. "I'm glad she's better now."

"She died two years ago."

For a second he lost his swagger and almost seemed to feel a stab of human sympathy. Then the second passed. "And how long have you been working as a security guard?" he asked.

"One day," I answered. "This was my first job."

"Really," he said, eyebrows raised. "Very interesting. And what made you choose suddenly to get into this line of work?"

I could see he was fixing me for a link with someone on the staff, a setup to get at the boss. Might as well squash that one before it even started to move.

"I didn't choose," I told him. "I got roped into the job by Gloria Gold, the president of Global Security." Then I decided that if Thorson wanted to put on the dog, I could show off a little, too. "It's a very select agency," I added, "and the clients expect the personnel to be carefully matched to their needs. I was the only person who fit this particular job profile."

He was unimpressed. "Any idea why your friend was so eager to bring you out of retirement for this special assignment?" he asked. "Any idea why this assignment was so special?"

"No."

Thorson waited for me to go on, but I didn't have anything else to say.

"Pardon me for prying," he said nastily, "but I find it a little odd that after three years of retirement you suddenly decide to take a job that is not exactly around the corner from your home. And then, on your very first night, when you believe you are the only person on the premises, you suddenly have a hunch to leave your dinner and check around, at which point you find a very recently murdered man."

I'd already told him once why I took the job and a lot more times how it was a suspicious noise, not just a sudden hunch, that had led me to Lombardo, but I could tell the facts weren't going to stop the lieutenant from reaching his own conclusions. The bored detective wasting his time questioning a minor witness had been replaced by the hard-driving investigator, determined to sweat a confession out of his suspect. I wondered if he had already used the same techniques on Janine. It was all so phony, like a bad movie, I could have laughed. Except that I was the suspect, and I had seen enough people like Thorson to know that he wouldn't care how funny things looked if he really made up his mind to get me. So I didn't laugh, and I didn't make the mistake of getting angry. Or at least I didn't make the mistake of showing it. Instead, I played dumb.

"Listen, Lieutenant Thorson," I said, "I don't exactly like finding corpses. It's not the first time I've seen a stiff, but it wasn't what I was looking for when I took this job. You want to know about the guard service, you ask Mrs. Gold, my boss. You want to know about any problems Lombardo was maybe having with people at the restaurant, you ask Mr. Lyder. I've only been here one night, and I've already told you everything that happened since I came in. Three times. If you have any questions about my statement, let me know. Otherwise I don't have anything to add."

At this point Powers finally came back. "You done yet, Thorson?" he asked. "I want you to take notes while I talk to Mr. Lyder."

While Powers was gone, Thorson had been the big man, all ready to close the case with a brilliant collar of the first person he talked to. Now he shrank back to size so fast I wouldn't have been surprised if he disappeared.

"Be right there, sir," he answered. Then he turned to me, with one last blast of hot air.

"Don't get any bright ideas about leaving town," he said, "because we'll want you again for questioning. For now, though, you can go home."

"No, I can't."

He looked at me sourly while he put the cap back on his pen. "What do you mean? I'm through with you. Go away."

"I still work here, remember? I don't punch out until seven A.M."

"That's really beautiful." He laughed. "The last real worker in America. Not even murder can keep him from his time clock. Okay, Jacoby. Stay and guard the tomatoes while we guard you."

We stood up together, and he waved me out before him and stood in the hall to make sure I went straight to the kitchen. I half expected him to have me tailed. Now it wasn't just two people who were accusing me of having murdered John Lombardo. It was three.

Chapter 10

While I was off in the dining room wasting my time with Plato Thorson, the kitchen had been turned into headquarters for all the different kinds of business that you get into after a murder. The police photographer was there, talking to the body snatchers who had come to take Lombardo to the morgue. A girl from the lab was unpacking her kit, getting ready to take prints and gather samples of anything that looked like it might prove useful later on. A plainclothes I hadn't seen before was writing up a report at the big table where I had started to eat dinner about three centuries ago. That would be Sergeant Hong, the extra man Thorson had been talking about. Kelly and Carter had vanished, probably back to their squad car, but another pair of officers had arrived to take their place. They were carefully going through the trash, packing it up to take back to headquarters where they would have the fun job of combing through it at their leisure.

And then there were the suspects. Janine DuPage was dressed now, back in the white suit she'd been wearing when I first saw her. She looked a lot the worse for wear, but at least she wasn't yelling anymore. She was sitting on a wooden chair pushed up against the wall, and you wouldn't even have known she was there except for the sniffly way she blew her nose every few minutes. The kid in black was sitting across the table from Sergeant Hong, but he had turned his chair around to face the stretcher where they had laid out John Lombardo. It didn't look like he had much to say anymore either.

I had insisted on staying partly out of curiosity but mostly to annoy Thorson. Now that I was there, I didn't know what to do with myself. The place was certainly full enough of law enforcers without my little bit of help. Hong looked up from his report when I headed for the coffeepot, but he didn't say anything, so I poured a cup of brew and took a chair, carefully away from either Janine or the handsome parsley chopper. I didn't want anybody to think I was conspiring with the other suspects.

I kept waiting for them to find the killer holed up in a closet somewhere, clutching a bag of loot, but the hours passed, and nobody turned up. All exits from the building had been sealed as soon as I called down to the front desk. Nobody had gone out through the garage. Nobody had taken the elevators in the lobby. The cleaning crew, which consisted of six oversize Polish ladies in stretch pants, had been mopping the stairwell on the sixty-fifth floor, and they all agreed that nobody had come down that way. I was in the kitchen when they made their statements, which took a while because they insisted on doing it in both English and Polish. I myself was ready to swear that the freight elevator hadn't budged, which meant the kid had been hiding there since at least before the restaurant closed. Nobody asked me, though, and after they finished with the garbage, the two uniforms searched the elevator, including the overhead cables to make sure nobody was hiding on top of the car. No helicopters had taken off from the ground to pick up a killer on the roof. Nobody was found crouching under any of the desks on the floors above or below. The guy at the desk in the lobby had been watching his monitors all night, and nobody could have come down from the restaurant to any of the residential floors without his knowing. He had confirmed Lyder's story, and so had Kelly, the patrolman who had nearly run him over. I thought some more about the scene in the wine cellar and finally realized why Powers hadn't bought the idea of an interrupted robbery. So there we were, in a giant skyscraper in one of the most densely populated cities in the world, faced with a murder in which only three people had any way of getting to the victim, and none of them had had a chance of escape. Janine DuPage. The kid in black. And me.

Right away I eliminated myself, which put me one-third ahead of the detectives. Until they got something more in the way of evidence, there was no way of knowing which of the other two had done it. It wasn't clear to me how either could have managed, given the layout of the joint, but one of them must have because there just wasn't anybody else.

Working in the order by which I had made their acquaintance, I first considered the case against Janine DuPage. As far as I was concerned, it made sense to put her on top of the list of suspects. She had known for sure that Lombardo would be staying at the Pinnacle after closing time, had what she thought was a guarantee that they would be alone, and could certainly count on sneaking up on him unawares. Most stiffs get murdered by their closest relatives or dearest friends, and there was no reason for Lombardo to be an exception.

There was one big problem with that explanation, though. If she and Lombardo had had some kind of lovers' quarrel, bad enough for Janine to turn on him while he was prying open a bottle of champagne, I doubted very much that she would have then beat it back to his office and lounged around in her underwear, waiting for the cops to come so she could show off her false hysterics. In stories that happens all the time, with the impulse killer suddenly going cold and rational, covering his tracks and figuring out alibis to crimes he hadn't even thought of committing until two minutes ago. But in real life people who get angry enough to kill are not in any shape for long-range planning. Either they stand there screaming until somebody notices and locks them up, or else they drop everything in a bloody mess on the floor and try to make like ostriches, hiding in some stupid, obvious place like behind the fire escape or under the bed.

On the other hand, maybe she hadn't been acting on impulse at all. She had to have known about the burglaries, and maybe—for whatever reason—Janine had seen them as her golden opportunity to get rid of the boss. Given another few hours, she could easily have made it seem a lot more convincing that Johnny boy had been killed while a robbery was in progress. Then all she would have had to do was wait around the empty restaurant until morning and slip out of the building while the Interdine office staff was arriving for work. It must have been a big surprise when I popped out of the woodwork, sending her scurrying with her alibi only half-worked-out.

Before I sent Janine up for life, though, I also had to consider my other suspect. What was his real tie to John Lombardo? Was he just some lonely kid working in the kitchen, cutting up vegetables and nursing his fantasies about the boss until the whole thing boiled over into murder? Or had Lombardo really been playing both sides of the street, carrying on with Janine and this kid, too? From all I'd heard about Lombardo, he had been one of those types who didn't care what they did as long as they did it with style, and it wouldn't have surprised me much to find out that he had liked men and women both. Though after seeing these two, I had the feeling that what Lombardo had gone for was anything exotic and beautiful, and the question of male or female had been secondary. If the kid was telling the truth about his relationship with Lombardo, then maybe he had murdered him out of jealousy when he had found his lover together with Janine, and pointing the finger at me had simply been an attempt to distract attention from himself. But if he had killed Lombardo, how had he managed to get back into the freight elevator, with the garbage and the laundry piled up against the door? That was the part I couldn't figure, no matter how hard I tried.

I had plenty of time to puzzle this out, sitting there in the kitchen while Powers and his crews searched for the evidence that would allow them to make an easy arrest. I guess they didn't find it, though, because around two o'clock Thorson came through and told Janine she could go home. He gave me his special I-know-you're-guilty sneer, but I just sat tight and looked right through him, and he didn't make any special effort to get me to leave. Then Sergeant Hong started in again on the kid. I held my breath and did my best to act invisible, but it didn't particularly matter, because there wasn't much to learn. His name was Angel Ruiz. He was nineteen years old, had lived in Manhattan all his life, had worked at the Pinnacle since it opened in June. Beyond that the main thing he had to say was that he loved John Lombardo, hated Janine DuPage, didn't trust me, and was ready to take the law into his own hands if the police didn't arrest either her or me right away. On that last point he was particularly loud. At least he'd broadened the range of his accusations.

As for more helpful details, there weren't many. According to Ruiz, he and Lombardo had been lovers for over a year, which might or might not be true. As far as I could make out, the kid was claiming that he had hidden in the elevator to spy on Lombardo, for reasons he refused to reveal. He also refused to explain what he knew about the robberies, except to keep on insisting that there hadn't been any that night. Hong worked on him for quite a long time while I pretended to be part of the wallpaper, but the kid never changed his story or added to it in any way.

Gradually the room cleared. At 3:00 A.M. Powers left, taking Angel Ruiz with him to see if he would be any more talkative down at the station house. At 3:30 there was a diversion when the cleaning women came back and got very insulted because the officer at the door wouldn't let them scrub away the evidence. Twenty minutes later the lab called to report that the bloody apron Kelly had found belonged to a cook who had had the bright idea of using his hand to jam some potatoes through the food processor. By 5 in the morning the photographers, the lab crews and all their ghouls were gone. The officer stationed in the kitchen had gone to the pantry to check something with Hong, and for thirty whole seconds I was alone. I was about to get up for yet another cup of coffee when new company arrived.

My first impression was that the guy had wandered in by mistake. Here it was, the middle of the night in the middle of New York in the middle of August, and suddenly this person appears looking like he's ready for a weekend in the country, complete with plaid flannel shirt and leather patches on his corduroy jacket. To complete the outfit he had neat gray hair that kept a part, a pink, well-shaved complexion, a straight, little nose that was just barely big enough to keep his tortoise-shell glasses from slipping down to his chin, and the kind of lean, well-kept body that had stopped changing at age eighteen and would just gradually dry up until he withered away at eighty, still wearing the duds he had bought for college. All I could figure was he had to be from out of town.

His first words showed I was right.

"I came up from Valley Forge as soon as I got the call," he announced. "Where are they?"

I was already standing, which took care of that formality. Leaving only the stickier one of still being a guard. It didn't matter much at that point, but I still felt that a job is a job and worth doing right if you're going to bother at all.

"I'm afraid I have to ask your name and business," I said.

"What?" he asked impatiently. Then he smiled, the way you would at a stupid puppy, and clapped my shoulder. "Sorry, fellow," he said. "Blount Harwell. President of Interdine. Own this restaurant. Own the whole building. Glad you're doing your job. Now," he continued confidently, "where are they?"

The man talked like a telegraph machine, but I got the message. I sent him up to the office, where Hong was still talking to Lyder.

Unless they'd moved it since I was in school, Valley Forge

was that place in Pennsylvania where George Washington froze his bunions during the Revolutionary War. It must have taken Harwell two, maybe three hours to do the drive from there to Manhattan. Either he got up at five every morning to make it into the office, or else he saw his wife on alternate weekends, with special appointments for lunch when the dog show was in town. I would have laid any kind of money you like that a man like that had a wife who raised dogs.

I had gotten only about three feet closer to the coffee machine when the door from the dining room swung open and Lyder stormed in, followed by Sergeant Hong.

"There is no way on earth I will put up with that," he shouted, while Hong trailed behind. "There is no way that Mr. Lombardo would have put up with that if he were alive. He built this restaurant out of his own personal vision of excellence, and the last thing he would have wanted was for his death to drive us out of business. This is not the post office or the schools, where you close down for a day of mourning. This is a fickle business, Mr. Kong, and if we're not open for lunch at twelve o'clock tomorrow, we'll lose thousands of dollars in immediate revenue, plus God only knows how much in the blow to our reputation. It's going to be bad enough when everyone finds out that Mr. Lombardo is gone and they start talking about how the kitchen is already going downhill. If we close, it will be a total disaster."

"It's Hong, Mr. Lyder. Sergeant Maxwell Hong, Detective second grade. And I'm not asking you to close for a day of mourning. I'm just telling you that the homicide unit is going to need time to go over all the evidence, and until we're through, we ask you not to disturb the scene of the crime."

"Right," agreed Lyder with heavy sarcasm. "Great. Wonderful. I open the restaurant, but with no liquor service. I suppose you want the reservation desk, too, since that was the last place Mr. Lombardo was seen alive. And then again he usually spent a lot of time in the kitchen, so perhaps you'd like to rope that off, too. But you're not asking me to close down or anything. Oh, no." He glared at the sergeant, clenching and unclenching his fists. Hong was still standing right beside him, but Lyder raised his voice again.

"Well, I won't put up with it," he shouted. "You've been here all night, with my fullest possible cooperation, but that is it! By eight o'clock tomorrow morning I want every one of your people out of my restaurant."

"That's eight o'clock this morning, Bobby. And technically, you know, it's my restaurant, not yours."

I'd been watching Lyder too closely to notice when Blount Harwell came back, just like Lyder had been too busy yelling at Hong to notice me. Now the whole scene seemed to deflate, like an overblown dream when you finally realize with relief that a dream is all it is. Lyder still looked dazed and stiff, like he hadn't quite woken up, but I could see Hong relaxing. I fought down the urge to stretch.

"Could I talk to you for a moment?" Hong said to Harwell, clearly relieved at not having to deal with Lyder anymore.

"Certainly. The dining room?" Harwell looked at me, then gave a little nod to Lyder. "Won't be long, Bob. Wait for me. Terrible business. Afraid it means a lot of work for us."

Lyder nodded dumbly and watched them leave the room. He looked like he wanted to smash his fist into the first thing he saw. Unfortunately, that was me. Fortunately, civilized meanness won out over brute force.

"What are you doing here?" he demanded.

"I'm on duty until seven," I answered. "You didn't say anything about going, so I thought I better stay."

"You thought wrong," he snarled. "Get out of here. And don't bother coming in tonight either. Or coming to me for a reference. You're a great guard, can't even keep a man from getting killed. Get out of here before I show you what I really think of you."

I was a couple of inches taller than Lyder and just as solid across the chest and shoulders, and for all his being younger, I could have taken him on if it ever came to that. But if it ever came to that, it certainly wouldn't be my doing. I picked up my jacket and left. Lyder hadn't signed my time slip, but Gloria would just have to deal with that however she wanted. I was going home.

Chapter 11

Six o'clock on a Tuesday morning, there wasn't a lot of walk-through traffic at the Interdine Tower. A man and a woman were stationed by the Washington Street entrance next to a pile of luggage, waiting for their limousine to the airport. A jogger in running shoes streaked through, out for sunrise exercise. A tired-looking man in a company uniform was standing by the central desk, glancing over his consoles while he talked quietly to a patrolman I had already seen upstairs. The sag end of a shift that had started out with murder. I went over to thank him for getting help up to me so fast, but he gave me the plague treatment. Gratitude from suspects is like candy from strangers, much too dangerous to accept.

I followed the jogger out onto Albany Street and ran right into a more familiar figure. It was Pierre, the wineman from the Pinnacle Room. Barely daylight, and he was already dressed for work. Except he was about four hours early, by my best guess, and he needed a shave. As soon as he recognized me, he grabbed my arm.

"Is it true?" he demanded anxiously. "I run right over as soon as I hear the radio, but I can't believe such a thing."

"John Lombardo's dead if that's what you mean."

"But this is so terrible. How can it be? The poor man. And in his special room!"

He was still clinging to my arm, like he was hoping I would tell him a different story. Then he looked over toward the building and straightened up a bit.

"I must help," he said. "There will be so much..." Before he even finished the sentence, he had forgotten all about me and was off to contribute whatever he could to salvage the glory of the Pinnacle Room. Seeing him made me feel even more tired and seedy than I had felt before, and more disgusted with myself. Pierre at least knew what his job was and how to do it. I should have stayed where I belonged, safe in retirement, where nobody would make the mistake of thinking he could count on me for protection. Before I crawled back into my hole, though, there was one more thing I had to do. Gloria was going to know soon enough about how I had messed up her new account, and I'd rather tell her myself than have it waiting for her at the office.

Besides, it was on my way. Since her divorce Gloria lived in one of those boxy apartment buildings off Washington Square. I walked over to Eighth Avenue and rode the local up four stops to West Fourth Street, thinking about how I would break the news.

The doorman wasn't too happy about letting in visitors at six-thirty in the morning, especially ones who were wearing yesterday's shirt and a day-old beard to match. To put it bluntly, he told me to get lost, and I had to convince him I worked for Global Security before he'd even consent to buzz Gloria's apartment. I started to tell him how good these clothes had looked twenty-four hours ago, but I was cut off by some barks from Gloria's end of the intercom. Finally the machine settled down and I could hear her voice, still fuzzy from the early morning, assuring him it was all right to let me up.

When I got up to her apartment, Gloria was already standing by the front door. "Morning, Quentin," she said wearily. "Come in. Have some coffee. Don't bother telling me about John Lombardo. I know already, and I can't stand to hear it twice." From the way she said it, I couldn't tell if the hard part was Lombardo's dying or her losing the Interdine contract. I decided not to ask.

I followed her back into the apartment, watching the orange terry cloth robe move against her body. She had just come out of the shower, and her bare feet left little wet spots on the carpeting.

"What did they say on the radio?" I asked.

"Radio? I got my news direct from headquarters. The First Precinct. They want to see me in a couple of hours, question me about what Lombardo said when he came in to hire a guard. Hell of a way to wake up in the morning."

It was becoming clear to me that Gloria was not one of those people who start the day with a song. I kept quiet while she padded around the kitchen, making coffee, putting up toast, setting out plates on a little round table in the corner. "Eggs?" she asked briefly, and looked relieved when I said no. The coffee perked her up, though, and she started giving me questioning looks over the rim of her mug. By the second cup she couldn't stand it anymore.

"If you don't tell me what happened, Quentin Jacoby, I'm going to explode."

"I thought you knew all about it," I answered, smiling for the first time since I'd found John Lombardo. It is impossible to feel grim while eating breakfast with a woman in an orange bathrobe.

"I know that John Lombardo was alive and well in my office Sunday morning, and now he's dead. I also know Robert Lyder canceled our contract because he called my night operator a half hour ago to make sure the message got through. But I don't have the slightest idea of what really happened, and if you don't tell me soon, they're going to have another murder on their hands."

I winced at her language. To Gloria it was just a distant horror, something that happened someplace else, to other people. But

90

I had found the body, and heard Janine's screams, and spent too much of the night with Powers and Thorson to talk lightly about killing. Gloria took one look at my face and apologized.

"I'm sorry," she said. "You've had a terrible night, and here I come on yakking like an idiot. You don't have to tell me anything at all."

Then, of course, I wanted to tell her everything. About Lombardo and Janine and finding Angel Ruiz in the elevator. About the cleaning women and how Harwell showed up and Lyder started attacking me just when I thought the nightmare was finally over. Then I started at the beginning again and told her the important things, stuff the police weren't interested in. Like the way Lombardo's blood had congealed when it hit the cold marble floor and how Janine had laid herself out like an extra-juicy morsel on some kind of sexual buffet. About how I wasn't used to being up so late, and just the fact of being tired had made it so hard to put up with Thorson that I'd been afraid I would try to hurt him.

Finally I even told her what I had just realized myself: that I had come to see her because what I wanted most right then was to be with a woman.

After that we just stared at each other for what seemed like a long time. "What am I supposed to do now?" Gloria asked at last. "Slap your face?"

"Not unless you want to," I answered, coming around to her side of the table. Then we were both standing up, and I was fumbling with the belt of her robe until finally Gloria had to help me get it off.

"You know how it is," she whispered. "I never could resist that cleft chin." The next minute we were over on the living room couch, as hot and hurried as a couple of teen-agers. Except it was much better than that because both of us knew exactly what we were doing.

Afterward Gloria was the first to say anything. "It seems a little late to be asking," she said, "but would you like to go to bed?"

The thought of cool sheets and a soft pillow was the nicest thing I could imagine. "Come with me," I urged, and before she could answer, I scooped her up and carried her down the hall. Gloria laughed when I stumbled on the pile of clothes by the door, but she didn't offer any arguments, and she was wonderfully warm and soft when I had her next to me between the sheets. And then I fell asleep.

I opened my eyes around noon and thought I was up, but the next time I looked at the clock it was two-thirty and the phone was ringing. At first I thought it was two-thirty in the morning and somebody must have died. Possibly me. Especially if heaven was a strange bed with yellow flowered sheets. Then I remembered everything. The Pinnacle Room. John Lombardo. The police. Gloria. Where was Gloria? Groaning, I reached for the receiver and mumbled something that was as close to hello as I could manage.

"You sound terrible. I just got back to the office and thought I'd better check to see if you were ever getting up."

At least that answered the question of where Gloria was. While I'd been sleeping, she must have gotten dressed and gone to work. It embarrassed me to think of her puttering around with me snoring away in her bed. I glanced around to see if I could find my clothes.

"Quentin? You still there?"

"Yeah, right," I answered. "I'm still here. And I guess I still sound terrible." I was more than a little embarrassed to talk with her now, but it wasn't Gloria's fault I was already regretting our little after-breakfast interlude. I tried to adjust my tone. "How did it go with the police?"

"All right. I talked to your Lieutenant Thorson—seems to be a whiz at dictation. All they wanted was a statement about how Lombardo had come to hire a guard and what were the terms of the contract. So much for my notion that they might want a

92

professional opinion on security problems at the Interdine Tower. Expert witness, isn't that what it's called?"

"Only at a trial."

"Oh. Well, I guess they have their own experts. Here's the reason I called," she said abruptly. "The police are looking all over the place for you. Powers wants you to come in for further questioning, and I'm afraid they were beginning to think you'd left town. I didn't want to give them my number, so I just said you were visiting a friend and I would make sure you got there. By four o'clock."

"Is that the only reason you called?"

Gloria waited for a good long while before she answered. "Stop by the office when you get out of the police station," she said at last. "We have to talk."

"Sure," I said. "But I have to tell you . . ."

"Later," she said quickly. "We'll talk later. Right now you have to shake a leg if you're going to make it to the station by four. Which I personally guaranteed you would." Now that she was back to being the lady executive, all the hesitation was gone from her voice.

"Yes, ma'am," I answered. "On the double." I had a sudden image of Gloria, just the way she had looked this morning, except now the orange bathrobe had epaulets. I hung up and started to look in earnest for my clothes.

By the time I found them, took a shower, and scraped my face with the ridiculous pink thing that Gloria seemed to use instead of a razor, it was three-thirty. Another minute or two wouldn't matter, though. Before I left, I went back and made the bed. Always clean up your private life before you talk to the police.

Chapter 12

Powers's squad room was in an old station house over by City Hall. It took me twelve minutes to walk over to the Lafayette Street station of the Lexington Avenue line, and another eight, turnstile to turnstile, before I was heading out the exit of the Brooklyn Bridge station. Say what you will about the graffiti and the crime, the New York City subway system is a miracle for getting around fast. I'd be there in plenty of time to honor Gloria's promise.

The station house was the typical pile of brick and sandstone, built when Theodore Roosevelt was commissioner of police and never touched since. Everything that wasn't painted beige was either gray or dark green, and all of it was grimy with a kind of dirt that had nothing to do with dustpans and mops and everything to do with time. Map boards, time blocks, duty rosters, and wanted posters were stuck all over the walls, each at the eye level of whoever had happened to do the hanging. Once they got up, they stayed there until the tape turned to brittle orange cellophane and the nails fell out of the walls. If what fell down was out of date, it maybe got thrown away. If it was something they still used, it got hung up again somewhere else, usually someplace conveniently close to the supply closet where they kept the hammer. I'd never been in this particular precinct, but the whole place was so familiar I practically punched in when I passed the time clock. Which was just where I knew it would be.

Powers's office I had to ask for. It was upstairs, a private room chopped out of the main office area when they had modernized the building about twenty years ago. *Modern* meant industrial carpeting over the old wooden floors, draperies that only reached halfway up the twelve-foot windows, lots of frosted glass partitions put in any which way, and even a plywood wall jammed into what had once been an open archway, to make a niche for file cabinets. It was dark and dreary, and it stank of stale coffee, but most of the people inside probably liked it a good deal better than they liked their own living rooms. Certainly they felt more comfortable in it. This was one place where nobody worried about getting ashes on the rug.

Powers's door had his name on it, which helped, but I still stopped at the sergeant's desk out front. Any other business in the world, they would have an intercom where you could buzz the boss. But this was the police station, office of the taxpayer-supported protectors of the peace, so the sergeant had to leave his work, walk over to Powers's office, and stick his head in to tell him I was there. Before he got up, he carefully put the stapler on top of his papers, so they wouldn't get blown around by the electric fan sitting on top of the file cabinet. Any other business would have air conditioning by now.

"Oh, yeah, Jacoby," Powers repeated, like he hadn't ordered me to show up. "Tell him to come in."

The inside of the captain's office was just as dingy as the outside, except that the partitioning had given him half a window with a view of the fire escape on the other side of the airshaft. On the metal balcony was a row of geraniums in pots and a wooden pigeon coop, currently empty. It was a nice view as long as you didn't worry about the neighbors getting out in a fire.

Powers was behind his desk, and my old buddy Thorson was

also on hand. They were wearing the same clothes I saw them in last night, and they both looked tired and impatient. Thorson was sitting in the single extra armchair the office had. That left me with a steno model on wheels, shoved over in the corner by a typing table. Steno chairs are not made for big men, and I skidded a few feet toward the file cabinets when I tried to sit down.

"Get another chair from outside," Powers ordered. We both waited in silence until Thorson got back with another oak oldie like the one he had just vacated. He plunked it down in the middle of the room, and I took a seat.

I had been a police officer for thirty years, and I had always prided myself on not taking advantage of the position to intimidate people during routine interrogation. What I had never figured, though, was that you don't have to do anything to be intimidating. Here I was, innocent as air, and my heart was racing and my palms were sweating like I had just pulled off the crime of the century. For the first time I understood those stories I'd always heard, about how people confessed to things they weren't even suspected of doing, just because they couldn't stand the strain of waiting around. And that was before Powers started talking. After, it got much worse.

In point of fact, it was Thorson who started.

"As you know, Mr. Jacoby," he began, "our investigation of the murder of John Lombardo has turned up a number of suspects. Without ruling out the possibility of outside perpetrators, we have naturally focused our attention on those persons who were on the premises at the time of Mr. Lombardo's death: to wit, Miss DuPage, Mr. Ruiz, and yourself. Although I admit that your own connection with the homicide appears tenuous, certain anomalies in your situation force us to give the circumstances our closest consideration."

I turned to Powers. "What's he talking about?" I asked.

"What Lieutenant Thorson is saying, Jacoby, is that we want

to know what you were doing up at the Pinnacle last night. Did anyone pay you to take the job, and what else went along with the pay? Who introduced you to John Lombardo, and how long have you known him?"

"But I told you all this last night," I protested.

"That's right," Thorson agreed. "And now we want you to tell us all over again, including any parts you might have left out, accidentally or on purpose. Like if someone set you up for that job, and what you got for playing deaf and dumb until after midnight, and where you were this morning. Also what your connection really is with Angel Ruiz. And how much you know about the penalties for conspiracy to commit murder. Little things we can't seem to find in your original testimony."

By then I was out of my chair and leaning over Thorson, one hand on the wall and the other ready to break his nose if he didn't sit still and listen. I, of course, was steely calm, but somebody who sounded a lot like me seemed to be yelling.

"Listen, you creep," the other voice said, "I was in uniform when you couldn't wipe your nose without your mother's help. You've got a hell of a nerve, insulting a fellow officer like this. You've seen my record. Thirty years on patrol. Two commendations for bravery. Not so much as a citation for coming in late. Is that the record of a cop who's conspiring to commit murder?"

Even to me it sounded like a pretty lame defense. I stopped and made a real effort to lower my voice. Thorson sat there, looking up at me like he was just waiting for the right time to spring up and pin me against the wall. I realized that it didn't matter what I said because he wasn't even listening. I kept going anyway, but slower now, more rational.

"If you want to work out a conspiracy case, go right ahead, but don't try to pin it on my hide. I came to work at the Pinnacle Room as a personal favor to the director of Global Security, and I'm happy to say that I've already been fired from a job I didn't want in the first place. As for bribes and payoffs, I'll be lucky if

97

I get my salary for last night. And frankly I don't think I deserve it. Thanks to the union we both belong to, my pension is enough to meet my needs. It may not stretch to cover the tab in joints like the Pinnacle Room, but as it happens, fancy French cuisine is not my style." Thorson stuck his pointy nose a little higher in the air, like he had his own opinions about my level of style, and I got angry again.

"And neither do I like dumb detectives," I roared, "brow-beating people without the faintest shred of evidence! If you think I'm going to put up with you and your cheap insinuations, you can start thinking again. If your brain can take the strain."

Just being around Thorson made me sink to his level. Disgusted, I sat back in my chair. "Get him out of here," I told Powers. "Get him out of here before I throw up."

All this time the captain hadn't said a word. He hadn't stopped Thorson when he launched into his insults. He hadn't budged when it looked like I was going to make hamburger out of his lieutenant's head. Now he just nodded in a way that could mean anything at all.

"That's fine, Thorson," he said. "I'll take over from here." Thorson didn't want to leave, but Powers pointed firmly at the door. "Close it behind you," he said. Reluctantly, Thorson got up and left.

Then I saw it. The classic ploy: good cop and bad cop working as a team. Thorson comes on as a sadistic bully, and I spill it all to Powers, giddy with relief at talking to a human being. But I could play that game myself, and I had the advantage of being all warmed up. While Powers was still leaning back in his chair, getting ready to be my buddy, I went ahead and stole his lines.

"The way I look at it," I began, "you and I are on the same side here. Last night John Lombardo got killed. I met the man only a few hours before, and you never met him at all, but we both want to find out who did it, and for the same reasons.

Because neither of us likes seeing people get away with murder and because we both get paid for making sure they don't."

I stood up, to have more room to expand on my theories of the holy brotherhood of cops. "You're a detective," I said. Powers nodded in agreement. "The citizens of the city of New York hire you to capture people who threaten them or otherwise violate the peace. It's your job to keep the city safe, and you won't be doing very well if a guy like John Lombardo can't even hang around his own restaurant without getting skewered like a piece of shish kebab. I'm a security guard. The Interdine Corporation hired me to protect its premises and its property, and I can't feel very happy about my record when the boss gets killed my first night on the job. Both of us, see, we're just doing our jobs.

"And between you and me," I continued, "there is maybe a little self-interest here as well. John Lombardo was a friend of a lot of important people. A buddy of the mayor's. If you solve this case fast, you'll probably get promoted. Maybe make inspector. If I solve it, I'll get you guys off my neck and maybe get back some of the business I lost for Global Security.

"So there we are, Captain Powers. Competitors, but still on the same side. You have the edge, of course. You have the manpower, the labs, and the official sanction of everybody down the line. You can follow me around the city, get a warrant to tear up my house, even slap me in jail if you really want to. I have to cooperate fully with your investigation because that's the law, and you don't have to cooperate with me at all. I know perfectly well that a former transit patrolman is less than dirt as far as you're concerned, and anybody working for a private agency just gets in your way. But if you want to cooperate, I'll give you all the help I can. And if you want to keep bugging me with that creep Thorson, I guarantee I will waste more of your time than you can afford to imagine."

I hadn't meant to end with a threat, being as how I had started with the idea of changing myself from suspect to policeman's pal, but it didn't seem to matter. As usual I had gotten things wrong. Powers had been willing to let Thorson try a little bullying, but he himself had no intention of trying to charm a confession out of me. Or letting me charm any concessions out of him. Buddying up to the public was definitely not his style. He heard me out, patient and watchful, and then he moved ahead to his own concerns.

"Mr. Harwell wants you back on duty at the Pinnacle Room," he said. "I am not legally empowered to stop him or to bar you from the premises, so unless you have any objections, you're back on the job. Don't look for any big welcomes, though. I had three detectives working all day, questioning the staff of the restaurant. Those people idolized Lombardo. General opinion of you, on the other hand, is not very high."

"Mr. Harwell wants me back?" I asked. "Why?"

Powers shrugged. "You tell me," he answered. "I advised him against it, but he says he wants to be sure there's somebody there at all times. Says he was impressed with the way you were doing your job last night when he arrived. Beyond that you'll have to ask him yourself."

The red light on Powers's telephone started flashing, and he picked up the receiver. He listened for a while, making notes on a pad, while I counted the flowerpots on the fire escape across the way. There were six. Four of them had red flowers. Two had pink. I liked the red better. Finally Powers told his caller he would be there in twenty minutes, wherever there might be. Then he hung up and turned back to me.

"I've been checking up on you, Jacoby," he said grimly. "I talked to O'Banion, and he told me how you stuck with those three juveniles who were jumping fares all over the city and finally tied them in with that series of holdups on the IRT. I talked to Abe Minelli about that tricky murder case in Westchester you helped him with last spring. I talked to a lot of other people, too, and everyone said you used to be an honest, solid enforcement agent." For someone who seemed to be singing my praises, he made it sound like a dirge. Then he leaned forward and planted his arms on his desk.

"The crime rate in the First Precinct is rising one hundred percent every six months," he said, "and I have exactly half as many men as I had ten years ago. An Austrian tour guide was raped and strangled last night in the garden of St. Paul's Chapel. Two fourteen-year-olds shot each other after holding up a bank on Twelfth Street. No one knows where they left the money. A convention of Spiderman freaks is coming to town, and they've already called the papers to announce that there will be surprise assaults on the city's six tallest buildings, half of which are in my precinct."

He waited for it all to sink in, then leaned back heavily in his chair.

"Last night a man got murdered on the sixty-eighth floor of the Interdine Building," he said, "in an assault that may or may not be related to a previous string of sophisticated larcenies. I could assign fifteen detectives to the Lombardo case and have it sewn up by the end of the month. But I don't have fifteen detectives for every stiff that shows up, not even a friend of the mayor's, and I don't feel like waiting around until the end of the month. I want this case closed now. You hear anything, see anything, smell anything that looks significant while you're up there at the Pinnacle Room, I expect you to let me know about it right away.

"But understand this: there's a very short list of people who could have killed that man last night, and you are on it. I don't have any hard evidence against you and your statement checks with Mrs. Gold's, but your presence on the murder scene is just too damn sudden and convenient for my taste. I don't know of

101

any good reason why you should be involved, but I've been working here too long to think that matters. So until I find out for sure who killed Lombardo, I'm going to keep checking you out. While you're up there at Interdine, just remember that we've got our eye on you all the time. Got that, Jacoby? All the time."

Chapter 13

I made my way out of the stale heat of the station house and into the moving heat of the street. It was just a few minutes past five, and all the municipal offices were emptying out at once. That was the summer that all the secretaries dressed like it was V-J Day and they were off to welcome the troops. I stood there, washed around by waves of tropical prints, pompadours, and high-heel sling-back pumps. They looked the way girls used to look when everyone was young and the world was up for grabs, and it was easy to imagine that we were all going home to dance to Benny Goodman records, drink beer, and boast about the great things we would do with the rest of our lives. But who was I kidding? Now it was all punk rock and dope, and I was retired. The future was behind me, and all the girls of my youth were gone.

Except, of course, Gloria, who was waiting for me at her office right now. My interview with Captain Powers hadn't exactly cheered me up, but at least it had distracted me from the mess I was making of my personal life. This morning had been a terrible mistake. It was one thing to know that, though, and another to say so to the lady involved.

I decided to take the subway the half mile to Gloria's office, which at that hour was a form of stalling. From Brooklyn Bridge

I rode south one stop to Nassau, where I changed for the Eighth Avenue line north to Chambers Street. The cars were packed, but I learned a long time ago that a nice crowded subway is a great place to be alone.

When we got to Chambers Street, I could have doubled back on the Eighth Avenue local for the World Trade Center station, but even for me that was too much of a stall. I got out and walked the two blocks to Global Security.

Out on the street it was still daytime, but the lights were on in Gloria's office. The only lights in the building. The place didn't look any better than it had yesterday, and it dawned on me that the fancy locks and intercoms were probably for her own protection and only incidentally to impress the customers. I knocked on the outer door.

"It's me," I called. "Quentin."

I could hear Gloria moving around inside, and in a moment the door opened.

"Come in," she said brightly. "Sit down. Relax. Mr. Harwell's secretary phoned me that they want you back, starting tonight. Great, isn't it?"

I didn't answer. Nobody, I noticed, had even considered the possibility that I might not want the job. Riding down here, I had decided to quit on Gloria. Get out of her life as soon as possible. It would be tough for her to lose the contract, but I figured a quick break would be better for both of us than any kind of long-drawn-out apology. Now that I was in front of her, though, seeing how happy she was with the news, all the speeches I had planned stuck in my throat.

"Can I take you out to dinner?" I asked instead. Which wasn't at all what I had meant to say.

"Lasagna," she answered, which I guess was an acceptance. "La Tavola, over on Liberty Street. You just enjoy the air conditioning for a minute while I close up."

Half an hour later we were sitting at a corner table at the kind of neighborhood restaurant I didn't know existed around that part of town. Gloria hadn't been kidding about lasagna, which was printed on the menu as the daily special. While we waited for it to arrive, I tried again to explain to her that a sudden encounter at an overwrought time didn't have to mean a permanent commitment.

"About this morning..." I began lamely. She waited. I waited. Then I gave up. "I don't know what to say," I confessed.

"So don't say anything," Gloria suggested, picking the olives out of her salad. She played with her food awhile more, then finally looked at me.

"I don't want you to think of me as some kind of a cheap one-night stand, Quentin, but I have to be honest with you. I've been on my own for going on fifteen years now, and for the first time in my life I feel like I can take care of myself. I like where I live. I like my work. I like my routines. Right now I don't need any complications to mess me up. Sure, it's hard living alone, but who said hard is always bad?" She studied my face for a while, but I had no arguments to offer.

"When I was a kid," she continued, "I used to dream that Mr. Right would come galloping along and sweep me away, take care of me for the rest of my life. But I found out a few things since then. I found out I'm not a kid anymore, so I should stop wasting my time on daydreams. And I also found out I like making decisions for myself. So even if Mr. Right arrived, we'd probably end up having an argument. This morning was this morning, and there's nothing about it I would have changed. But this is tonight, and you're on your way to work. You've got to learn not to mix business with pleasure."

All afternoon I'd been nervous that Gloria was expecting me to move in with her or something. Now I was stung that instead she wanted to forget the whole thing. Maybe not forget exactly. After all, she had called it a pleasure. But she was certainly making it clear that I didn't have to worry about her making a lot of demands. Well, that was what I wanted, wasn't it? Sure it was. On those terms I was even willing to go back to work. I decided to settle in and enjoy the present, which was a nice dinner with an attractive woman I had been acquainted with for forty years but who I felt like I was only just getting to know.

"All right," I agreed. "Let's talk about business."

"It's about this murder," she began, stabbing a tomato. "It doesn't look good for Global Security when we send up a guard and the boss gets killed."

That was putting it mildly. I nodded my agreement, and Gloria went on. "Blount Harwell is the president of Interdine. I don't mean to sound like a ghoul, but he's a much bigger catch than Lombardo even—if we can land him as a client. Working through Harwell's office, we've got instant access not only to the restaurant arm of Interdine but also to the hotel division, the time-sharing outlets, the food services franchises, the whole company. We still have to prove ourselves, though, and the best way I see to do that is to solve this murder ourselves."

"You sound pretty cheerful about our prospects of doing that," I observed.

"I always sound cheerful," Gloria answered, though in fact, her voice was glum for the first time that day. "My therapist says it's a neurotic need to be loved. I'm afraid people won't like me if I don't sound happy all the time."

"So now you have a therapist," I said. Gloria had traveled a long way since the old days at Morris High.

"Yes, I have a therapist," she snapped. "Also a lawyer, an accountant, and a personal physician. Not everybody wants to be the Lone Ranger, you know."

I had hurt her feelings. I stumbled over an apology, but Gloria waved it away.

"The point is, with you rehired we've still got a wedge in the Interdine market. The thing is to widen the wedge, and the way to do that is like I said: find out who killed John Lombardo."

106

She settled back in her chair, pleased as punch with her view of the situation, then spoiled the effect by pouncing on the lasagna that had finally arrived. Not that I had been dazzled in the first place.

"In case you haven't noticed," I said, "there are a lot of other people concentrating on that very issue. They belong to a group known as the New York Police Department, and while they're not as great as the Transit Police, they are still good enough to get this particular job done without us."

"Of course they are," Gloria agreed. "They're fantastic. They've got people who can look at a bloodstain and tell you which way the wind was blowing on the day of the crime. It's amazing."

"Forensic pathologists," I said.

"Huh?"

"Forensic pathologists. That's what you call them."

"Right. Thanks. Anyway, the point is that with all their expertise and forensic pathologists and all, I'm sure the police can find who was stealing from the restaurant and just how Lombardo was killed. But it's going to take them awhile to do all those fancy tests and all, and if we could just beat them to it, that would make a nice little stroke for Global Security. After all, Interdine isn't going to give a contract to the New York Police Department no matter how great a job they do—so the credit might as well go to someone who can use it, right?"

"Meaning you?" I asked.

"Well, why not?" she said defensively.

"No reason at all," I answered. "Just tell me one thing. Why did Harwell put me back on the job?"

"Because he knows that you're a good guard from a reputable agency. That's one reason why." She poked around her plate for a while, like she had lost something under the noodles. Then she came out with the other reason. "Maybe also because I said we would work without a fee for a week, kind of a free sample from Global to Interdine. Don't worry," she added. "I'll pay your salary. But, Quentin, you've got to do it. I'm not crazy enough to think I can handle this myself. I know the security business pretty well by now, but only as an administrator. The closest experience I have with crime is getting my wallet snatched at Saks. And as I have told you before, there is nothing like a big guy like you when it comes to throwing a little weight around. Alone I barely weigh enough to donate blood. Together we'll make a hell of a team."

I considered explaining to Gloria exactly why this was a dumb idea, but it would have taken a couple of hours, and it wouldn't have done any good. Once Gloria had a plan, it would take dynamite to change her course. Instead I clued her in to my big realization of last night. Powers had seen it right away, but at least I had caught up with his thinking. All you had to do was look around. There was no way Lombardo could have been killed because he had stumbled into a robbery in progress. The victim had been standing in the center of the room, an open bottle in his hand. He had been stabbed from behind. When he had turned to see his assailant, he had been pushed back against the statue, which conveniently bashed in his skull. It was no accident that John Lombardo had died last night. What we were dealing with was deliberate, premeditated murder.

Chapter 14

That quieted Gloria down a bit, but not for long. All the way back to Washington Square she kept on talking about how we were going to steal the Lombardo case from the NYPD, until finally even she got tired of it. Or maybe she just got tired. When we got to her apartment, she patted my arm.

"Thanks for dinner," she said sleepily. "Be careful tonight." And then she closed the door in my face.

It was worse than being a kid out on a date. Then at least I would have gotten a kiss and maybe a quick feel up against the mailboxes. Not that that was what I wanted. Or at least I didn't think so. Confused, I turned around for the trip back to the Interdine Tower.

When I got there, I was amazed all over again by the beauty of the building and by the number of people who came to that run-down part of town. My first look at the pileup of cars and limousines by the main entrance, I thought that someone else had died. After my stomach finished turning over, I realized it was just the normal traffic for the night.

Inside, the lobby looked like a marble desert, with well-dressed caravans moving from one expensive oasis to another. Down from the restaurant and into the waiting car. Home from some other night spot and up to the luxury apartment. The Interdine offices were closed, though, and at that hour the Pinnacle Room traffic was all going in the other direction, so the elevator man put me in a car all by myself.

I had already pressed the button and moved to the rear of the car when the doors opened again to let in another passenger. Blount Harwell had traded his tweeds and leather patches for a tuxedo and a black satin bow tie, but he still looked more like a gentleman farmer than a corporate president. Nodding blindly in my direction, he took a leather key case from his pocket, selected a small brass key, and turned the lock for the executive offices on the sixty-ninth floor.

Gloria would never forgive me if I wasted an opportunity like this.

"I appreciate your confidence in rehiring me, Mr. Harwell," I said. "I think you'll find you can rely on Global Security."

He twirled around, startled, then seemed relieved when he recognized me.

"Jacobs, isn't it? New man at the Pinnacle Room?"

"That's right. Except it's Jacoby. Quentin Jacoby." In a strange way I was flattered he'd remembered even part of my name.

"Sorry, fellow. Wife says I'm going deaf. Glad to run into you. Talk to you in my office before you report for work."

Without waiting for an answer, he turned to the front of the car and pressed his palm over the button that keeps the doors from opening. The elevator stopped at the sixty-eighth floor, but the doors stayed closed, and a second later we continued up a flight to the executive offices.

It was a good thing he told me we were going to his office, because I never could have guessed from the looks of things. We got out into a kind of giant living room, with wood-paneled walls, slipcovered sofas, lots of rugs, and little tables next to every chair. There was even a fireplace with a picture hanging over the mantel, a portrait of an old-fashioned gent in a white wig. It was the kind of room where George Washington would have felt right at home.

Harwell walked through without so much as a glance at the candlesticks, and I followed to what turned out to be a whole string of rooms that made up his private office. First there was the place where the secretaries sat, full of typewriters and telephones and computer hookups. Then there was Harwell's inner sanctum, with leather armchairs, a big marble-topped desk, and a wraparound window looking south over the harbor and west to the highways of New Jersey. On the desk was a framed photograph of a plain-looking woman with cropped gray hair, smiling down at the shaggy pooch I knew all along would be there. Something to keep the missus company back in Valley Forge.

To the side I could see another room where the walls were covered in long panels of mirrors that reflected back a spectacular view of upper Manhattan. There was a dining table in the middle of the room, and two of the mirrored panels had been folded back and were swung open, showing a closet-size version of the wine cellar downstairs, minus the pink marble but with a small, well-stocked bar built into the wall. It occurred to me that one of the definite perks of Harwell's job was that he didn't have to order out for lunch.

"Sit down," he said. I picked one of the leather armchairs in front of the desk and was surprised when Harwell sat down in the other.

"Ugly business last night," he observed. "Damn shame— Lombardo, I mean. Never had anything like that before."

I nodded, wondering if he had hauled me up here for a sympathy call. He looked like he had lost the thread of the conversation and started fumbling in the pockets of his coat. Finally he found what he was looking for, a short, chewed-up brown pipe. There was another minute or two while he demonstrated his technique for packing in the tobacco, and then he just stared out the window, puffing away.

"Eternal happiness," he said softly.

"Beg your pardon?"

"Sorry, fellow. Woolgathering. I was just hoping that Johnny Lombardo has found eternal happiness."

I nodded, trying to imagine what kind of happiness Lombardo would have chosen if he'd known it would be eternal. Was Harwell going to turn religious on me now? His next words were a total change of subject, which was a big relief.

"I understand you were the first one to find poor Johnny's body," he said.

"That's right," I answered. "I wish I had been fast enough to find him while he was still alive."

"Tut, man," Harwell answered. "Can't blame you. Nobody could have known. What had to be had to be. Damn shame," he said again. Reaching for a bowl of nuts on the table between us, he hollowed out a little nest and rested his pipe inside. "Smoked almonds," he joked. Then he straightened up abruptly and got to the point.

"You're probably wondering why I've rehired you," he said. I shuffled awkwardly in my chair, trying to act like it was a reasonable thing to have done.

"Captain Powers was not very happy with the idea," he added dryly. "Said it was like asking one of the rabbits to guard the lettuce. Quaint turn of phrase for a city detective, don't you think?"

I squirmed around a little more. The whole conversation was getting beyond me. Luckily Harwell didn't wait for an answer.

"Well, I'll tell you why I want you around," he said. "John Lombardo hired you. I don't know why he decided to go beyond our regular security force. but I'm sure he had a reason, and I'm hoping you'll help me find out what that reason was. I also hope you'll help discover who killed him, because I don't think you did. Whatever other faults he had, John was far too clever a man to hire his own assassin. It is my opinion that he was murdered by somebody on the Interdine staff, and I want to know who it was. The two principal suspects you already know. Others may turn up. In any case, I want somebody to be in that restaurant after hours, making sure that nothing gets altered and also that no gossip goes unreported. They can't be talking of anything else down there. Captain Powers suggested planting one of his people in the kitchen, but I hardly think a new arrival would go unnoticed right now. Everybody has already seen you. All you have to do is arrive a bit earlier in the evening, keep your eyes and ears open, and report to me anything you find out."

"Shouldn't I report to the police then?" I asked. Harwell studied the view for a while before he answered.

"This is my company," he said. "Everything that goes on in it is my concern. Including murder. The police are doing their best, but you might say their methods don't always mesh with Interdine policy. They're tearing things apart, trying to uncover the culprit. I'm trying to put the pieces back together. The Pinnacle Room represents a considerable investment, both in money and in personnel. I want to make sure it continues to prosper even without its creator."

"What about Mr. Lyder?" I asked. "I don't think he's gonna be very happy to see me back."

"Mr. Lyder was tired last night. Strained. Shocked. You were hired on a weekly contract, and I've already told him you'll be working through to the end of it. No need to tell him about our conversation tonight. Quite enough to be nervous about, taking over so suddenly and all. Don't want to make it worse by making the new man feel like he's under suspicion. Catch my drift?"

He peered at me over the bowl of his pipe, and I realized that for all his tweed clothes and his absent-minded airs, Blount Harwell was a very sharp fellow. He was cooperating with the police, but he was already looking beyond Lombardo, thinking about the future of the restaurant and the people who worked there. I had no illusions about how Harwell respected my judgment or anything like that; the odds were good that he was talking this frankly because he assumed I was a fool. It didn't matter. He

113

was working with the tools at hand, doing his best to keep the Pinnacle Room going without its star attraction, but also watching out for his staff, making sure nobody crumbled from the combined pressure of the police investigation and the sudden change of management. There was calculation there, but also real concern.

Yesterday morning, when Lyder had been feeding me his line about the Interdine system, everybody part of one big corporate family, I'd thought it was just a lot of fancy language, like forcing a speed-up on the assembly line and calling it Pep Week. After I talked to Harwell, though, it was possible to imagine that he really did take the trouble to get to know his people, if only to figure out how to get them to work their best. No harm in that, I thought, watching him pick up his pipe and start to puff away. A nice change from the cutthroat style you usually hear about.

It was also a considerable contrast with what I'd seen of the management style of John Lombardo. Lombardo was all flash and dash, in love with the world and happy to let everybody else bask in the warmth of his personality. Harwell was so quiet and restrained you had to keep reminding yourself that he was the boss. Lombardo made a better first impression, but I suspected that Harwell might be the stronger figure in the long run. Everybody admires a genius, but not too many people want one for a father.

I was lingering over my vision of the happy Interdine family when Big Daddy himself interrupted my thoughts with a reminder that they were waiting for me downstairs. It was while I was making my way back across the living room with all the antique furniture that another thought struck me. Did Blount Harwell know more than he was telling about the death of John Lombardo? When the company president calls in a lowly security guard for a private conference, it can only mean he doesn't trust the people between them in the ranks. How far, I wondered, did the president's concern for his corporate family stretch? Was it far enough to cover for a murder?

Chapter 15

Whatever else he had on his mind, Harwell could stop worrying about losing customers. Ten o'clock is about four hours past my idea of the right time for dinner, but there were enough people who disagreed to keep the Pinnacle Room plenty busy for a Tuesday night. Lombardo's murder was front-page news in all the afternoon papers, and it looked like a good number of his devoted followers hadn't been able to resist coming by to see how the empire was managing without its king.

Robert Lyder was standing at the top of the stairs, greeting people as they came up from the dining room and doing his best to imitate Lombardo's style. It wouldn't have been easy under any circumstances, given that the new manager was about as suave and elegant as a half-grown boxer puppy, and it was just about impossible with the ghost of his predecessor hovering over his head. Plus Janine DuPage had chosen not to show up for work, which was understandable but left something of a hole in the staff. Pierre, the wineman, was trying to cover for her as assistant greeter while also supervising the wine cellar and the bar, but mostly what he managed to do was look harried and exhausted. Not that he wasn't entitled, having been there since six in the morning. Still, the net result was hardly the atmosphere of pampered luxury that had made Lombardo's operations so famous.

What it was like was a well-fed wake. Instead of all the hand kissing and cheek rubbing I had seen last night, there was a lot of sad shaking of heads, but I wondered how genuine it was. When I got there, Lyder was comforting a huge brunette in a purple tent of a dress who had buried her fat face on his shoulder. When she passed me on the way out a moment later, she had made a miraculous recovery.

"Served Johnny right, dying *en brochette*," I heard her whisper to a friend. "I always said he did too many dishes with skewers. Strictly tourist." Her companion giggled briefly, then tried to look shocked.

From the amount of chitchat going on upstairs, I could understand why Harwell thought I might pick up some dope by hanging around the kitchen. What he had forgotten, though, was that everyone who worked there was by that time both very tired and very scared. If they didn't think I had actually been the one to stab John Lombardo, they certainly blamed me for not stopping whoever did, and in the meantime, nobody was too eager to hang around while there was still a murderer on the loose.

In point of fact, most of the kitchen staff had left by the time I arrived. The few who were still there had already talked themselves out, both to the police and to each other. One by one they finished their jobs, shucked off their aprons and jackets, and threw them in the big canvas bins by the elevator. I tried to imagine Angel Ruiz crouching down behind the piles, waiting to jump out and surprise John Lombardo after everyone else had gone. What had he thought when he heard me wheel the laundry bins in front of the doors? Had he been able to get around them? I was staring at the layout, but one of the cooks must have thought I was watching him. He detoured over to where I was standing.

"You the one who find Monsieur Lombardo?" he asked. Like

a lot of the people who worked here, he had a French accent blunted by several decades in New York.

"Yes," I answered. Now everyone in the room was looking at us. Whatever was coming, I knew it wouldn't be a medal.

Reaching into his pants, he took out an enormous red handkerchief and blew his nose in my face. So much for my standing with the regulars on the Pinnacle staff. If that were the worst attack I got, I'd consider myself lucky.

By eleven-fifteen the kitchen was empty. I could hear Lyder off in the pantry, talking fast and low with Pierre. Lyder's end of the conversation I couldn't make out, but for answer Pierre was giving his boss what sounded a lot like a pep talk.

"Of course, you will succeed," he said, raising his voice to show how confident he was. "You must not worry so much about the appearances. You are the manager now, you can do as you like. There is no need for you to be another Monsieur Lombardo. You must continue as you have started—that is the way to make your celebrity. There is risk, yes, but maybe also triumph. That is what matters."

Lyder mumbled something in a doubtful kind of voice and came around the corner into the kitchen. He stopped short when he saw me, then flushed a dark brick red that quickly faded into an unhealthy-looking pallor.

"Forgot about you," he said curtly.

Up close, I could see why Pierre felt like Lyder needed reassuring. The man was in terrible shape. He looked like he hadn't slept in thirty-six hours, which was probably true, but at his age that shouldn't have mattered. It was more than lack of sleep that had put shadows under his eyes and started a nervous twitch around the mouth. Plain and simple, Robert Lyder was scared.

Well, who could blame him? Yesterday he'd been the bright young man of the company, flexing his muscles under his jacket and looking forward to a rosy future and meanwhile having to do

117

nothing more strenuous than check out the time sheets and talk sports with the customers. Now all of a sudden the boss had been killed, and little Bobby Lyder had to start making decisions for himself. And taking the flak if he decided wrong. It couldn't help any that the first move he'd made as manager had already been reversed by the big boss upstairs. Lyder had been pretty emphatic about firing me last night, and I hadn't been looking forward to seeing him again.

I guess the feeling was mutual. He made a couple of skittish passes around the room before he finally came to a stop about six feet from where I was sitting. There was a warming cart in front of him, a portable rig for wheeling food around the dining room. Lyder clutched it like a barricade and gave me a look like he was daring me to jump over the line.

"You have a contract here for a week," he said grimly. "You may last that long. But only if you're very careful. Do you understand?"

"I guess so," I answered, but it wasn't true. Did Lyder think he was doing me a favor, reminding me that I was up there alone while Lombardo's killer was still on the loose? He glared at me awhile longer, then went through the room just like he had last night, turning down the lights and making sure all the stoves were turned off before he went home. I wouldn't have been surprised if he had counted the knives.

After he left, I became the perfect night watchman. Twenty minutes of experimenting with the laundry bins convinced me there was no way Angel could have slipped out of the elevator without my hearing or gotten back in again either. Then I began my rounds. Every hour I made a tour of the premises. At 12:00, 2:00, 4:00, and 6:00 A.M. I made my way through the pantry to the big dining room, went to the Coronation Room, rattled the door of the wine cellar, climbed up to the bar, stuck my head in the phone booths, inspected the bathrooms and the fire exit, checked the manager's office, and went back down to the kitchen by the service door near the elevators. At 1:00, 3:00, and 5:00 I reversed it, starting with the office and working my way around through the dining rooms and back to the pantry. I always took a deep breath before I got to the wine cellar door. It was always locked.

Either direction, the kitchen was my last stop. That's where I sat between rounds, and I always looked around good to make sure nobody had tunneled through to the meat locker while I was out of the room. The whole business took about twenty minutes, including checking the blind spaces inside the bathroom stalls and behind the draperies. That still left plenty of time for doing nothing.

Even without my finding a dead man the night before, the setup would have gotten on my nerves. The simple fact was that I wasn't used to a job that stayed put. On the trains you were always moving—car to car, station to station, up and down the platform—and the whole world was moving with you. Even when there was nothing much happening, you always felt like you were going somewhere. And you were never alone. You might want to be, especially if you were working a rush-hour tour, but even on the graveyard runs there was always somebody around, and not just creeps, though of course they're the ones you keep your eye on. Say there's a hophead jiving in the corner, fingering his pocket like he's trying out a knife; you can't arrest him for just thinking, and meanwhile, you're standing there watching the rest of the car with plenty of chance to see the couple snuggling in the last seat, coming home from who knows where and impatient to get into bed together. You can listen to the kids, keep up on their world and what tales they're passing around. You can see where the dames who live in the subways are getting their shopping bags and check how much underwear the girls are leaving off this season. There's always something going on. Not a bit like guarding a lockerful of cold food.

At least there was one advantage to my current locus. Working the trains, you were always chasing someone who had instant access to the world's largest urban getaway system. By the time you got to a victim, your assailant would be way the hell out in another borough. Up here everything was wonderfully simple. Angel or Janine. Janine or Angel. Making my rounds, watching the cleaning crew come through, tracing the dawn as it lit up the distant reaches of Queens, I repeated the names over and over until neither of them made any sense. Then I went back to the kitchen and waited for the bakers to arrive. My first night on the job had been full of excitement, all of it the wrong kind. On Tuesday I put in the most boring eight hours I had ever endured.

Chapter 16

Upstairs I'd been dead on my feet, keeping awake on coffee and confusion, but as soon as I hit the sidewalk I came alive again. It was a beautiful morning, the sun just up and the air still cool with the breeze off the Hudson River. It made me feel like a kid again, like when I used to sleep out on the fire escape with my brother to get away from the heat. The delivery trucks would wake us around 5:00 A.M., and we'd sit up in our underwear and take our time watching the day arrive. Forty years slipped away with that first taste of the early air, and suddenly I forgot all about the fact that I hadn't been to sleep since yesterday or changed my clothes since the day before. The time had come for action, and the first thing I planned to do was pay a call on Miss Janine DuPage.

A quick consultation with my favorite reference book, the telephone directory, informed me that she lived on Lexington Avenue up around Ninety-second Street. As far as I could guess, she was halfway between Bloomingdale's and the heart of Harlem, which struck me as a pretty accurate placement. Unfortunately I would have to take three trains to get there. I bought a roll of mints to keep me cool on the trip. A cold shower and a complete change of clothes would have been more to the point, but I try not to spend too much time wishing for things I'm not about to get.

I flashed my pass for a free trip through the turnstile at the World Trade Center station and waited on the uptown platform for the Broadway local to Times Square. From there I switched to the shuttle for Grand Central station, where I got hemmed in by two women who had been working all night at Chock Full o'Nuts. One of them was telling the other how she should have done better dealing with a junkie who was nodding out in her station.

"I tell you, Shirley, you let that cokehead sleep in your section, he'll come there every night and bring his friends. How long you think you gonna last on the job when the manager see you running a flophouse?"

"So what am I s'posed to do with him?" Shirley demanded. "Twice as big as me and all shot up with junk so he don't care what he do—guy like that would knife the good Samaritan out of the Bible, and Lord knows what he'd do to me. They want him outta my station, they hire a bouncer like the good Lord knows we need." Her friend nodded emphatically, and Shirley leaned back to expound some more of her views on social life at the all-night coffee counter.

"You know what gets me," she said confidentially. "It's not the junkies or even the hookers. What *turns my stomach* is those kids with the green hair and the safety pins through their cheeks. They come in for coffee or what all, and I gotta stare at them for ten minutes while they sit at the counter, and it just make me so sick I can hardly work. I had one the other night, tried to put a razor blade through his friend's ear while they were sitting right there. One of those narrow single-edge blades, you know? Well, I just told him to pay up and clear out because I wasn't having no *surgery* going on at my counter. Can you imagine?" Then they both burst out laughing, and Shirley's friend changed the subject to whether it was warmer to get a hat for the winter or buy a wig. I tuned out and didn't bother staying with them when we all changed at Grand Central for the Lexington Avenue line.

Neighborhoods change fast in Manhattan. Janine's was as stylish as the lady herself, the cutting edge of the shoe box modern apartments that were steadily pushing out the tenements of East Harlem. Across the street you could still see narrow walk-ups that dated from the days when nobody worried about providing cross-ventilation because poor people were used to sweat. The folks who live there get around the heat by sitting out on the stoop, playing on the sidewalk, or hanging around the corner making a breeze with their mouths, which a lot of them were already doing when I came by. The developers had gotten to Janine's side of the block, though, and put up a row of apartment houses with doormen in the lobbies and rents that were four times as high for half the space. They were the kinds of buildings that appealed to airline hostesses and young executives whose mobility was still waiting to get upward—people who didn't mind having to store their shoes under the sink as long as they'd never be humiliated by a naked light bulb in the hallway or a bathroom that didn't have a shower built into the wall.

Janine's building was in the middle of the row, a tall, skinny number just like the lady herself, faced in light blue ceramic tile with an ugly mosaic over the door. The lobby was a tiny cubicle with an enormous mailroom in back. The man on duty was busy sorting letters, but he buzzed Janine's apartment for me quickly enough, and when she didn't answer, he volunteered the information that she should be back real soon. I would have to compliment Gloria on having a much more protective doorman.

There were two wooden armchairs in the lobby, with a plastic plant in a tub on the floor between them. I was admiring the way they had put real dirt around the plastic roots when the outer door opened. It was Janine, clutching a paper bag in one hand and the end of a leash in the other. She held the door open so the rest of the leash could follow. At the end was a very large

German shepherd. Janine was dressed in baggy blue jeans, a faded cotton shirt, and a big straw hat that flopped down all around her face, but as an effort at going into hiding, it didn't work. No matter what she wore, there was no mistaking those good looks.

Janine recognized me right away, too.

"What the hell do you think you're doing here?" she demanded.

"Looking for you." It was a dumb thing to say, but the truth.

"Paying a condolence call from the gang downtown?" she snapped. "I've been wondering if anyone at work remembered me. But I don't see any flowers. No cake. No basket of fruit. What's the matter? Didn't your mama raise you right?"

I had started to feel sorry for Janine, skulking around in a fifth-rate attempt at a disguise, but at this point I stopped. The lady could take care of herself.

"I came to talk to you about John Lombardo."

"Did you now? Well, isn't that sweet? I've already made my statement to the police, and I am not discussing it any further. Now get out of my way before I get somebody to move you for me."

"I think I may be able to help you," I said, blocking her path to the elevator. I looked around. The doorman had vanished back to his mail.

"Who says I need to be helped?" Janine countered. "You see me in jail? You see any police officers hanging around? I'm free as a bird."

"Is it because you're so free that you didn't show up for work last night?"

"Whether or not I go back to work is up to me," Janine said, pulling back on the leash before Fido could reach the piece of my leg he was aiming for. "For your information, I have decided to give up the restaurant business. As soon as I wind up my affairs here in New York, I am moving to Chicago, where I have a long-standing offer from a leading agency for photographic models. I'll be earning at least fifty dollars an hour. You can tell that to all those sad sacks down at the Pinnacle Room, slaving away for nothing and dreaming of working their way up in the so-called Interdine family. In fact, you'd better tell them because I'm not coming back to any company reunions to do it myself. Now, for the last time, out of my way!"

It sounded good, and for all I knew, it was true. Janine could certainly make it as a model. She had the build, the bones, and the style. But for somebody who was totally innocent, she sure had changed careers fast.

"Looks mighty suspicious," I observed, "your leaving town right after the murder. I don't think Captain Powers is going to like it at all."

"Listen, big boy, you just leave Captain Powers to me." Janine jerked on the leash, and the pooch started growling unpleasantly. Tired as I was, she could have driven me off with a chihuahua, but I didn't tell her that. I planted myself in front of the door and tried another approach. Lying.

"I think I have a way to put you completely in the clear," I said, trying to sound like I meant it. "But first you have to talk to me. Sitting down. I've been up all night, and I am getting very tired."

"I don't need your tricks," Janine snapped. "I *am* in the clear." Then she thought for a while, wavering. Finally I guess her curiosity got to her. Or her self-interest. "Not upstairs," she said abruptly. "There is no way I'm going to let you inside my place."

"Right here is fine," I answered, pointing to the two chairs in the lobby.

She perched stiffly on the edge of her seat, the dog lying at her feet as a gnawing, growling reminder not to try anything funny.

"You know what happened Monday night?" I asked tentatively.

"Johnny died," she answered. "We had a date, and he never

125

showed up. Somebody killed him instead. Now he'll never show up again." She shook her head from side to side, as though she wanted to emphasize how thoroughly she'd been stood up. It was an interesting way of viewing things, like she'd been the most injured party. I started over.

"I was up at the Pinnacle Room Monday night," I began, "and last night, too, and in between I've been in to see Captain Powers. In addition to which I used to be a police officer myself, so I know how this investigation is being run. But I'm not an enforcement officer anymore, and right now I've got my own interests to protect. Play ball with me, and there's a good chance that I can get you off the hook. But first I have to know."

"Know what?" Janine asked. There was a nervous, mocking tone in her voice, like she wasn't too impressed with my fancy credentials. Neither was I, but they were the best I could do. I kept trying.

"Know if you killed him or not, of course. Odds are that you did, you know. You're a tall woman, Miss DuPage. Taller than Johnny Lombardo was, and probably stronger, too. It would have been easy for you to pick up one of those fancy little skewers from the vase in the hall. Easy for you to stab him from behind, and no sweat to knock his head in against that marble pedestal either. You had the means, and you had the opportunity. And maybe you also had the motive."

It was dark there in the lobby. I could barely see Janine's face under the brim of her hat, but I could feel the tension in her body. The dog could, too. He stood up by her legs and started growling. Don't walk out on me, lady, I thought. Stick with me. I need you.

"Down, Lobo," she said tensely. She didn't move to leave, though, so I kept on talking.

"How did you feel when you found out Lombardo was cheating on you?" I asked. "Mad enough to kill? Or was that only when you wised up that he was two-timing you with another man?"

I hadn't exactly expected Janine to pop right out with a confession, but I hadn't been ready for her to start laughing either.

"You think I imagined I was Johnny's one true love?" She snorted. "What a joke. I knew all about that little Ruiz kid, knew about him all along. That didn't stop me and Johnny from having some good times. So maybe Johnny was using me, taking me around so people would see us together and not imagine there was this other side of his life. Nothing wrong with that."

There was plenty wrong with it in my book, but now was not the time for a discussion of moral values.

"What was in it for you?" I asked. "Or was that the problem? Maybe you weren't getting enough out of the deal, and when Lombardo refused to give you something you wanted, you got mad and killed him. Was that the way it went?"

"You know perfectly well I didn't kill Johnny," Janine said sharply, the laughter all gone from her voice. "You're as bad as that creep Thorson down at the police station, trying to trap me into saying things that aren't true. 'Are you sure you don't wish to change your statement, Miss DuPage?'" she whined, imitating Thorson's phony gilt-edged way of talking. "'Are you aware that we realize you were using your affair with Mr. Lombardo to further your own career?' Sure I was using Johnny," she said in her own voice. "But that doesn't mean I didn't love him, too. Just because you respect a man doesn't mean you can't want something from him, you know. Hell, what would you want from somebody you *didn't* respect? Just because a person's got ambition doesn't mean she can't have feelings, too. You men are all alike. You can't handle the idea of a woman having it all. You see someone like me, someone with a chance of making it for real, and you just can't wait to put me in jail, I'm so scary!"

"Calm down," I said. "I don't want to put you in jail." Not unless you killed Lombardo, I added to myself. "I just want the truth. And believe me, I'm not a bit like Plato Thorson."

It took Janine awhile to get her breath back, she was so upset.

We must have made an interesting triangle, sitting there in the lobby—me staring at Janine, Janine studying the rubber shower thongs she was wearing instead of shoes, the dog keeping his sights on my neck, just waiting for the order to spring. When Janine finally looked up, she seemed more disgusted than angry.

"I don't know why I'm even talking to you," she said. "I guess I keep hoping somebody will understand. The police certainly didn't. You probably won't either, but I'll try. At least it will get you off my back," she added, just in case I'd been getting any swell ideas about her respect for my powers of comprehension.

"You want the truth?" she continued. "I'll tell you. The truth is, I meant to take over the Pinnacle Room. I was going to be the first woman manager at Interdine, the first black woman to manage a major restaurant in America. Bob Lyder may know all about accounting and have a graduate degree in corporate loyalty, but the man has no style at all, and after a while even Mr. Harwell would have noticed that. Hanging out with Johnny, I was learning the ropes, meeting the right people, moving up so I'd be front and center in a couple of years when everyone saw that Lyder couldn't cut it. By then Johnny would be long gone."

"Gone?"

"You know. Blown. Gotten out. There was no way he would have stayed around the Pinnacle for more than another year, tops. That man was always off on some new sport. But God, it was exciting to be with him!" She smiled at some private memory. "Wherever he went, you suddenly knew that was the place to be. Whatever he did, it was fun. Life was a great big party for Johnny Lombardo, and everybody was invited.

"That's what those management types at Interdine never understood," she added. "Harwell and his cronies, they thought they could buy him forever, stuff him with profit sharing and pensions and medical benefits and get him so fat and lazy he'd never move on. But that wasn't Johnny, not at all. Johnny was newness and dreaming and never doing the same thing twice.

128

He was playing with them, was what he was doing. And when he got tired of the game, I planned to be there to take over, because I like profit sharing a whole lot. But that wasn't for another two years, according to my timetable, and rushing things up only got me Bob Lyder in the way. In two years I would have known enough to bump Lyder right out of the running, with Johnny's blessings. But now I'm nowhere because it all happened too soon. I ask you, why would I want Johnny dead?"

A good question. But then I had spotted Janine right off as a smart girl. And it would certainly have taken at least two years of proving just how smart she was before she could have hoped to convince Interdine to let a woman manage one of its fancy-pants restaurants. Especially a black woman. As for taking over right now, it was the kind of idea that makes sense for only a second, and then only if you've been up all night. In terms of her career Janine had no motive at all to kill Lombardo and every reason to want him alive. The jealousy angle didn't seem to make much sense, either. After I talked to Janine, it was easy to believe she didn't care what Lombardo did with the rest of his time, as long as she got what she was after. Which left me with Angel.

"Thanks for talking to me," I said, pulling myself out of the chair. "I'll be getting back to you."

"Hey!" Janine exclaimed. "Where you going? You said you had something that would get those detectives off my back!"

"Did I?" I asked. "You're a big girl, Miss DuPage. You should know better than to believe everything you hear."

Chapter 17

I would like to say that I went straight from Janine's to hunt down Angel Ruiz. The truth is, I beat it home and went to sleep. Except for a few hours the day before when I passed out at Gloria's, I hadn't been to bed for over fifty hours. Little lights were exploding inside my eyeballs every time I blinked, and when I got outside I noticed right off that the sidewalk had started to buckle and the lines in the pavement were dancing around. Plus it was raining again, the hot, thick summer rain that hangs on you like a weight. I'd be wet to the skin before I got home, if I even made it that far. I might pass out and just ride the trains forever.

There are only two seasons on the subway, and rain makes both of them worse. In the winter it's dank, and the tunnels stink of wet wool and rotting rubber boots. In the summer it's muggy, and every ride seems like a trip on the *African Queen*. It took me forty minutes to get to Baychester Avenue, which still left a ten-minute hike over asphalt that holds the heat and sends it back up through the soles of your shoes and right into your brain. By the time I got to my apartment, I was ready to climb into the refrigerator.

Instead I turned the bedroom air conditioner on high and went to take a shower. Then I sprawled on the bed and dried off in the draft from the cooler. After an hour or so I crawled under the bedspread, and that was the last I saw of Wednesday.

When I woke, it was getting dark out. The digital clock on the dresser said it was 6:18. I lay there and watched the numbers change a few more times before I finally got up and put on some clothes. Clean pants, a white shirt, the same tan jacket I took off that morning. Pulling the shades was too much trouble, so I dressed by the light coming in from the streetlamps outside. Sodium vapor moonlight. Even in the shadows I could tell that black oxfords didn't go with the rest of what I had on, but after thirty years in uniform they were a habit I couldn't break. I laced them up and turned on the light to find a tie.

After I got dressed, I tried to call Gloria, except she wasn't home or at her office either. Just as well, I told myself. After her big speech last night about independence I didn't want her to think I was trying to cramp her style. I switched on the television to see if they had anything to say about Lombardo, but the so-called newscasters had already finished up with the hard events and moved on to their usual mush of jokes and features. Tonight they were yapping about all the funny groups that come to town this time of year. The International Brotherhood of Embalmers at the Hilton. The Spiderman League, members' whereabouts unknown. A trade show for manufacturers of natural hair wigs. A family gathering of two thousand Gypsies camped out at Flushing Meadow for a week. Who cares? The only straight information you get on the news these days is the ball scores, and even there they like to make like the reporters are just palling around, making bets and predictions while they talk about the games. No clue to whether they'd arrested anybody on the Lombardo case. At least they hadn't tried to collar me. Not yet.

By this time I was getting hungry, except I couldn't decide if it was for breakfast or dinner. I made some coffee and was just sitting down in the alcove that passes for a dining room around here when Sam Fuentes started pounding on my door. I could tell it was him because he was also singing, and when Sam sings, you can hear it even through a reinforced steel fire door. Even through pounding. Doorbells are one of the things Sam doesn't believe in, along with green vegetables, income tax, and the reality that the Brooklyn Dodgers are not ever going to come back from L.A.

I went to open the door before he had a heart attack. Sam is one of those skinny little guys who looked forty when he was twenty and then never seemed to get any older, but the truth is he's pushing seventy and not as strong as he used to be. Of course, he'd kill anyone who said so. Or threaten to kill him. Sam's as big on talk as he's slow on action.

Tonight he was at the top of his form. "Good evening," he sang as he sailed through the door. "Good evening, my *amigo* who doubts both miracles and science." He set his portable radio down on the table next to the afternoon paper, then headed into the kitchen to help himself to coffee prepared according to his own special system. First he took a mug down from the rack, filled it halfway with light cream, then up to the top with hot java and four spoons of sugar. Sam likes his coffee the same way he likes his women—light and sweet.

Usually I like to talk to Sam. He's funny and he's been around. He's also very relaxing to be with, since he almost always talks about himself and doesn't really care if you don't contribute much to the conversation. Unless the subject is handicapping horses, on which I usually have a thing or two to say myself. Tonight I had other things on my mind, so I cut short his description of Hector's teen-age daughter and what happened when she bent over to get some beer from the bottom of the icebox. Not that it wasn't interesting. They do amazing things with short shorts these days.

"Anything special you want?" I asked. "I was just heading out."

Sam looked at me reproachfully. "*Mi amigo,*" he said, "this is not very good hospitality." Then he brightened. "Hey, you gotta date? Where you goin'? She gotta friend, likes little guys?" Sam is the last of the great optimists.

"Sorry, Sam. The truth is, I'm going to work."

"No!" He couldn't have been more shocked if I told him I was going to move upstate and take up farming. "What you need for to work? You put in your time, man. You got the pension. Now you enjoy yourself before you're too old. Hey," he demanded sharply, "you in trouble? You need extra bucks?"

"Nah. Not really. We could all use a little more, I guess. But this is more in the line of a favor, a friend who needs some help at the office."

"In the middle of the night?" he asked skeptically. "You need money, *amigo*, you follow my advice. Forget this job. Drive you loco. I work forty years on the street, honest work, and I don't end up with *nothing*. A lousy stinking pension from the government, a crummy little chicken coop of a place to live, always worried about the inflation and the fees and what happens if I get sick. That's what *work* gets you. You need money, you come in with me and the other guys. That's what I come up for, give you a second chance."

John Lombardo's murder had knocked Sam and his horse-talking swami clear out of my mind, but I'd known when I heard the race results Monday night that he would be back sooner or later. And that I would have to hear him out. Checking the clock, I decided there was time to go out for dinner before I headed downtown. After Monday night I'd kind of lost my appetite for the midnight meals at the Pinnacle Room.

There aren't too many restaurants in Co-op City, it being a middle-income family-type housing project. Middle-income people with families can't afford to eat out. What there was was mostly coffee places, like Maybelle's Donut Shop, or else it was fast food, which gives me heartburn. Besides, I like to get out whenever I can, to see what's beyond the highways that protect us from the rest of the Bronx.

133

Not that the choices were so lush on the other side of the street. We finally settled for the Chicken Kitchen, which is better than average because they actually cook the food there instead of bringing it in frozen and warming it up under a red light. The mashed potatoes are anemic and the vegetable du jour is always lima beans, but you can't expect miracles for $3.29, including beverage.

All the way over, Sam was bending my ear about this Faerbrother character, waving his newspaper and shoving the radio in my face like a mouthful of plastic was going to make me swallow his story. Monday night Sutpen's Hundred had scratched, just like Faerbrother predicted. Tuesday Reluctant Suitor broke the track record at his morning warm-up, just like Faerbrother said he would. When I tried to mention to Sam that the first horse was nursing a sprained leg from Saratoga and the second had won every race he'd entered since May, he wouldn't begin to listen. Faerbrother had predicted in advance what the paper and the turf reporters told him later, and as far as Sam was concerned, that was that.

"Is for real," he insisted, shaking his radio again to prove the point. "That man has the power, and we all getting rich!"

We went inside and placed our orders at the counter, and Sam didn't stop jabbering for a second. I let it wash around my head, a vague mambo rhythm behind my real thoughts. Two days ago, this kind of hash house had been the highest I ever aimed. Now I was spending half my life at the Pinnacle Room, a joint where I couldn't even pronounce the names of half the things they served, supposed to be a security guard but acting more like a detective. The job, the setting, even the crime were all way out of my league. What was a patrolman doing messing with homicide?

"When you gonna stop being a chalkie?" Sam was asking. "Betting the favorite to win? Bet five dollars, make fifty cents, where that gonna get you? When you gonna loosen up? Take a chance? After you dead is too late, baby."

I thought about John Lombardo, surprised by death on his way to a tryst with Janine DuPage. A man my age, but living at twice my pace, with five times my style. Whatever had happened between him and Janine at the end, I was pretty sure he'd had fun while it lasted. He hadn't been afraid to take chances. He'd known all along that the party could end at any moment, and he'd made sure to grab the good times while he could.

Or was it taking chances that had left him dead on the wine cellar floor? I sat down next to Sam and stared at my dinner, wondering which of us was better off. Then the lima beans vanished in a blur of newsprint, and I realized Sam was showing me the racing column, the proof of his miracle right there in black and white.

"One question, Sam," I said, pushing the paper aside. "Why me? Why are you so hot to sign me up?"

"Because you my friend," he answered proudly. "You pass this up, man, you gonna be one sorry *hombre*. Sorry and poor. I don't like to see my friends like that."

"Why me?" I asked again. "For real."

Sam put down his drumstick and bowed his head, like he was going to make a little prayer. "Because he won't do it unless we get five thousan' dollars," he confessed. "Faerbrother, see, he gets ten percent of the pot. But it's not his money he cares about. He says he don't want to waste his powers unless he bring at least that much joy of winning to the world." Sam paused, awed by such nobility. Then he got back to business. "Hector's sister in Miami, she promised to come in, too, but we're still one thousand bucks short. Who else I know with that kind of money but you?"

It was flattering to know that Sam Fuentes considered me a rich man, though it was also depressing to think of where that put the rest of his acquaintances. Did Sam really imagine I had a hoard stashed away in a shoe box somewhere or that I'd blow it on a scheme that didn't even deserve to be called a long shot? I let him down as gently as I could, but he still touched ground with a thud. He didn't even cheer up when I promised to go to the track with him every night the next week. First he started complaining that I had no sense of friendship. Then he switched over to whining about how Faerbrother was unhappy using the World Trade Center for his practice, worried that the crowds were breaking his concentration and sapping his psychic powers. Sam has great stamina as a complainer. After he alternated between his two themes for a while, it sounded like it was my cruelty to a pal that was causing the crowds.

"Tell you what," I said in desperation. "How would you like to take Faerbrother up to the top of a real tall building where he can be all alone to practice as long as he likes? You want to try that, I think I can make it happen." I wasn't sure how, but there had to be some way to get them up to the Interdine roof.

"How come you do that for me?" Sam asked.

"Like you said, Sam. Because you're my friend. And also," I said slowly, "because you can do me a favor, too." I sat back, dazzled by the flash of the great idea that had just come my way. If I were ever going to find out who killed Lombardo, it wouldn't be by spending all my waking hours cooped up in the Pinnacle Room on the sixty-eighth floor of the Interdine Tower. So far I was working on nothing but hunches and vibrations, which added up to just plain nothing without some facts to back them. But with Sam and his buddies doing the legwork for me, I stood a chance of finding out at least some of the things I wanted to know.

"That's it!" I exclaimed, caught up in the beauty of my plan. "You, Hector, and Ysidore help me out for the rest of the week, and in return I will not only get you up on the roof but will also contribute one thousand dollars to the pot."

"Help you out with what?" asked Sam suspiciously. "This part of that *job* you talking about all the time? Because I don't want to have nothing to do with no *job*. Is forty-five years ago next May I become a Newyorican. Thirty years I push around that goddamn cart, selling the sno-cones, plus five years over the river to Jersey to work in the factory." His face took on an exalted expression, so I knew he was about to quote from somebody's campaign literature. "I have earned the right to retire with *dignity*," he announced with a flourish.

"Let me put it differently," I said. "How would you three like to get that money by riding around in taxis and chasing pretty girls?"

"Well..." Sam considered, his body swaying back and forth to show me his mental uncertainty. When he decided he had hesitated long enough to preserve his precious dignity, he made up his mind.

"For you," he announced generously, "anything. Cash up front, of course."

"Nothing doing," I answered. "Work first, money after. That way you'll maybe even have a little left for the Hampton Stake." If everything went according to plan, Faerbrother would be in jail by then and he wouldn't get to spend it at all, but I didn't go into that with Sam. That was for me to know, just like the fact that I didn't have a thousand to give him.

What I wanted was simple enough. Someone to follow Angel Ruiz. See where he hung out, who his pals were. While I was at it, I also gave Sam a description of Janine. Ysidore lived up that way, and with all his kids it wouldn't be hard to keep track of her movements. We were almost out the door when I added Robert Lyder to my list of people to be watched. I wasn't sure what I suspected him of doing and I had no idea what I expected to find, but I knew that nobody could be that nervous without a reason.

137

Chapter 18

Sam and I split up outside the restaurant. He headed home to change into the special good-luck shirt he likes to wear to the track; I made my way downtown to work. I checked over the racing forms, thinking I might place a wager at the OTB office on my way out of the subway, but it was hard to concentrate on a claiming race for two-year-old pacers when all the time I was wondering what Captain Powers was up to. I hadn't noticed anybody trailing me when I got on the train. I hadn't seen anybody hanging around Janine either. So what kind of investigation was he running anyway? Had they already picked up Angel and closed the case, or had I lost the knack of spotting a tail?

I checked out my fellow passengers, trying to figure if any of them was working undercover, but the main thing I noticed was that everyone in my car was terrified of everyone else. The cleaning woman going downtown for the night shift clutched her shopping bag to protect it from the tough-looking girl in pink jeans who had dyed one side of her head purple. But the girl was carrying a skate bag, just a kid on her way to the roller disco, and she was concentrating on keeping her distance from the guy with sideburns and slicked-back hair who was staring at her from his post by the door. Lover boy was scared of me, smelling a cop even though I was three years off the force and out of uniform, which was why he was leaning back instead of coming closer and trying to make some time with the roller queen. I had my eye on a weirdo muttering to himself in the middle of the car. Someday he might get through reciting his list of the ways the world had screwed him, at which time he would take the knife from his pocket and try to get even. Tonight, though, he was still tuned to his inner demons. A typical late-night crowd, the elegant party hoppers of the glittering after-hours scene, hurtling along in their public limousine with its hand-painted graffiti interior. No wonder most people favored those Guardian Angel kids who rode around the trains in uniform. They didn't do a damn thing, but at least when you saw one, you could check him off as probably not about to get hostile.

The fares were sparse to begin with, that hour on a weekday night, and they got thinner as we got lower into Manhattan. When we got to the World Trade Center, I was the only person getting out, and I don't mind admitting I did not linger over the vacant stretches between there and the Interdine Tower.

Up at the Pinnacle Room it was a different story. Lombardo's obituary had been top news all day, padded out with rave descriptions of all the restaurants he'd ever built, and it was beginning to look like his death might be the best thing that had ever happened to the food end of the Interdine Corporation. Next week, of course, might be a different story. Like Lyder had said, this was a fickle business he was in, and sooner or later he'd be standing on his own.

Not tonight, though. It was a repeat of Tuesday, with people piled around six deep to offer their condolences. Then I noticed that one of them was Plato Thorson. He looked even damper than usual next to the regulars, their suntans deepened by the flush of a good dinner. If he took off his jacket, I wouldn't have been surprised to see moss stains on his shirt.

As soon as he saw me he came right over, and Lyder broke away to join him a minute later. Very flattering, all that attention coming my way, except that none of it was cordial. Lyder started in on how I was ten minutes late. Thorson interrupted to ask a whole lot of questions about my height and weight and which hand did I use to brush my teeth. Lyder countered with a long story about an antique corkscrew that was missing, and the two of them together managed to imply that I was guilty of everything from a burned steak to John Lombardo's murder. Especially John Lombardo's murder. I hightailed it in to the kitchen as soon as I could, but all I picked up for my efforts was a lot of talk about Lombardo's sex life and speculation on who would take over Janine's job if she kept on calling in sick every day. Yesterday everyone had been in shock, but now the gossip had started.

Everybody had known all along that Janine had had her eye on the boss, it seemed, but no one had been wise to Lombardo's affair with Angel until word filtered through in the news reports. "Longtime companion" they called him in the *New York Times*. MALE PATOOTIE A SUSPECT went the headline in the *Post*. I couldn't wait to see what the weekly tabloids came up with. And in the meantime, the story going around the kitchen was that Janine and Angel had gotten into a screaming brawl over the boss's body. Forty-eight hours ago John Lombardo had been next to God in that kitchen, or maybe a little higher, and now already the busboys were entertaining each other with dirty jokes about their old boss's different appetites. Instead of picking up any inside dope, I got a lot of cheap misinformation about events that I had witnessed myself.

Plus I still wasn't winning any popularity contests with the staff. The only person who even acknowledged my existence was Pierre, and he was so busy running around giving orders that it was a tossup if he even knew who he was nodding to. After a while he slowed down, though, and I grabbed him.

"Got a minute?" I asked.

"Is terrible here," he countered. "Everything so confused. The service so dismayed, the cellar in such a disarray. I try to provide the direction, but I am helpless. Such a tragedy!"

"All I want is a list of the wines that are missing."

"But certainly. I have already done this for the police." Pierre looked at me thoughtfully, then moved a few steps over to the side of the room. "You are not any longer under their suspicion?" he asked. "I am very content to hear that. I feel sure always you are not the man."

"You think it was Angel?" While he was trying to provide the direction, as he put it, Pierre must have picked up some of the gossip that wasn't coming my way.

As though in answer, he pulled the napkin off his arm, smoothed out the folds, and put it back.

"Perhaps," he said at last. "Perhaps him, perhaps Miss Du-Page. I think probably this person who is doing the stealing, no? But for certain we must look for someone who could profit from Monsieur Lombardo dead. That is the question for sure." He patted his napkin again for emphasis, then made an apologetic little bow. "You will excuse me now?" he said. "I must help Mr. Lyder with sending the after-dinner cordials to the tables. Our special customers, he does not know what they like."

After he left, I sat down by the wall, waiting for the place to clear out. When John Lombardo died, it was like my own life had gotten turned around. During the day all I could think about was the case. I rode the subway home in the morning trying to figure who had been stealing from Lombardo. I brushed my teeth thinking about his relationship with Janine and with Angel. I dreamed about him when I got into bed, and I woke up depressed before I even remembered why. Everyone I talked to lately was somehow involved, and if they weren't, like Sam, I dragged them in as soon as possible. Then, at ten o'clock at night, I showed up at the Pinnacle Room, the famous scene of the famous crime, and for the next nine hours I was helpless. If they had locked me up at Rikers or put me in a holding cell in the Tombs, they couldn't have done a more effective job of keeping me away from finding out who had really killed John Lombardo.

My mind went around and around the same old circles, getting nowhere. Why hadn't the police made any arrests? Did they know anything about Angel or Janine that I didn't? Had the sneak thief really reappeared? Maybe it was Lyder who had been taking things. Maybe it was Lyder who had killed Lombardo. Getting rid of the boss had given him an overnight promotion, and under the kind of circumstances where everyone would make lots of allowances if he wasn't so great in his first few weeks on the job. Think about who would profit, Pierre had said.

So I sat there thinking, and meanwhile, the subject of my thoughts came through to close up the shop. He rattled the lock on the freezer, wiggled the oven knobs, stuck his head in the dumbwaiter to be sure it was empty, checked the sink for drips, and swept the counter for crumbs. When there was absolutely nothing else to do, he turned to me.

"I'll be here for two more hours," he announced, making it sound like some kind of challenge. "You can find me in the manager's office upstairs."

Lyder acted like he expected me to show up with a pair of dueling pistols. I thanked him for the information and went back to counting the dots in the ceiling tiles, hoping he wouldn't be too disappointed if I didn't come by.

For the next two hours, exactly, he stayed in his office. When I made the rounds I could hear him pacing the floor, flipping through the books, muttering to himself to a background of little beeps that I finally figured were the noise you made when you hit the buttons of a calculator. Around 12:30 it sounded like he took a break to do a little decorating. First the protesting whine of furniture being dragged across the floor, then the sound of nails being pounded into the wall, and then a lot of banging I couldn't identify. I was getting up for my 2:00 A.M. circuit when

I heard the elevator arrive and then descend again. He hadn't bothered to wish me good-night.

As soon as I was sure he was really gone, I beat it over to the office to see what he'd been up to. The door was locked, but that didn't matter because I'd brought the passkey from the kitchen. Lyder himself had told me it was there.

The only other time I'd been in the room was Monday night. Even with the powerful distraction of Janine DuPage, I'd been struck by how much trouble Lombardo had gone to fixing up the place to his taste. The walls were painted the color of peach ice cream; the bookshelves were filled with handsome pieces of silver and crystal; the desk was topped with some kind of tortoise-shell stuff that matched the frames on all the photographs on the wall. Even the account books that sat on the desk were covered in brown velour instead of the usual red and black cardboard.

Over the last forty-eight hours, though, Lyder had managed to turn Lombardo's pretty little sitting room into something that looked like an extension of the Wall Street YMCA. The silver gewgaws had been pushed off the shelves to make room for an impressive set of athletic trophies and plaques. The celebrity mug shots were down from the wall, replaced by a huge framed poster of a snow-covered mountain so steep even the goats hadn't made it into the picture. The account books were still there, jumbled into a pile on the desk, but the desk itself had been moved to the center of the room to make space for a strange-looking contraption that was now attached to the wall. After a minute I recognized it for one of those executive exercise machines they advertise, with springs and pulleys and weights for adjusting the resistance so you can pack a full workout into a coffee break.

The exercise machine explained the banging and the furniture moving, though it seemed queer that Lyder had suddenly developed this urgent need to install the thing at one o'clock in the morning. Maybe he thought body building would help him run

143

the restaurant. Last night Pierre had been assuring Lyder that his personality would draw as many customers as Lombardo's had, but if this was a sample of the changes the new manager had in mind, the Pinnacle Room could be in for some rocky times.

I walked over for a closer look at the trophies. Ten years ago Lyder had been winning medals as a track star for the University of Pennsylvania. He had piled up a respectable number of medals for the 100-meter dash and the 440 relay, which looked to be his specialty. Lately, though, it seemed he had switched from running down roads to climbing up mountains. Little brass plaques set on wooden shields announced that he had been to the top of Mount McKinley, camped on the summit of Mount Shasta, been second man over the wall of El Capitan. Just to clinch it there was a fancy piece of parchment, framed, declaring him a member of the American Mountaineering Society and a phony cartoon certificate that said Robert Lyder was now officially qualified to climb the walls. The guy must have suction cups on his toes, I thought. Probably felt right at home working here, way up above the cloud line.

Looking around, I was struck by what a wholesome type Lyder seemed to be. Hard-working, clean-living, reverent, loyal—the guy was a regular Boy Scout. So what was there about him, I wondered, that made me distrust him? It's easy to be suspicious of people when you're all alone in the dark. At three in the morning there isn't a soul on earth who doesn't seem capable of murder. But there was more to it than that. Whenever I saw Lyder, my first thought was that the man had something to hide, the question being what.

I went back to the kitchen to see if I could figure it out better there and ended up falling asleep with my head on the table. The cleaning crew woke me at three-thirty, coming through like a demolition derby out of Krakow and leaving a stink of Lysol in their wake. I jumped out of their way and ran to make a tour of the premises, terrified that Lombardo's killer had come back

144

brandishing the missing corkscrew, but as far as I could tell, I was all alone.

By five in the morning my system had given up complaining about the hours and settled into just feeling lousy. There was no point in the world in my being there, and I meant to tell Gloria that I quit, first thing in the morning. Then Powers. Then Blount Harwell. Let them all do their own investigating if they were so keen on secrets. Let them stay up all night waiting for Lombardo's killer to return to the scene. I sat down on the couch by the entryway and told my troubles to the Statue of Liberty, out the window. And then I started hearing noises.

It was just the ordinary whirring and creaking of the elevator coming up from downstairs. Nothing strange about it at all. Except the elevators weren't supposed to be running at that time of night. When I got dressed for work, I had decided to pack my gun and let Gloria's insurance take care of itself. Now I pulled the revolver out from under my jacket. I hadn't been expecting company, but I planned to be ready if it arrived.

I could hear the click the car made when it brushed the doorway on the floor below and then the louder knock against the landing when it got to me. I released the safety catch on my gun, took the ready position in front of the door, and stood there a good long while until finally I realized the elevator wasn't stopping. Putting the safety back on my revolver, I pressed my ear against the elevator doors. I could hear the car passing Harwell's office, then going up beyond the executive suite on the floor above. Finally it whirred to a stop at the roof.

Why would anybody be going up to the roof? If they ever got it finished, it would be a health club, but right now there was nothing up there but an empty swimming pool and a lot of sky. After a few more minutes with my ear pressed up against the elevator door, I decided to let the Pinnacle Room fend for itself. I slipped through the fire door to the stairs and climbed the three flights fast but quiet, stopping every few steps to make sure nobody was coming down from above. When I got to the top, I was standing in a wooden shed that protected the stairs until they got the plastic dome in place. Very slowly I opened the door.

It was already well into daylight by then. Across the roof I could see the elevator boxes and the beginnings of what would someday be a reception area, the whole area wrapped in a giant piece of heavy-duty plastic like some kind of mutant sandwich bag. The empty swimming pool was out in the open, its metal diving board still giving off a pink reflection of the rising sun. And at the very edge of the roof, standing next to a huge metal crane that had been left there to lift up the final pieces of the builder's puzzle, was Robert Lyder.

He was facing away from me, one hand braced against the crane as he peered down the side of the building. I pulled the door almost all the way shut and watched through the slit, waiting for Lyder to do something that would clue me in to why he was up there. Unfortunately Lyder had other plans. He stood there awhile longer, studying something down below, then abruptly turned to pick up an orange knapsack that had been leaning against the base of the crane. Quickly pulling the straps over the shoulders of his business suit, he made his way across the roof and vanished under the plastic tarp that shrouded the elevators. I gave him plenty of time, then sprinted down the stairs back to the sixty-eighth floor. It wouldn't be polite to let the bakers arrive without me there to greet them.

Chapter 19

Courtesy doesn't have to take a long time. At seven sharp I
ushered in the flour and sugar boys, and ten minutes later I was
on my way to see Gloria. Strictly business, of course. With me
working nights and sleeping through the day, this was about the
only time I could count on catching her when we'd both be at
least semiconscious.

The doorman remembered me from Tuesday and had already
buzzed upstairs when I got to his desk. He gave me a sour smile
and waved me on through to the elevator. For Gloria's sake, I
wished I had thought to shave before I came over. It couldn't be
helping her standing with the service people to have this bum
keep showing up first thing in the morning.

She was waiting by the door to her apartment, already dressed
for the office in a gray plaid skirt and a white shirt that hadn't
even had time to get wrinkled. Seeing her made me feel even
seedier than I had before. I must have looked it, too, because
right away she started making sympathetic noises about how tired
I looked, and wasn't it terrible that I had to stay up all night
working when everyone else was home in bed? She stole my
lines, was what she did, so instead of complaining like I had every
right to do, I started right in on what I'd found out since Tuesday:
first my meeting with Janine, then the sudden changes in the

manager's office, and finally the big puzzle, which was Lyder's trip to the roof.

"What do you think he was doing up there?" she asked. "Do you suppose it has something to do with the murder?"

"I don't know," I answered. "One idea I had was that maybe he'd been stealing things from the restaurant himself and hiding the stash on the roof, letting it cool off for a while before he took it onto the street. That would explain the knapsack anyway."

"Yeah," Gloria agreed, but not like she meant it. "But wouldn't the police have found that out when they searched the building right after the murder? And all that exercise stuff..." Her voice trailed off as she concentrated on some new possibility. "Hey!" she exclaimed suddenly. "You think he could have climbed down from the roof on a rope, come in a window, killed Lombardo, and then climbed down to the garage?"

It was a nice idea. So nice I'd thought of it myself, which was how I knew right off that it was impossible.

"You're living in the past," I said. "Windows don't open nowadays, haven't you noticed?"

"I bet there's a transom somewhere," Gloria countered stubbornly. "Think how great it would be if we could prove that Lyder was really the killer! Not only solving the murder but also discovering a dangerous criminal right inside Interdine! Harwell would hire us for sure after that."

Trust Gloria to be working the angles on someone else's killing. Then her voice changed.

"Two things I have to tell you," she said. "Number one, Lieutenant Thorson spent yesterday afternoon going through my files, trying to make a case for some prior connection between Global and Lombardo or somebody who knew Lombardo. He kept bringing up that work my ex-partner did for that friend of Johnny's, trying to make it the basis for some grand murder conspiracy or something. What a creep!"

Creep was right. I had been planning to call Captain Powers

to spill my ideas to him, but I was sufficiently steamed by the idea of Thorson pawing through Gloria's files to consider that little obligation no longer binding, at least for now. Any suspects I handed over to the police were going to be gift-wrapped with the name of Global Security all over the paper, so there could be no mistake about where the credit was due.

"What was the second thing?" I asked.

"Last night they arrested Angel Ruiz. I heard it on the eleven o'clock news."

"What!" All night I'd been thinking evil thoughts about Robert Lyder, and meanwhile, Ruiz was already in the stir. I felt like I'd been cheated.

"But they didn't say anything about having found the killer," Gloria said. "The way they were telling it on the news, the cops brought him in only for the *robberies*. It didn't sound like a real strong case to me. Just a lot of jazz about how they hope to have something to announce in the near future. Don't worry, I figure we've still got a shot at it."

It was irritating that Gloria could read me so well, but I had to admit she was right. What was getting to me now was that maybe Powers was going to close the case before I had a chance at it. I was convinced that something was going on at the Pinnacle Room that had nothing to do with Angel Ruiz, though the news about the robberies did surprise me. What kind of case did Powers have against Ruiz? I wondered. For sure, a better one than I had against Lyder. What had seemed clearly suspicious at dawn was a lot harder to make out in broad daylight. Something was there, though, and it was worth finding out what.

"Are you serious about seeing if it was someone besides Ruiz who killed Lombardo?" I demanded.

"Sure," Gloria answered, sitting down. Her voice was a little shaky, but she looked determined.

"Good. Here are the things I want you to do today." I outlined the calls she was to make—to the garage; the mountaineering clubs, and the personnel department at Interdine. "Tell them anything you want," I said, "but find out that information."

Gloria had been taking notes on a memo pad she brought over from by the telephone. Now she put down her pencil and her coffee cup, too.

"You think we can do it?" she asked. She sounded like the odds had just suddenly struck her. "Two little people trying to beat the whole police department at their game. You think we've really got a chance? We keep kidding around, we're liable to get ourselves killed."

"Make that five little people," I said. As briefly as I could, I explained about how I had enlisted Sam and his friends to help us out. Unfortunately I wasn't brief enough. Gloria exploded.

"Are you out of your mind?" she yelled. "Here I am, worrying about your getting hurt, and you're off hiring your railbird friends to do legwork! As if those guys were going anywhere except to the nearest betting parlor. And a thousand dollars! For that kind of money you could get real help, instead of those zeros. I don't know about the other two, but I've met your pal Fuentes, thank you, and I wouldn't trust him with anything worth over fifty cents. If that's the way you operate, forget the whole thing!"

"Well, if that's the way you run your business," I shouted back at her, "I'm not surprised you're going broke!" Here I'd been turning myself inside out to help her, and all she could do was criticize my methods. So far I hadn't heard one word of thanks from her since I'd agreed to take the job. What was she waiting for? After I got dead?

"You talk a good line," I told her, "with your custom service and fancy customers and all, but the fact is that I got three people working on the job while you're sitting back waiting to bail out your company with pennies from heaven. If you have better people on hand, let's see them. And as for the money, don't worry because I'm paying them myself!" It was going to wipe out my savings account for sure, but right then I didn't care.

At that Gloria stomped out of the kitchen and down the hall to her bedroom, slamming the door behind. It seemed to be my signal to leave, but before I could do it, she was back.

"Here," she said angrily, sticking a pile of twenty-dollar bills in my hand. "It's two hundred dollars, just in case you end up having to pay those guys. But tell them they'd better come up with something fast because there's no more where that came from." Then she reached into her pocket, pulled out a pair of keys, and stared at them for a while.

"These are for you," she said finally, shoving them at me. "You're busy. I'm busy. We're also playing around with a lot of people we don't know, and it could be dangerous. Anytime you need a place to go, you can come here. Don't worry about the hour. Don't worry about letting me know or if I'm here or not. Just come. The brass key is for the front door; the silver, for the apartment." She looked at me like she thought I was going to pick an argument, but I didn't say a word. "I never gave those to anybody else," she added softly.

"That's none of my business," I said.

"Right," she answered, slamming her purse up under her arm. "I'm going to work now. The cleaning woman gets here at nine. Clear out before then, or make your own introductions. And, Quentin"—she hesitated, then suddenly smiled, "take care of yourself."

She was out the door and down the hall to the elevator before I could begin to think of an answer. I stared at the space where she had been. Then I put the cash in my wallet and the keys in my pocket and headed out myself. Gloria hadn't exactly given me a lot of answers for the questions on my mind, but at least she'd gotten rid of my grogginess. There's nothing like a good fight first thing in the morning to wake a person up.

Or to make him hungry. Detouring around the subway entrance, I walked south from Washington Square, looking for a place to pick up some breakfast. It was pretty early yet, every park bench still occupied by a sleeping bum, and I had trouble finding a place that was open. On the outskirts of Chinatown I finally settled for something that called itself the East-West Dim Sum Deli, where for $1.79 I got the breakfast special. Two rolls stuffed with sweet orange paste, a ball of rice with some fish in the middle, and a whole pot of green tea. It was awful, but at least it filled me up.

While I ate, I tried to figure out the story over at the Pinnacle Room. Janine DuPage had been having an affair with John Lombardo, but instead of being shocked at his murder, she acted like she'd been jilted. John Lombardo, while having a good time with Janine, had also been fooling around with Angel Ruiz. Angel Ruiz, who said he loved Lombardo, had also been stealing from him, at least according to the police. Blount Harwell had built Interdine's reputation on the glamour of Lombardo's restaurants, but now he seemed perfectly willing to have the newest one run by Robert Lyder, who had as much charisma as a bowl of oatmeal. Robert Lyder had just gotten a really fast promotion, but instead of its making him happy, it seemed to make him nervous. Not so nervous that he tried to learn the business, though. When you would have expected him to be practicing his white sauce and learning about wines, Lyder instead spent his time moving furniture and popping up in odd corners of the building at even odder hours. The only thing I could say without any qualification or contradiction was that none of it made any sense.

Having come to this brilliant conclusion, I downed the last of my tea and stepped outside. On the other side of the street the tiniest woman I had ever seen was struggling with a pole at least twice as tall as she was, trying to unroll the awning over her store. I crossed over to give her a hand and eventually managed to unfurl a length of red canvas covered with faded Chinese letters. The proprietor chirped something that might have been thanks and hopped inside, behind a clear glass door practically painted over with more Chinese letters and even a few English ones, too.

What really caught my eye, though, was the window. From the size of the pane I'd have expected either a fortuneteller or a jeweler, but what I saw was a display of rental notices, neatly lettered in Chinese and English and stuck in the slots of a homemade display board. "Good location laundry," I read, "$1,600 per month. Equipment extra"; "Small room for family, share bath, $250 per month"; "Basement apartment near school. Three good rooms, kitchen. $500." The window on the other side of the door had a similar board, but these were mostly business offers, and many of them were only in Chinese. Even the ones I could read were mysterious. What did it mean to offer "Key money loans, good terms"? Who would pay $500 for "room for apprentice waiter"? And what about the offer to "share one BR Hong Kong apartment, $3,000 per month"? Anybody willing to pay that kind of money for only a slice of an apartment would hardly do his real estate shopping in a joint like this one. Not from what I could see of the inside, which consisted of a couple of battered desks, an old travel poster of Chinese barges in the bay, and a whole wall of red metal file cabinets.

Meanwhile, Thumbelina had been watching me from behind one of the desks. By now she was making urgent gestures for me to come inside. Instead I walked away quick, before she could talk me out of any key money. I had enough problems, I told myself, without burdening my brain with the mysteries of Oriental real estate procedures. Which turned out to be one of my many wrong assumptions.

Chapter 20

Right then all I knew for sure was that the day was hot and I was tired. An endless ride on the subway did nothing to improve conditions. When I got home, it was past 10 o'clock. I pulled the blinds, set the alarm for 6:00 P.M., took off my clothes, and got into bed. Ninety seconds later I got out again and called a man I knew on the bunko squad, to get him to put a tracer on Ezra Faerbrother. I wasn't back in the sack for a minute before I was up again to check that I hadn't lost Gloria's money.

It was a day of thrashing and dozing, with no real rest. Every time I closed my eyes I fell into a nightmare. I imagined Angel escaping from jail on an endless rope of knotted tablecloths. I dreamed that Lyder was a giant spider, hanging over everyone who worked in the restaurant and dropping down on them whenever he thought they weren't being loyal, until I woke in a sweat, slapping the pillow to knock the bugs from my face. Next I dreamed that it was dinnertime at the Pinnacle Room. John Lombardo was still alive, and everything was fine, except that Janine was wearing her filmy undies while she did the seating. Nobody seemed to notice but me, though, and nobody noticed me at all. I kept on trying to warn Lombardo to stay away from the wine cellar, but every time I tried to talk to him he just brushed me away.

When I woke up from that one, it was after four o'clock, and I gave up on further shut-eye. I got dressed and went downstairs to see if I could catch Sam before he headed out for the evening races.

The blare of the television met me halfway down the hall, which was a good sign that Sam was still around. I rang the bell and waited, knowing from experience that it would take him a while to find his shoes and hide his glasses. For a guy who used to make his living selling flavored ice chips from a wagon, Sam is very vain.

Eventually he opened the door, his shirt billowing in the blast from the fan he kept by the couch.

"Buenas tardes, Jacoby, baby!" he exclaimed. "Wanna go out to the track tonight? They got some good claiming races. Maybe we buy a horse, you and me."

"What are you planning to use for money?"

"Don't you remember? Sunday we gonna be rich men. Buy all the trotters we want. And their drivers, too!"

"That's right," I agreed. "But I don't think the track will give us a horse on credit. Besides, I'm still working nights. Come with me to Maybelle's; we'll talk while I get something to eat."

I hurried him out as fast as possible. Sam's apartment is furnished entirely in red plush, which is okay for December but more than a sane man can bear in the middle of August.

All the way over to the doughnut shop Sam was talking at his usual speed—mostly about how he was planning to spend the money he won through Faerbrother, partly about this blonde with dynamite legs he'd seen a lot of about thirty years ago, but not at all about what he'd done to help me on Lombardo's case. Probably he'd forgotten all about it, he was so caught up in his telepathic race fixer. Just before we got to Maybelle's, I managed

155

to stop the flood of gab long enough to ask if he'd ever gotten through to his fellow investors. Sam winked and headed for his favorite seat at the counter, right opposite the tray of chocolate doughnuts.

After he was comfortably settled and had finished flirting with the waitress, he was nice enough to consider my question. The big surprise was that he actually had some answers. As soon as he got home last night he got on the horn to Hector and Ysidore, and the three of them had gone to work right then and there. Sam had come downtown right after me and hung around until Robert Lyder went home. Lyder had gone straight to his apartment on East Fifty-third Street, at which point Sam gave up and went home himself. I tried to explain that he had quit right when it would have done me some good to know what happened next, but Sam didn't even notice. He was still flushed with the excitement of getting in a taxi and telling the driver to follow that car. I dug out fifty dollars of Gloria's money and told him to call me at work if Lyder went anywhere else tonight. I also told him that Faerbrother could have his morning on the roof anytime he wanted. If he ever took me up on the offer, that would be soon enough to mention the stairs. Then I asked what news Sam had from the others.

Like I expected, Ysidore had set his family on what amounted to a twenty-four-hour stakeout of Janine's building. So far she had come out of her apartment once. At eight in the morning. To Gristede's. Only one little bag of groceries, he added, and on the way back she stopped to look in a hardware store window. After this thrilling piece of information Sam settled down to his food, clearly satisfied with his first night as a private eye. I wished I felt as happy. "What happened to Hector?" I asked.

Sam shrugged and took a bite of his doughnut. "Hector, he go down by the apartment of your Angel Ruiz," he said. "Way in Little Italy, you know? So he stand outside for a while, watching the windows, and then all these police cops arrive and haul

156

the man away in their cars. Hector, he figure that makes it time
to go home. I tell you, Jacoby, baby," he added earnestly, "this
job of yours is nothing fun. You keep working nights like this,
you *never* gonna get out to the races."

"Truer words I never heard," I said, sliding off my stool and
toward the door. The kid should be out by now, I thought. Time
for a personal visit.

"Hey, baby," Sam called after me, "don't forget you owe Hector and Ysidore, too. Not my fault we following people going
nowhere."

I didn't bother to answer. A call downtown confirmed that
Angel Ruiz had posted bond and been released, which left me
with the simple problem of finding where he had gone. Angel
hadn't struck me as a real deep thinker. I decided to start with
the obvious and made tracks for his apartment just off Spring
Street, fifty-eight minutes due south of Co-op City on the Lexington Avenue line. The address turned out to be a three-story
brick building, a single-family house that had been chopped into
apartments about the same time the landlord installed indoor
plumbing. Angel had the top floor, which doubtless meant Lombardo had been paying the rent. Now to see if the little cherub
was at home.

He wasn't. Twenty minutes of hanging around the mailboxes
inspired me to pry open the door, which was ridiculously easy
to do. It's amazing how many people won't pay the extra twenty
dollars for a dead-bolt lock. I crept up three flights, not wanting
to meet the neighbors, then settled myself at the top of the stairs
to wait for Angel.

It took another hour of waiting to get rid of the last of my
scruples about breaking and entering. If Angel came back and
saw me on the stairs, five would get me ten he'd just turn around
and run out of my life. And what if he never came back? Either
way, a waste of time I couldn't afford to lose. Whereas if I waited
inside his apartment, I could catch him by surprise and mean-

while maybe nose around the premises and see what I could learn. I had my credit card out and the door open before you could say criminal trespass. If I ever did catch up with Ruiz, I meant to give him some tips on upgrading his home security.

After all that waiting I should have known I would get only about three feet inside the door when I heard someone coming up the stairs. I just had time before the door opened to wonder if Angel was the type to press charges. Unfortunately I didn't have a chance to find out because when the door did open, it wasn't to let in Angel.

There were only two of them, but each was big enough to seem like a crowd. The one in front was an enormous hulk of a guy with curly blond hair and pale gray eyes the color of cataracts. He was wearing black, just like Angel had been the other night, except he was about twice as big and his muscles pushed out of his T-shirt like they were looking for something to hurt. He jumped with surprise when he saw me, then got much too calm.

"Hello, fuzzface," he said, smiling in a way that made me extremely nervous. "You here all alone? Don't bother telling me what you're doing. Snooping around, is what. Or maybe you came back to put a little extra pressure on Angel, real private, like. It's a real shame we showed up instead. Isn't it, Roger?"

I started to explain about how there was a terrible mistake and I wasn't a police officer at all, but I stopped wasting my breath as soon as I caught sight of Roger. He was built along the lines of King Kong, only slightly bigger, with a huge round jaw and beady little brown eyes under a sloping forehead that made him look like the missing link. A natty dresser, though. You could tell by his black and white saddle shoes and the white beaded cowboy belt that was holding up his black lizard trousers. A real Ivy League type.

"Move it, buddy," he said by way of introduction. I was amazed he could talk. Actually he was a very convincing speaker. "I've got a knife," he went on, "and I'd love to add a piece of your ass

158

to my collection." I was about as old as the two of them together, and each was twice my size. Whatever they had in mind, I wasn't going to argue.

What I got was a quick hustle out the back way, down the fire escape, and into the alley. It was a textbook demonstration of a beating, with me posing for before, during, and after. Especially during. First Roger held my shoulders against the brick wall while the blond punched me in the jaw and the guts. This went on until my knees buckled, which didn't take long. At that point they let me slide to the ground so Roger could practice his foot-work. He didn't like it when I started puking on his shoes, though, so they went back to Plan A, up against the wall.

"I'm not police," I gasped.

Blondie stopped banging my head. "Of course not," he agreed. "You're a cute old ass-twitcher in from Kansas, come to check out the action in the big city." When he started hitting me again, I pulled my best move of the evening. I blacked out.

When I came to, I was lying in the alley, nose to nose with a banged-up metal Dumpster. Roger was going through my pock-ets. I decided to keep on playing dead. As though I had a choice.

"There's a gun in his jacket," he called up to his buddy. "No ID, though."

"Try the pants. But no loitering."

They both laughed. I concentrated on staying relaxed when he rolled me over. Then they were flipping through my wallet, and suddenly the atmosphere changed.

"Jesus Christ," Roger muttered worriedly. "You see that?"

I tried to imagine what they had found that was so upsetting. Two charge cards, one expired. A gun license. A picture of Bea, taken twenty years ago. Gloria's phone number on a piece of paper. A lifetime pass to the subways. An employee ID to the Interdine Tower, signed by John Lombardo. A card for the Co-op City branch of the public library. Nothing there that could possibly scare anyone.

At least they weren't hitting me anymore. There was a low buzz of talk, but I didn't have the energy to try to listen. I could feel the blood coming from my nose every time I breathed: a warm, salty trickle down my throat when I inhaled; a messy bubble when I exhaled. When they hoisted me up from the pavement, I tried to break loose, but Roger gave me a gentle hug that reminded me I was much too old for this kind of exercise. Once more my body was sending my brain urgent messages to pass out.

The next thing I knew I was sprawled in the back of a car, going for a ride to I didn't know where. Roger was driving, and Blondie was sitting next to him up front. They were talking low, and they were worried.

"We made a big mistake on this one," I heard Roger say. "He worked for Johnny. What are we gonna tell Angel?"

"How about we tell him nothing? No big loss if we off this customer and somehow lose his remains. Make like nothing happened and hope for the best."

"You know what?" Roger said. "You are a real sadist." He sounded delighted.

How much of it was real, I wondered, and how much was just passing the time? It had been real enough when they dragged me from the apartment and more than that in the alley. Something had scared them off, but now they were getting back their nerve. Everything hurt too much for me to focus on what they were saying, but it all sounded like bad news for me.

If they really thought I was a cop, it made no sense for them to be attacking me unless they planned to get rid of me for good. And if they didn't think I was a cop, there still wasn't any advantage to them in leaving me around and every reason for getting me out of the way.

I thought about where we might be going. Every city in the world has its dumping ground for superfluous bodies, and in Manhattan the odds-on favorite is over the edge and into the

160

water. It doesn't matter if it's the East River, the Hudson, or the Gowanus Canal—whichever you choose, it's one quick splash and out of sight, out of mind. For some reason I was more upset about going into that filthy water than about getting attacked. I imagined the liquid muck closing over my head, washing through the cuts where my face was all torn up, getting into my bloodstream and in my lungs. I started moaning at the idea. They must have heard me because the car pulled to a stop and Roger loomed over the front seat. I closed my eyes, but I couldn't stop the moans. When he leaned over to grab me, I started to scream, and then I blacked out for the third time.

Chapter 21

When I came around this time, the gorillas were gone. I was still in the car, my blood no more full of garbage than is standard for anybody breathing late-twentieth-century urban air. For a minute I thought I was already dead, gone to heaven in the back seat of a Dodge surrounded by big-eyed black-haired angels. Then the world stopped spinning, and I saw it was only one angel, the one who hung out with John Lombardo. The one who had vowed to kill me for sticking his boyfriend. Better they had dumped me underwater and gotten it over with.

Or maybe not. Angel was sitting in the front of the car, in the passenger seat, and when I finally sat up in back, he looked positively relieved.

"You okay?" he asked hesitantly.

I checked over my body, twitching the different parts to see how loud they objected. I wouldn't be doing any sit-ups in the near future, but there didn't seem to be anything broken inside. My face hurt like crazy, and my lower lip felt about three times its usual size, but things weren't nearly as bad as they could have been. So I wasn't quite ready for the old folks' home after all.

"You all right?" Angel asked again. He sounded distinctly nervous. I tilted my head toward the door, and he hesitated. "I don't think you better move for a while, mister," he said.

I couldn't have agreed with him more, but it was comforting to know he thought I had a say in the matter. I tilted my head again and opened my mouth just enough to gasp out, "Air."

Angel smiled in relief and bent over the back of his seat to roll down the window beside me. It was gradually penetrating my thick skull that the guy was pleased that I was still alive.

I craned my head out the window to gulp in some fresh air and right away started retching again. Nobody had told me that we were parked by the Fulton Fish Market, but there was only one place in town that smelled like that. Nothing like the aroma of yesterday's mackerel to set a fellow up.

"Get me out of here," I groaned.

Angel nodded but just sat there. "I don't know how to drive," he said finally.

Neither did I. Only an idiot kept a car in New York, and I was a great champion of public transportation, which as an ex-policeman I got to ride for free. Right then I would have settled for being an idiot. I checked my bones again and decided anything was better than the fish.

"I'll walk," I told him.

Walking was too good a word for it, but the smell wasn't so bad once I was out of the car. Leaning on Angel pretty hard, I managed to lurch up half a block to the outside edge of that fancy new tourist trap they built around where the big old sailboats are parked. Just far enough to find a place to sit down and still be out of range of the night life. I sank onto a bench in front of some schooner left over from the Boston Tea Party and tried to sort out what had happened.

Over on the Brooklyn side of the river there was a billboard with a clock built in. "Time to Prepare," it said, with a picture of a young couple smiling at each other while they planned their retirement savings. It felt like the middle of tomorrow, but the clock said it was only ten after ten. If I didn't slow down soon,

I'd never get to enjoy those golden years they talked about on the poster.

"You want anything?" Angel asked. "Glass of water? Something to drink?"

"Yeah," I answered thickly. What I wanted was a month in the country, starting yesterday, but I was willing to settle for some information. "I want to know what the hell is going on. I went to see you, nice and peaceful, hoping we could maybe have a quiet talk without a lot of detectives listening in, and the next thing I know Heckle and Jeckle are pummeling me out in the alley. That the way you treat all your visitors?"

"They were just trying to help me out, man," Angel said anxiously. "Protect a friend. Cops crawling all over me since Monday night, what they supposed to think when they find you inside my place? Then they saw you worked for Johnny. Big mistake, that's all. You gonna press charges?" From the way he asked, I could tell he'd already had more than enough of police stations.

"That depends," I answered, taking advantage of his worries to brush over the little matter of my own illegal entry. "You tell me what was going on between you and John Lombardo and what happened Monday night, and maybe I won't file a complaint. But I want to know everything, and that includes the parts you haven't gotten around to telling the police."

I had trouble talking, but the words seemed right. Not right enough, though. Angel wasn't that glad to see me alive.

"Sure, man. Sure." He sneered. "I bring you back from the dead, and for thanks you want my life story. Maybe you're gonna sell it to the movies, we'll both be famous. I don't have to tell you nothing."

I sighed. Talking made my mouth hurt, and the wind off the river wasn't helping my ribs any either. Already it was 10:24, and the young couple under the clock hadn't gotten any further into their retirement plans. When would they quit smiling and get to work? I wiggled my mouth a little, just to get it loosened

164

up, and then started informing Angel of some of the basic facts of life.

"You're out on the street tonight," I said, "but that doesn't mean you're free and clear. There's still the small matter of John Lombardo's murder to be settled, besides all those stolen bottles of wine they probably found in your apartment. You told me yourself that Powers's men are still keeping tabs on you, and your friends with the iron fists must be even dumber than they look if they think a beating in the alley is going to make any of them go away. You, pal, are in deep trouble."

"Wasn't no wine," Angel muttered. "Was that big old silver duck press Johnny was so crazy about. That's what they found."

"Okay. Fine. You still don't get it. As far as the police are concerned, there were three people at the Pinnacle Room Monday night. Me, Janine DuPage, and you. I know I didn't kill your sweetie, and right now I don't think Janine did either. So that leaves you. Unless, of course, we can prove there was somebody else on the premises, which is my private theory. So you can cooperate with me, or you can leave the police to draw their own conclusions."

Angel wasn't the brightest light in the world, but he got the point. First came a repetition of what I had heard Monday night, with some elaborations that had come after the police bustled Angel away. He had hidden in the elevator toward the end of dinnertime, planning to stay there until after closing and then jump out and surprise Lombardo two-timing him with Janine. A real dramatic scene, with lots of screaming and crying, and at the end Johnny would give up the evil woman and come back to his own true love. But then I'd shown up and started pushing barriers in front of the elevator, and Angel had been trapped there until the police hauled him out and showed him Lombardo's body. At which point he'd gone berserk.

The way he told it, it was all tragic and beautiful like an Italian opera, only instead of Lincoln Center, we were over on South

Street with the fern bars behind us and the rumbling engine of a garbage scow for chorus. I was ready to cry, except the story wasn't getting me anywhere near where I wanted to be by way of information.

"What about the robbery?" I asked. "All that champagne in the sack, remember? Was that part of your big scene too?"

Angel stared out over the boats. Down the block I could hear the trucks pulling in for the fish market, but where we were it was very quiet.

"I told you already," he said. "We weren't stealing no wine. Not that night, not never."

"Who's we?" I demanded. This was the first I'd heard about a partner.

"Who you think, man? Johnny! It was his idea, stealing from the job. He thought it was a big laugh, you know? Said they'd never dare call the cops if they ever found us out."

So that was it. Lombardo had been stealing from himself. Suddenly I understood the funny way he acted when he hired me and the strange puzzle of why he'd gone outside Interdine to get a guard. Paid for it himself, too. Like they said, honor among thieves. Or maybe just an extra tickle to the joke. Meanwhile, Angel kept on talking.

"We took some decorations, see, for fixing up my place," he explained. "And sometimes food, like if we were having a party. It was kind of a game, you know? Lift it from the restaurant, use it at home, watch that dumb stiff Lyder get all nervous about the loss. Johnny was real proud of that wine cellar, though. We never messed with that. Anyway, it was all over."

"What do you mean?"

"I mean, it was all over. We weren't going to do it anymore. That's why Johnny hired you, see. We'd make a big deal, hire a guard, and then stop taking the stuff, so it would seem like the thief was scared off. No one would ever be the wiser. It wasn't

166

for the money. It was fun. Johnny was even talking about taking the duck press with us. A kind of souvenir, like."

"Take it with you? Where were you going?"

Angel straightened up, the downcast punk buoyed up by a wave of hope. "You don't know, man," he said smugly, "I'm not gonna tell you."

"I don't know," I agreed. "And the police don't know about your two pals in black who tried to reorganize my ribs. Doesn't look good, you having such violent buddies. Tell me where you were going, and maybe I'll forget to mention your friends."

Angel took his sweet time thinking over my terms. If I didn't get up soon, I had the feeling I was going to need a stretcher. I stared at the clock across the river, where 10:51 became 10:52. There was no doubt about it. For the first time in my life I was going to be late for work.

"So what?" he said at last. "Nothing wrong with planning a little trip. Who says we had to stay here forever?" Then he sat back and told me a tale of magic and romance, just like the weepy movies Bea always loved, except in this one both the leads were men. While he talked, Angel stared out over the water, but that wasn't what he was seeing. The words came out all perfect and polished, a story he'd thought about every day, memorized from the dreams that Johnny Lombardo had fed him.

They were going to go to Italy, to a coastal city Johnny knew about. A run-down summer resort on the Mediterranean, outside Rome. They'd buy up some property near the water, shabby and cheap, and then transform it into a replica of the ancient baths, with goldfish swimming in green marble tubs and the kind of cooking that would bring people swarming out of the city. They would make a fortune and live on Sardinia and commute by private Hovercraft from a villa overlooking the sea.

The plan was Lombardo all over, romantic and commercial and likely to work for as long as he didn't get bored. To a poor kid like Angel, never out of New York and hustling since before he could remember, it must have seemed like a vision of heaven. Now I understood the wail he had let out when he saw Lombardo's body. It wasn't just the cry of grief for a lover, though a lot of that was there, I suppose. It was the anguish of a dream dying. Kids like Angel knew all about how opportunity doesn't knock twice. For him it was a miracle that it had knocked at all. What I didn't understand, though, was why it had taken him so long to talk about it. Usually you don't have to threaten people to get them to tell you their dreams. Not in my experience.

"So what was the big secret?" I asked. "If Lombardo was going to open a new operation overseas, I'm sure somebody at Interdine must have known about it." Not that anybody had bothered to mention it to me.

Angel looked blank. "Interdine?" he asked. "No, man. This wasn't for Interdine. This was for us. That's why we were keeping quiet. Only our real close friends were in on it. But not the bosses, man. That was gonna be one big fake-out surprise on them."

Suddenly I felt like I was back talking to Sam Fuentes. Was I the only person in the world who still thought you needed to have money to make investments?

"If John Lombardo wasn't going to be working for Interdine," I asked, "how were you two planning to finance this place? I don't know much about restaurants, but it costs plenty to buy waterfront property, and you don't get those marble fishbowls for nothing either. Where were you two planning to get the dough?"

Angel shrugged. "Johnny always said not to worry. Eternal happiness would take care of us."

Eternal happiness. Harwell had talked about that when I was up in his office the other night. Had Lombardo been some kind of mystic, like my aunt Sadie, who went off the deep end when the banks failed in '29 and spent the rest of her life insisting that

God would provide a free chicken dinner for everyone who believed enough to ask? But Sadie's voice had always had a little tremble in it, the fervor of the true religious crazy, and Angel sounded completely matter-of-fact.

"Eternal happiness?" I asked tentatively. "That some kind of a church you guys belong to?"

Angel was a good-looking kid, but nobody could ever accuse him of having a gift for gab. Talking about Sardinia had been easy. It was probably all he ever thought about, and the words poured out as frothy and clear as that champagne Lombardo liked so much. This was different.

"Wasn't no church," he said slowly. "I know that." He turned to face me, then turned quickly back to the river. I guess I wasn't such a pretty sight.

"He talked about it all the time," Angel continued. 'Eternal happiness is everywhere,' he would say. Or, like, 'I have a plan for eternal happiness.' Things like that. Johnny said eternal happiness would follow us to Italy, so we didn't have to worry about bills."

Eleven-twenty by the clock. Time to wind this conversation up.

"Money may buy happiness," I said, "but how was happiness going to bring you money?"

"It would, man. That's all. Johnny said so."

There it was. The quiver in the voice that meant blind faith. Faith is something about which you don't bother to argue. I learned that from my aunt Sadie. There was another question I'd been chewing on. I'd been afraid to bring it up, but now was definitely the time. While I could still talk.

"Angel," I said, "Monday night you were sure I killed Lombardo. Me or Janine. Now you don't seem to care about either of us. How come?" I knew something must have changed his mind. After all, I was still alive.

"After it happened," he answered slowly, "I thought about it for a long time. Johnny hired you. He didn't tell me you were coming that night, but I knew somebody would be showing up. I was there all the time, in the elevator. I heard the crash out in the dining room. I heard you get up and leave to check it out. And then after, I could hear that stupid broad upstairs, screaming like she wouldn't ever stop. So if you were with her, like everybody says you were, it must have been somebody else came through the kitchen after you left."

So my guess was right. There had been somebody else around. Thorson or not, this was something the police had to hear.

"Did you tell this to Captain Powers?" I demanded.

"Didn't tell it to nobody. Powers knows what he can do before he finds out anything from me."

"Go to the corner," I told Angel, "and find me a cab. I'll talk to you in the morning. I won't press charges against your pals for assault, but I think we have to go talk to the police."

"You promised we wouldn't!"

"I promised nothing. I said maybe. Go find me a cab before I croak on you, or you'll have police in plenty."

It was eleven-thirty already, but if I hurried, I could probably get to work while there was still something left of the night. For the first time this week I was very eager to spend some time alone at the Pinnacle Room.

Chapter 22

Angel took his time getting back with a taxi. Maybe the restored
seaport wasn't such a boom town as the investors had hoped.
Maybe only Lombardo could get the crowds to come for dinner
in a ratty old warehouse. Too bad for the slums, now that their
savior was gone. Every once in a while it crossed my mind that
the kid might have just cut out and left me there, but mostly I
thought about the fish market. All those nice fish with their clear,
fresh eyes, lying on crisp beds of crushed ice. If I could just lie
down with them, I thought, how much better my body would
feel. Maybe if I walked back to Fulton Street, somebody would
let me stretch out in the back of his truck. Just for half an hour.
I wouldn't even mind the smell.

   I was still dreaming of life as a tuna when Angel got back
twenty minutes later, in a cab he had practically shanghaied from
the off ramp of the Brooklyn Bridge. One look at me and the
driver demanded payment in advance. Angel stayed behind to
wait for his pals to come back for the car. I didn't even want to
know where they'd been.

   It was well past midnight by the time I got to the Interdine
Tower, and there was nobody in the lobby but me, the elevator
starter, and the machine watcher at the desk. They were both
real impressed with my looks. The elevator starter went so far

as to suggest that I should maybe go home or even see a doctor, but I gave him a song and dance about how much I needed the job, so he finally opened up the car and sent me up to the sixty-eighth floor.

The first thing I did was head for the bathroom to check out the damage Roger had inflicted on my face.

It looked even worse than it felt. I knew my left eye was swollen, and I figured I had a split lip from the way it hurt to talk. What I hadn't realized was that my whole face was covered with dried blood, with stiff clumps where it had gotten into my hair. I looked like an ad for a horror movie, pale blue eyes staring out of a puss like a smashed tomato. No wonder the boys downstairs had been a little shaken.

I found a towel, soaked it in cold water, and draped it over my face while I sat down on the little stool the valet uses when he's not brushing the lint off customers' jackets. The water felt real good where it dripped down over my chest. If I'd had the energy, I would have taken off my shirt and soaked that, too. It couldn't have made it in any worse shape than it was already.

It took a few more towels to do it, but I finally got cleaned up enough so that I only looked terrible. I took a couple of aspirin from the bottle in the closet and went down to the kitchen to rustle up some ice for my lip.

Propped up on the table was a note from Robert Lyder, informing me that lateness would not be tolerated and that he was docking me thirty percent of my salary for the night. As a footnote he added that Captain Powers wanted to see me in the morning. I pocketed the message, wondering why he hadn't just fired me and gotten it over with. Then I remembered that he'd already tried that once before. I went and fixed an ice bag and held it over my mouth while I made the rounds. By that time I didn't think I would have been more comfortable lying down with the fish on Fulton Street. I knew it.

After talking to Angel, I was pretty sure I wouldn't find any more evidence of the phantom thief, and I wasn't disappointed. If Lombardo was stealing the fixtures to play house with Angel, he probably used the wine for when he saw Janine. I admired his way of keeping the two adventures separate. At least now I didn't have to worry that the sneak thief would pop out and bash me over the head. Which gave me plenty of time to concentrate on the burning question of who Angel had heard when he was holed up in the freight elevator Monday night.

As soon as I finished the rounds, I got inside the freight elevator. It smelled pretty crummy, packed tight with the garbage and all, but I wanted to check if you really could hear anything from inside. I left the kitchen radio turned on and discovered that I could at least make out the noise, if not the actual words. Probably it would be different when the kitchen was busy, but there hadn't been anyone there but me on Monday night. I could well believe that Angel had been keeping his ears open, crouching there in the dark. So maybe there was something to his story after all.

When I heard the crash Monday night, I'd gone up the ramp to the entry level and checked there before I found Lombardo in the wine cellar down below. If Janine killed him, she must have heard me charging around and would have had plenty of time to dash over to the pantry and through the kitchen, waiting till I was down in the wine cellar before she went up the ramp and back to Lombardo's office. I traced the route to confirm that it was possible. Could she have been loud enough for Angel to hear her when I didn't? There was no way for me to know.

But what if it wasn't Janine? What if there had been somebody else in the restaurant after all, somebody who had made his escape through the kitchen? How could he have gotten out? It would have to have been in those first few minutes before the police arrived, because after that, the kitchen was occupied continuously throughout the night. And searched. And searched again. In the Saturday afternoon thrillers I used to see at the Loew's Paradise,

173

the villain always escaped by crawling through the heating vents, hanging onto the window ledge for fourteen hours, or scaling a blank wall. Which brought me back to Robert Lyder. I hobbled over to the side of the kitchen and dialed Gloria's number.

The first thing I heard was the crash of the receiver being dropped, and then a couple of words I hadn't realized Gloria knew.

"Hello," she mumbled at last.

"Gloria," I said. "This is Quentin."

"Oh, my God," she groaned. "Quentin. Are you all right?"

I thought about it. "Yes," I answered finally. "But I need to find out what happened on those phone calls you made."

"For crying out loud," she wailed. "Do you realize what time it is?"

"One-thirty in the morning," I answered. "You busy?"

"Right. I was just entertaining the Sheik of Araby. Threatens to throw himself off the Empire State Building if I won't be his queen. Think I should do it?"

At least she was waking up. "I'm sorry about the time," I apologized. "This is important. I have to know what you found out."

"Okay." She sighed. "Hang on a minute. I have to find my notes."

It took more than a minute, but when she got back, Gloria was awake for real.

"Here it comes," she announced, sounding like the recording at the bus station that reels off the departures for Albany, Schenectady, Utica, Syracuse, and points west. "First the personnel department. Angel Ruiz has been an employee of the Interdine Corporation since last April. He is nineteen years old and to the best of their knowledge has no criminal record. Janine DuPage has been with the company for two years, first as a receptionist in the restaurant division offices and then with the Pinnacle Room

174

since it opened. She is a graduate of Hunter College with a degree in public administration. Robert Lyder is a graduate of the Wharton School of Finance and Commerce and spent eighteen months in the accounting department of the Pennsylvania Paper Box Company before coming to Interdine three years ago. Salaries they will not divulge, and about Lombardo they've been instructed to say nothing, even to an adjuster from the Global Retirement Annuity Association, which is what I claimed to be."

"That's fantastic, Gloria. What else?"

"Next I became a secretary for the NYPD homicide squad to check the time when Robert Lyder arrived at the Interdine garage. I had to call the night attendant at home, but I figured it was better to wake him up than have him alert enough to wonder who I was. He was pretty mad, but he did say Lyder came down a few minutes after he got the call from the front desk that Lombardo was dead."

A few minutes. That could be anything. "Did you manage to get through to the mountain climbing club?" I asked.

"Well, it took awhile, and I'm not sure this is what you wanted, but I did get some information." There was a clunk when the receiver hit the table, followed by the noise of shuffling papers. Then Gloria was back on the line. "The guy who climbed the World Trade Center did it in twelve hours," she reported. "It took fourteen to get to the top of the Sears Tower in Chicago. The American Mountaineering Association does not in any way sanction these nuts, and furthermore, they disapprove of the way they make use of the rails that are built in for the window washers. The man I talked to seemed to feel it was cheating. Also, Robert Lyder used to be a member of the New York chapter of the Everest Society, which is a branch of the American Mountaineering Association—except he resigned last month in a policy dispute over artificial surfaces. Don't ask me what that means. I only report."

175

"That's great, Gloria. You are absolutely wonderful!"

"I know," she answered. "Do you need help? I can be there in half an hour."

"No. Go back to sleep."

I could hear her head hit the pillow before she even hung up the phone.

The personnel information confirmed what I knew already. The garage report was inconclusive. As for the data on the building climbers, there was some good news and some bad. The good news was that I'd been right in suspecting that Lyder was more interested in climbing walls than mountains. The bad news was that I had also been right in thinking there was no way he could have gone up and down the side of the Interdine Tower Monday night. Not with the time he had to do it in. I went up to his office to see if any new equipment had turned up since last night.

Everything was the same, down to the ledgers scattered across the desk. From the looks of things Lyder hadn't even been in here. The couch by the window was very tempting, but I was afraid I'd never get up again if I let myself relax. The desk chair looked safe enough. Gingerly I lowered myself into the seat, trying to concentrate on something besides how much my body hurt.

The first thing that caught my attention was a pair of the rubber squeeze balls Lyder used to build up his hand muscles. He had left them on the desk, ready for use whenever he was stuck on the telephone. Not for the first time, I wondered what Lyder was training for so hard. Then I got distracted by a much bigger puzzle. Lyder had left one of the ledgers open, the pages held flat with a pocket calculator. I'm no math whiz, but it didn't take an advanced degree in accounting to notice that most of the entries were on the debit side. I turned back to the front of the book. It was the accounts for the Pinnacle Room, and a few minutes of looking down the columns confirmed that they'd been losing money since they opened. The income was good, but the expenses were out of sight.

I looked through the other ledgers, for all the other restaurants Lombardo had opened. When the great man was still alive these had been his trophies, the record of his past triumphs just like Lyder's silver cups and brass plaques. Now they were just account books, and instead of packing them away with all the other personal junk, Lyder had stayed late to see what they had to tell him.

They all showed the same story, and it wasn't a good one. Huge outlays at the beginning, then a surge of business as the restaurant became the rage, but never enough to cover all the expenses. At the end of every month Lombardo entered the accountants' reports and circled the bad news in bright red ink. At the start of every year he began a new book, piling up the rows of plush-covered volumes like a set of diaries. Anybody else would have been embarrassed by the record, but Lombardo seemed to have been proud. Anybody else would have been out of business long ago.

So why wasn't John Lombardo? Had killing him been a way of stopping the flow of red ink? I knew Lyder was big on cutting expenses, but would he kill a man just because he refused to pay attention to costs? Maybe the restaurant was losing so much money he was afraid he would have no job to inherit.

Or had Lyder even known about the losses? From what I'd seen of Lombardo's management style, it hadn't included a whole lot of sharing of ideas. Maybe these late-night sessions were the first chance Lyder had had for a real look at the books. If he had killed Lombardo to take over his job, it must have been a real shock to find out what he had risked so much to inherit. Unless my first notion had been right and Lyder had been contributing to the losses. Angel admitted that he and Lombardo had taken that crazy duck press contraption, but that didn't mean that Lyder couldn't have been helping himself to some of the goodies, too. Following in the boss's footsteps, so to speak.

So now I had three maybes about why Lyder could have killed Lombardo but not a shred of evidence. Plus, I reminded myself, the man had a perfect alibi. From the time he'd been showing me the kitchen, when Lombardo was still alive, to the time he'd stumbled out of the elevator practically into Captain Powers's arms, Lyder's movements were all accounted for. Except for those "few minutes" between the lobby and the garage, when Lyder had stepped outside to admire the stars. Then I remembered that the patrolmen had confirmed seeing him out on the sidewalk when they entered the building. How long had he been there before they arrived? And what had he really been up to? I was still wondering when the telephone rang.

"Pinnacle Room," I said, picking up the extension on Lyder's desk. "Jacoby here."

"Buenas noches," sang out Sam, in the quavering tenor he always uses when he's drunk. "I am having a *great* time," he added. As if I couldn't tell. I should have known he'd feel obliged to spend the money I'd slipped him. The question was: Had he ever followed Lyder or had he just gone out on the town? For sure he wasn't spending the night at home.

"Where are you, Sam?" I demanded. "Are you in a bar?" If I didn't find out fast, he'd use up his dime serenading me with the top tunes of 1959, and I'd never know.

"I am in a telephone booth. The most *hermoso* telephone booth in the world. You know what *hermoso* is, Jacoby? Is 'beautiful.' This beautiful telephone booth has a little red roof, like a house, and the corners point up like the breasts of a beautiful woman I used to know. Crazy 'bout me, this woman was. And what legs! Like a jackhammer! Also, this telephone booth has a gold door that you can really close, with a picture of a dragon, and inside is a little red seat where I am sitting down right now. I think I

178

will leave my stinking apartment in Co-op City and move in here, is so beautiful."

"Okay, Sam." I sighed. Forty years in New York, and the man had just discovered Chinatown. "Give me the telephone number of your *hermoso* booth."

"Is a beautiful number. Is Five. Five. Five. Four. Three. Five. Zero." Sam read the numbers real slowly, which meant he wasn't wearing his glasses. It gave me plenty of time to write them down.

"Now hang up, Sam," I instructed. "I'll call you right back."

I dialed the number, and for a miracle he answered. *"Buenas noches,"* he repeated, starting the conversation all over again. "I am having a *great* time."

"What about the man I asked you to follow?"

"I follow him," said Sam, sounding insulted. "That is why I am having a great time. He take me places you wouldn't believe."

"Try me."

"What you mean?"

"I mean, for God's sake, tell me where you've been all night!" My mouth was starting to hurt again from the talking. I reached over for a trophy and held it to my jaw like a compress.

"Sure, I tell you," answered Sam. "But first I sing you the wonderful song I learn from this wonderful girl. So little, so sweet, this girl. She tell me she just here from China, never met nobody in America so nice as me. And Jacoby, she had on this dress, the skirt was slit so high you could see everything, man. And nice satin, it feels good to rub your hands on, you know?"

"Right, Sam," I agreed. "Just a simple village girl from China, happy to meet an honest guy in the big city. But where *were* you?"

"Okay, baby. Don't get angry. I skip the song. I'm gonna tell you everything. Then I'm gonna sit back and enjoy this most *hermoso* telephone booth. I think I sleep here tonight."

179

And get picked up for vagrancy in the morning, I thought. But I didn't say so. Sam was old enough to take care of his own life, which included spending the night in a phone booth in Chinatown if he was so inclined. So I let him ramble on, singing me a song here and describing a girl there, and after fifteen minutes I had at least a good part of the picture.

While I had been sitting down by the East River discussing the meaning of life with Angel, Sam had been staked out in the lobby of the Interdine Tower. After Bob Lyder closed up the Pinnacle Room, he hadn't gone home. Instead he had walked out the front door, turned east on Exchange Place, and then gone north on Broadway until he got to City Hall. From there, Sam reported, he cut across several parks and ended up in Chinatown. Over a mile, through business streets that are deserted after dark. This was not a route that a person like Lyder would be likely to take just for the exercise, and I wasn't surprised that he had company. He had been met in the Interdine lobby by two Oriental men in business suits, and the three of them had gone on their summer evening stroll together. Sam swore they never even spotted him, but that seemed unlikely. Probably they had taken him for a panhandler too feeble to catch up and make his pitch. In any case they hadn't turned on him, which was the main thing.

It was after they got to Chinatown that the great times began. According to Sam, he trailed the three men through a series of secret pleasure palaces, each one more exotic than the last. The sense of progress may have been the effect of the beer, though. Even in clip joints fifty dollars will still buy a fair amount of brew. Sam's absolute limit on beers is three, and it takes only two to start him singing.

The way Sam told it, they were touring scandalous opium dens run by the insidious Fu Manchu himself, but to me it sounded like Lyder had taken a couple of overseas customers out for a night on the town. It was quite a comedown, going from classic

French cooking to sleazy Chinese bar girls, but there was nothing illegal about it that I could see. Certainly nothing that seemed like a motive for murder. Then, at the end of the evening, Sam reported, the three men had all gone to look for an apartment.

"What did you say?"

"I said they went to find an apartment. They ring the bell, a woman answer, they all go in. So I figure it's for a private club. Hot stuff, you know? But then I go up close, and in the window there's nothing but ads. Apartments for rent, stores for rent, things like that. Lots of stuff I can't read. Then I hear someone coming from inside, so I hide in this phone booth. They all come out and get in a car. Now I can't follow no car, *amigo*, not with my feet. So I call you."

"Did you get the license of the car, Sam?"

"License? Baby, I don't know nothing about license. Just a big black car, one of those German ones like we drive after we hit it rich." The word jiggled a switch in Sam's brain. "Two nights now I give up the races to follow this Mr. Lyder for you," he complained. "When you gonna give me the money for Sunday? When you gonna take us up on the roof?"

"Soon, Sam. Soon. This place they went into, is there any kind of sign out front? What's it called?"

"Sure, there's a sign, baby, but I don't know what it's called. You think I read Chinese, maybe?"

"There's nothing anywhere written in English?"

"Nah. Yeah, wait, something on the door, little letters. I go look."

There was a thud when he dropped the receiver, then a long period when I got to listen to the noise of late-night traffic in Chinatown, which sounded a lot like late-night traffic in the Bronx. Finally Sam returned. I could hear him complaining to himself while he settled back into the seat. Then he picked up the receiver.

"Is a realty company, baby," he said, except he pronounced it *reality*. "Happy New Year Realty Company, it says. And that is all I'm doing for you tonight. Now be quiet. I'm going to sleep."

And that's exactly what he did, with the receiver right up against his mouth so I could hear him snore. After a while I cut the connection by hanging up. All night he'd be dreaming about recorded messages asking him to please replace the receiver, and when he woke, he'd probably be convinced there'd been a mysterious passionflower in the phone booth with him, nibbling at his ear. And wearing a dress slit way up to there.

Sam was lucky. The only thing I was convinced of was that I'd spent a lot of Gloria's money and gotten a beating it would take me a week to get over. As for the rest, every new thing I discovered just seemed to scramble up the picture. Angel's arrest. Lombardo stealing from himself. The move to Rome. The ledgers. Chinatown. The Happy New Year Reality Company. Was there really a connection that would bring them all together? Maybe I already had the explanation of why John Lombardo was murdered. And how. Maybe it was right in front of my nose, just waiting to get noticed.

I sat there the rest of the night, not even pretending to make my rounds. I just sat and thought, waiting for the brainstorm that never arrived. And then, at five in the morning, when everything was supposed to be shut down tight, the elevator slowly went up to the roof, just like it had the night before.

Chapter 23

By seven o'clock, when the bakers arrived, I still hadn't made any progress in the detective business, but I had managed to get my thinking straight on one point. The main result of my working at the Pinnacle Room was that it kept me from being anyplace else. Not out with Angel, finding out how much he really knew about Lombardo's murder. Not following Lyder into Chinatown. Not up on the roof, checking to see what was going on there. Not even home in bed, which at least would have allowed me to be alive, alert, and nosy when the rest of the world was going about its business. If it hadn't been for Gloria, I would have quit long ago. Not that I was doing her any great favor staying on. If she thought Blount Harwell was going to give Global a fat contract on my account, the lady was more of a dreamer than I'd imagined.

As it was, I waited until I got outside to call Angel, by which time he was not answering the phone. I hoped he hadn't been stupid enough to try to leave town. According to my calculations, he and Janine were still the leading suspects for Lombardo's murder, and Angel was already in big enough trouble without skipping bail. All he had to do to get behind bars was to stick his big toe in any airport, train terminal, or bus station in the city.

Maybe the kid was just a heavy sleeper. I decided to go by his apartment and haul him out of bed. As soon as I got near Angel's place, I knew it wouldn't be that simple. Two police cars were parked outside the building, and a hospital van was just pulling out. There was a knot of people standing in the schoolyard across the street, looking at the police cars and talking over whatever it was that had happened. I joined them to see what I could learn.

Two minutes' eavesdropping confirmed my fears. After he left me last night, Angel had gone home and spent the next eight hours working up the nerve to shoot himself. Most people put the gun in their mouths, which is messy but very effective. Angel had aimed for the heart and missed.

"Such a pretty boy," said the woman with the dog. "It's a mercy he didn't hit his face."

"If we had better gun laws, this kind of thing wouldn't happen." The old man tugged at the buttons of his cardigan and looked around for confirmation. His attention shifted when he saw my face.

"What happened to you, buddy?" he asked.

"Muggers," I said. They all nodded knowingly and moved back to the more interesting topic of attempted suicide.

"What happened to that other man who used to live there?" asked a woman with a stroller. "Lots of silver hair, you know?"

The dog walker looked at her with scorn. "Don't you know? He got killed a couple three days ago. Walked into a robbery at work."

"No! Really? Well, then, that explains it."

The group held on for a few more minutes, but it was clear the party was over. I oozed away with the crowd, just in case anybody from the homicide squad who might recognize me was hanging around. I'd come there to bring Angel down to see Powers with me, but the last thing I wanted was to be caught hanging around without Mr. Ruiz available to back me up. From

184

the way people were talking, it sounded like Angel would make it, but I doubted he'd be taking any visitors today.

If Angel hadn't shot himself, we would have told Powers all about the extra person coming through the Pinnacle Room kitchen Monday night. By the time we were through, he would probably have known about the trip to Italy, too, and that Lombardo had been stealing from his own place. If he didn't know that already.

But Angel did shoot himself. Was it because talking to me had exploded his dream for good and he couldn't face life without it? Angel was not the most valuable asset to society I had ever met, but I couldn't get around the fact that one way or another I had pushed him over the edge into self-destruction. I wanted to think things over before I went shooting off my mouth anymore. I walked a couple of blocks to the Bowery station and took the BMT all the way out to Queens Boulevard, looking for that famous new perspective that was going to make everything clear.

Who, what, where, and when I'd known all along. John Lombardo had been stabbed to death in the wine cellar of the Pinnacle Room at approximately 12:15 A.M. Tuesday. So far I'd been concentrating all my attention on the question of how the killer had gotten in and out of the premises, a line of inquiry that had gotten me exactly nowhere. It was time to shift my attention to why.

It went against my training. The first thing you learn when you work as a cop is that you shouldn't waste your time looking for motives. Most times, anyway, the motive is so obvious you don't have to look. A rider gets knifed because he wasn't fast enough in handing over his watch. A token seller gets blown away protecting the till. Rival gangs decide to fight it out on the train that crosses both their turfs. A junkie turns police informer and they find him in the tunnel, already starting to smell.

Even when the reasons behind an action are not so clear, it doesn't really matter. The real issues are opportunity, means, and enough solid evidence to close the case. Especially the last. Like my old captain used to say, a police officer's job is to catch the perpetrator and make sure he doesn't commit his crime again. The question of motive is to give the lawyers and the shrinks something to argue about.

But now I wasn't a cop anymore, and I was getting smart to the fact that trying to close on a homicide was different from stalking a purse snatcher operating out of the Eastern Parkway station of the BMT. Especially because I wasn't a cop anymore. I didn't have access to testimony, or lab reports, or any of the other information that makes it at least faintly possible to proceed. And for assistants I had Gloria Gold and Sam Fuentes, which was somewhat better than nothing but still not nearly good enough. My chief assets were still common sense, persistence, and a certain amount of experience of the world, and the only way they were going to help me find my murderer was if I could figure out who had a stake in getting John Lombardo dead.

I reached this conclusion at Queens Boulevard, which is a very boring station and also the end of the line. It was almost noon. I'd been up for the better part of twenty hours, and the closest I'd been to a meal was an order of French toast at Maybelle's Donut Shop yesterday afternoon. I had a black eye, a split lip, a king-size pain all around the midsection, and a set of clothes that was fit only to be burned. As long as I was feeling terrible, I might as well go talk to the police. I had the feeling if I didn't show up soon, Powers might send somebody out to find me. With my luck it would be Plato Thorson, and he'd arrive just as I had finally managed to go to sleep.

The trip back was steamy but interesting, since several of the women on the train were running around in less than my mother wore to take a bath. When I got down to City Hall Park a lot of people were taking their lunch breaks stretched out on the grass, snoozing or reading or otherwise goofing around. Over on the southwest side of the park, six deputy assistant types had put down newspaper to protect their pants and were practicing making a human pyramid, which they would have done much better except that one of the guys in the middle tier seemed to be ticklish. A woman in a business suit stopped dead in the middle of the grass, put down her attaché case, took out three felt balls, and started juggling. August is a month when everybody skips lunch and grabs something from the ice cream wagon instead, and I think all the extra sugar goes to their brains.

When I got inside the station house, the circus stopped. A new sergeant was stationed in front of Powers's office, but Thorson came bustling over as soon as he saw who had arrived. Didn't the man ever go home?

"Is Angel Ruiz going to be all right?" I asked.

"I am not at liberty to divulge his condition." As usual, he managed to talk like a robot reading from the manual of police procedures. An unhelpful robot.

"Tell me if he's all right," I repeated, "and I'll tell you where he was last night."

Thorson thought for a minute, but I could have told you in advance that he was one of those people who never say yes to anything without authorization from above. So instead he told me to cool my heels until I could make an official statement to the appropriate authority, by which he meant Captain Powers.

The captain was at a meeting, so Thorson parked me inside the office. Keeping the door open, of course. And watching like a hawk to make sure I didn't try to steal anything from the files.

I settled into the chair by the window and checked out the geraniums across the way. They were still there, but one of the pink ones had fallen over on its side. While I was watching, a bare arm reached out to straighten it, then faded back into the darkness inside. "Disembodied," I said out loud. That word gave my old man a lot of trouble when he was learning English. Then it became one of his favorites when he finally figured out what it meant. "What disembodied little mouth ate the last of the cheese?" he would demand, going for a snack that wasn't there, and all the children would giggle. "Disembodied," I said again, rolling the word around my tongue the way he used to do.

"Is that a confession or a hot tip?" Powers asked. I hadn't even heard him come in. His eyes widened when he got a look at my face.

"I had a friend once," he observed, "put a tomcat into a pillowcase and then stuck his head in to see how the kitty was doing."

"Something like that," I agreed, "except this cat was wearing rings."

"He says he knows where Ruiz was last night," Thorson interrupted.

Powers nodded and looked at me expectantly. "Well?" he asked. "Where was he?"

"He was with me. At least part of the time. Will he pull through?"

"Ruiz? Sure thing. Shot himself through the shoulder. Aimed in a mirror, I ask you, and didn't even allow for the recoil. We'll have him on the stand yet, with his ass in a sling to match his arm if that's what he deserves. What were you two doing together? Two days ago you said you were total strangers."

I hesitated, and Powers nodded to Thorson. Reluctantly, the lieutenant left the room. When I heard the door click shut behind him, I gave Powers an abbreviated version of my adventures last night, leaving out the thugs and the seaside restaurant and putting most of the emphasis on Angel's story about somebody coming through the kitchen right after Lombardo was killed. I also decided not to mention my ideas about Robert Lyder until I had something more definite to say. As it was now, I would only get into trouble for breaking into his office.

Powers was noncommittal. "What do you make of it?" he asked.

"What do I make of it! I make it that somebody else was in that restaurant Monday night. Somebody who killed John Lom-

188

bardo and then escaped through the kitchen. Somebody you haven't even thought of yet."

I wasn't expecting a medal or anything, but I had thought Powers would at least be interested. Instead he just leaned back in his chair and gave me the same careful once-over he gave to everything that might prove useful to remember later. Every time I saw him it was the same shock, seeing the probing intelligence of those eyes caught in the body of a fat friar out of Robin Hood. I took a deep breath and told him what was really on my mind.

"The way I see it," I began, "there had to be somebody else around. Because all the suspects we've got had a lot of good reasons for wanting Lombardo alive, and none at all for wanting him dead. Janine DuPage was using Lombardo as a kind of private training school for the restaurant business, and by her own calculations she wouldn't be ready to graduate—which is to say, take over his job—for another two years. And even if she was, there was no point in killing him to get the job—he was the one who was going to back her promotion and give her all the advice she needed to make her a success. Her mentor she called him."

Powers nodded in agreement. I guess he'd had just about the same conversation with Janine that I had.

"Then there's Angel," I continued. "Like Janine, gorgeous and grabby. Not nearly as smart, I'd say, with none of her long-range planning, but basically the same type. I don't know much about people like Lombardo, and frankly I don't really care, but my sense is that he shopped for sex the same way he shopped for food—approach the market with an open mind, and pick out the very best of whatever you find there. And you don't have to like the taste yourself to agree that both Angel and Janine are very luscious goods. Lombardo probably got a kick out of alternating between them. Angel was too dumb to notice, and Janine was too mercenary to care as long as she was getting what she wanted. Did you check out the villa on Sardinia?" I asked.

189

Powers raised his eyebrows but didn't bother asking how I knew about the plan to relocate in Italy. Of course Angel had been a fool to think it was a secret, a big move like that. If they hadn't found Lombardo's killer, I knew Powers and his men must have been doing *something* with their time.

"I checked it out," he answered. "They were planning to go all right. Even had their tickets to Rome. And I also see where you're leading, because now none of this is going to happen. Without John Lombardo, Angel Ruiz is just a pretty little hustler in a town full of competition. Like you said, no motive for having him dead, every reason for wanting him alive. Next?" he asked. "Or is it getting to be my turn?"

"Not yet," I said. At least he wasn't bored. "Next, I think, is me."

"Ah," said Powers, letting out a sign of satisfaction. "I was wondering if you'd come to that."

"Of course, I came to it. Don't you think I know how it looks? I show up out of the blue, take a job I don't need and don't want, and the minute I'm alone with the boss he gets murdered. Who's to say I really heard a noise, went looking, and found a body? Maybe I found a man and turned him into a body, for some crazy reason you'll never know. If everything else fits, you don't need a motive to make an arrest.

"But look at it the other way," I continued. "Why would I kill a man and set myself up as the most likely suspect? I may not be any intellectual giant or anything, but I'm smart enough to know that's no way to get away with murder. Besides, I'm just like the other two. I had a stake in keeping the guy alive. Maybe not as big a stake but a stake nonetheless. Here I am, just starting a new line of work, hand-picked by Lombardo to test out a new security agency. And the first night out I foul up beyond all description and let the boss get killed. I happen to have a personal interest in Global Security, and keeping Lombardo and his company happy was all to my benefit. I had no reason on earth to want him dead."

"I've been checking out your personal interest," Powers said. "Nice little piece, holding up well. Seems to be legit, too. Anyway," he added calmly, "you're built all wrong. Too tall. Left-handed. I'm not saying you couldn't have done it, but according to the coroner, it would have been a hell of a trick."

So that was what Thorson had been up to with all his questions the other night.

"You mean I'm not a suspect anymore?" I asked slowly.

"You're a suspect until somebody else gets convicted," Powers answered. "For now let's just say Thorson had some theories, but I wasn't surprised when they didn't check out."

I didn't know how worried I'd been. Not until I felt the relief and realized I'd been carrying around in the back of my mind a picture of myself as a permanent no-rent tenant of the state of New York. I couldn't help it. I started to smile.

"Don't go moving out of town," said Powers sharply. "We may still want you as a witness. You may as well know. An hour ago we arrested Janine DuPage."

I sat dumfounded. Finally I found my voice. "Janine DuPage! But I was just telling you why she couldn't have done it."

"You were telling me why it wouldn't have been a smart move for her to have done it. Killers are well known for acting stupid, Jacoby. Murder is a stupid crime."

"I think you're making a mistake," I said.

"Maybe," Powers answered. "It wouldn't be the first time. But we've turned up some interesting things at the scene of the crime. DuPage's fingerprints are all over the wine cellar, including on the bottles that were scattered on the floor. We found marks of her fingernails on the victim's neck. Some of the kitchen help report hearing arguments between the two of them a couple of days before the murder. In addition to which, DuPage is the right physical type and had ample opportunity to be alone with Lombardo. It's not an airtight case, but it's good enough to make an arrest on, and we had to move fast once we found out the lady was up and leaving town. If you've got a better candidate for Lombardo's killer, you've got forty-eight hours to come up with him because we can't have a bond hearing until Monday. But I want proof, Jacoby. Not just hunches and suspicion. Proof."

"So that's really all you're after," I said bitterly. "A better candidate. I thought it was just that stooge Thorson who was bucking for promotion and who cares about justice, but I see now where he learned his ideas." I was mad, and I didn't care if Powers knew it.

"Listen, Jacoby," said Powers, wiping his face with a piece of paper towel. I listened, but for a long time he had nothing to say. He got up and went over to the window, and I wondered how many times he had counted the flowers. Then he started to talk.

"A few days ago you were in here spouting off about how we both were in this together because neither of us could stand to see a crime go unsolved. In a way you were right. Being a cop, any kind of cop, changes a person. I see it in the rookies every year—six weeks on patrol, and they've picked up a kind of professional nervousness they'll never get rid of. When you're a cop, you've always got your antennae out for trouble, and it's not something you can turn off at quitting time or when you retire."

Powers turned away from the window to face me. "But there's something extra that happens when you're a detective, Jacoby. It's not just that they give you a gold shield and let you wear your own clothes." He sat down on the edge of his desk, so close I thought for a second he was going to collar me. But he just studied my face for a while and then walked back to the view. "When you're a cop, you're always on the lookout for the bad guys. When you're a detective, you learn fast that you can't spot them just by looking. Here, in this room, I've seen directors of charitable foundations who were making a business of arson for profit. I've seen baby-faced kids who plugged their mothers after an argument at breakfast and then went off to hold the incense at early mass. I've had nursery school teachers making porn movies in their classes and leaders of the block improvement association who were dealing cocaine when they weren't lobbying for stricter enforcement of the dog nuisance laws. I like you, Jacoby. I listen to what you say, and it all makes sense. But I also know that Janine DuPage was up there on the sixty-eighth floor last Monday night, with plenty of time to kill John Lombardo if that's what she felt like doing. Don't let yourself get fooled by a pretty face. Some of the most attractive people I've met have been killers."

Chapter 24

Fingerprints. Scratch marks. The evidence against Janine could have come from anywhere. Working in the cellar, playing around with Lombardo after. But would forty-eight hours be enough time to turn my ideas into something approaching proof? I crossed the street for the downtown entrance to the BMT. It had occurred to me that there were a few things the president of Interdine might like to know about his new restaurant manager. It was only two stops to the World Trade Center station and two blocks to the Interdine Tower, and I had nothing to lose but sleep.

I got on at the end of the train, stood at the back of the car, and scanned my fellow passengers for possible deviants, snatch artists, and other assorted cruds. Like Powers said, you don't stop being a cop just because you've punched out for the day. Then I saw a patrolman giving me the eye, and I remembered how truly crummy I looked. I wondered if I had enough cash on me to buy a new shirt.

For once things fell my way. Right outside the Trade Center was a guy selling dress shirts out of a suitcase open on the sidewalk. Genuine designer seconds, only seven dollars, no tax. The merchandise was as hot as the weather, but I bought one anyway and put it on right there in the street. Nobody even blinked when

I shoved my old clothes in the corner trash bin. New Yorkers are a very tolerant, sophisticated bunch.

Nonetheless, the receptionist on the sixty-seventh floor wasn't exactly encouraging about my getting in to see Blount Harwell. Somehow she seemed to think the president of a major international corporation had more pressing things to do than chat with the night watchman. I sat around anyway and finally had the satisfaction of proving her wrong. By then it was pushing two o'clock and I was holding my eyelids up with toothpicks, but it was a triumph just the same when they unlocked the elevator for the executive floor.

The room with the George Washington furniture was a lot more populated than it had been Tuesday night, and Harwell was a lot busier, but eventually I got my chance to sink into one of the big leather chairs and speak my piece. I made it as snappy as I could, starting first with my notion that Janine DuPage had wanted to keep Lombardo alive and then moving on to the observation that Lyder had been a little too quick with his accusations and a lot too ready to move into the manager's office, like he'd been prepared for the promotion in advance. Then I told him about Lyder's early-morning trips to the roof and his after-hours jaunt to Chinatown, which didn't mean anything to me but might to him. Not that Harwell was rushing in to back up my ideas with other suggestions. He just sat there, listening and fiddling with his pipe, until I got to the part about someone else coming through the kitchen Monday night.

"Wouldn't put too much faith in that Ruiz fellow," he interrupted. "Suppose you know he was stealing from us? Not to be trusted, not at all. Doesn't help a bit in solving the larger crime, unfortunately. Only circumstantial evidence against him, don't you know? Sad, really. Promising future with Interdine, all gone now." He made it sound like crime was a form of investment and Angel had made a bad move in the market.

"Anyway," he continued, "hard to imagine Robert Lyder doing

anything that would hurt Interdine. Very responsible young man. Reason I decided to give him a shot at the Pinnacle Room in the first place. Tremendous sense of company loyalty. Obsessive about eliminating waste. Excellent qualities for a manager. Just the counterbalance we needed. Of course, he'll have to find his own style now that Lombardo's gone. Rather different when you're in charge, don't you know? Terrible loss. John Lombardo was a very gifted man. Made a lot of money for Interdine."

Harwell stopped talking as abruptly as he had begun and shifted his gaze over my shoulder to show that the conversation was over. Sitting behind his desk, he could see skyline in every direction, once through the windows and then again reflected in the unbroken row of mirrored panels that lined the dining room wall. I got in one more question before he booted me out.

"If Lyder wasn't up to something fishy," I asked, "what was he doing on the roof?"

"Excellent question, Jacoby. See if you can find me an answer."

After that there wasn't anything else to say. I made my way out of the building and back into the full heat of the afternoon. A Con Ed crew was tearing up the street, the way they always seem to be doing, and the machinery sent ripples through the heat waves rising from the pavement. I was tired of noise and heat and tall buildings, tired of smelling tar instead of grass, tired of treating everyone I saw as a suspect. Maybe my problem was that I had an overdeveloped sense of responsibility. Maybe I would be happier if I were a dreamer like Sam, chasing after crazy schemes for profits that would never come, always thinking that tomorrow some young chick was going to fall for me for sure. Or maybe I should be a mystic, like Lombardo had been, trusting in Providence to preserve his genius for food and his psychic talent for putting restaurants where everyone would want to come. Eternal happiness would take care of everything, he said. What was that supposed to mean? A family plot in a prairie cemetery? One sweetheart in the hospital and another in jail? Wherever

196

Lombardo's eternal happiness lay, I hoped he had found it by now.

Walking back to the train, I peered in the window of a travel agency. Right then I was fed up with New York. I would have gone anywhere anybody offered.

This place was pushing Hawaii. The window was lined with plastic hibiscus and rubber pineapple, and in the middle was a big picture of a blond couple in his and her matching sarongs hugging each other under a waterfall. "Experience the magic of Hawaii," the sign said. "Not a place but a state of mind."

I stared at the words, reading them backwards and forwards until they lost all meaning. And then I stared at them some more because suddenly they started to mean a lot. Eternal happiness wasn't a state of mind. It was a place. A place I had already seen, except I had been too dumb to notice. Who needed Hawaii? I had suddenly developed a violent craving for Chinatown.

The office looked just like it had two days ago. Same crummy rental notices in the window, same wall of file cabinets inside, same faded English lettering on the door. Eternal Happiness Realty Company, it said. Except now I was paying attention. And now I knew where Lyder had ended up last night. Gone to look for an apartment, Sam had said. In the state he was in, it was easy for Eternal Happiness to turn into Happy New Year before he got back to the phone. And there on the corner, just like he had said, was the most *hermoso* telephone booth this side of Shanghai.

But what did it all mean? How was a run-down real estate office in Chinatown going to pay Lombardo's expenses in Italy? Why had Lyder come here, bringing along two other men? And why had Harwell been so unconcerned with Lyder's moonlighting? I tried to think up a line to inspire the tiny rental agent to spill it all to Papa Quentin until I saw the place was empty, the door locked. A big pile of mail was tumbled on the floor inside the door, like the postman had been pushing letters through the slot for days. I pounded on the glass just in case, but nobody answered. Whatever help Eternal Happiness had given Lombardo, it wasn't doing zip for me.

Meanwhile, it was Friday afternoon, and I hadn't been to sleep for a long, long time. Parts of my body that I hadn't thought about in years were sitting up and complaining. My head was throbbing from a combination of heat, pain, and fatigue. I went over to Sam's favorite phone booth and called Joe Reilly to see if the rackets squad had turned up anything on Faerbrother, but the bad news was that his record was clear, at least under that name. After I got through talking to Joe, I staggered north to Gloria's building. I didn't know how serious she'd been about using her apartment as a rest stop, but the time had definitely come to find out.

Chapter 25

I let myself in with Gloria's key and felt like a Peeping Tom as I went through the rooms. Gloria had been gone for hours, but traces of her were littered everywhere. Neat as a pin, the lady wasn't. A cup of coffee abandoned on the kitchen table. Cigarette stubs in the ashtray by the bed. A damp towel on the bathroom floor. I hung it on the bar and hunted around until I found a fresh one in the linen closet. Then I turned the shower on to a nice lukewarm temperature, took off my clothes, sat down in the tub, and let the water wash over my body. In my condition I wasn't taking any chances about passing out and knocking my head against the tiles.

I sat there a good long time, soaking away the grime and soreness. When I had had enough, I dried off and went back to the bedroom. Gloria had changed the bed since Tuesday. Today the sheets were pale blue with little white stripes. I eased myself into horizontal and instantly fell asleep.

When I woke it was well past eight o'clock, and I wasn't alone. While I was snoozing, Gloria had come home and slid in between the sheets beside me. She hadn't bothered with a nightgown, and she seemed to be having a very happy dream. As soon as I saw her, I forgot Powers, and work, and all my aches and pains.

199

A gentleman never disappoints a naked lady. I touched her shoulder gently with my fingers. Time for Sleeping Beauty to awake.

She stretched happily, then opened her eyes. And started to scream. I had also forgotten what my face looked like, and I'd been too buried in the pillows for Gloria to know.

"Oh, my God!" she shrieked. "What happened to you?"

"Nothing. Just ignore it."

"Nothing! Quentin, this is no joke! Should I get a doctor?"

Last night that would have been a good idea, but by now I'd done my own first aid. Nothing was broken, I knew. No internal injuries. Just a split lip, a black eye, and a lot of sore muscles.

"I'm fine," I assured her. "Or at least I will be soon. Unless I'm very wrong about what you had in mind." I reached out my hand again and lightly traced a finger across her shoulders and down her arm.

"You sure you're all right?" she asked hesitantly.

"Positive."

"Then turn off the light. I got into bed with Quentin Jacoby, not the Phantom of the Opera."

I did what she asked and then proceeded to have a thoroughly good time. Rest isn't the only cure for sore muscles. Sometimes exercise helps a lot, too.

It was nice and cool in Gloria's bedroom. It was pleasant to lie there and hear the air conditioner hum away and feel Gloria's foot brush against my leg as though we couldn't quite let go of each other completely. But much as I tried to concentrate on the here and now, my mind kept on going back to the Interdine Tower. And Chinatown. And Janine, locked up somewhere without even a proper pair of shoes. If I knew Lombardo's connection to that real estate office, maybe then I would understand why he had been killed. And from why to who and maybe from there to how. All within forty-eight hours, too, unless the answer really was Janine. What I needed was to talk to somebody who knew about real estate. An expert. I was staring at the ceiling so hard I didn't notice for a while that Gloria was sitting up.

"What's this about a real estate expert?" she demanded.

"Sorry," I said. "I must have been thinking out loud."

"About real estate. Tell me."

Instead I slid a hand over her hip, to where the bone stuck out a little to make a nice contrast with the surrounding plumpness. Gloria picked up my hand in hers and held it in the air, palm to palm. I felt like we were making a truce, except as far as I was concerned, the war had ended some time ago. When I tried to slide my hand down again, she grabbed me by the wrist and held on tighter. "Real estate," she repeated firmly.

Real estate. Murder. Business. I sat up in bed and pulled the sheet up under my armpits. I could be just as cool as Gloria if that was what she wanted. I traced back over my thoughts of the last ten minutes. Would it make sense to her?

"Try me," she said, reading my mind.

"All right," I agreed. "The question is the same as ever—who killed John Lombardo? Nobody's telling. Nobody's left any nifty clues. According to the coroner's report, Lombardo was killed by a right-handed person between five feet six inches and five feet ten inches tall. Unfortunately that describes about half the adult population, including Janine DuPage. Except that she had good reasons for wanting to keep Lombardo alive and none for wanting him dead."

"None that we know about," corrected Gloria.

"Right," I agreed. "None that we know about. So what don't we know? John Lombardo was a smash success in the restaurant business. Everyone adored him, everyone copied his ideas. But there was something else about all his ventures. Every time he opened up a new place, it was in some dumpy part of town that suddenly became real fashionable, right? Five years ago, who went to Yorkville at night? Just a few tourists who took a wrong turn looking for Munich. Ten years ago it was worth your neck to go under the Triborough Bridge after dark, and now you can hardly see the river for all the art galleries and flashy bars tucked in between the girders. Or take the Interdine Tower—Lombardo's company had an option on that property before the World Trade Center was even under construction, when that stretch of Manhattan was just a run-down wasteland east of New Jersey and west of civilization. Now they're building a whole new city over there along the Hudson, and the property values must be going through the roof."

"So?" Gloria asked. "I understand what you're saying, but I don't see where you're going."

I gave her a quick history of my discovery of Eternal Happiness, skipping a lot of wrong guesses along the way. Wrong guesses seemed to be my specialty lately, but I didn't have to say so to Gloria.

"Here's my thinking," I finished. "Lombardo worked for Interdine, but maybe he was also dealing in real estate on the side. Scouting out properties near where he was building a new restaurant, buying them up at depression prices, and then making a nice killing when he put the area back on the map. The guy was a natural for it, a kind of human divining rod for profits."

Gloria thought it over. "That may be true," she said at last. "But why would it make anyone want to kill him?"

"I don't know," I admitted. "But there's something going on that has to do with buying and selling property. Maybe Lombardo was cutting out too many other people or getting in the way of someone else's plans for a piece of property. Maybe Lyder found out that the boss was working his own angles on company time and they had a fight about it that ended up with Lombardo dead. That would explain how Lyder knew about the place anyway."

"Maybe Lombardo double-crossed Janine DuPage in some way and she killed him, like the police think," Gloria added.

"That's possible," I agreed. "It's possible, it's easy, and it's neat. But I don't think it's true. And I can't help feeling that if I knew more about the real estate angle, it would make more sense. After all, what *was* Lyder doing, taking those overseas investment types to a grimy rental office in Chinatown? Why did Lombardo say it would pay for his restaurant in Italy? And now that I think of it, how much did Blount Harwell know about what was going on? He said something about Eternal Happiness, too, the night after Lombardo was killed."

Gloria hesitated. "If you really want to consult a real estate whiz," she said slowly, "I might be able to help. Rachel's roommate claims to be one of the biggest experts on real estate investment in New York."

"Your daughter's roommate?" I asked.

"If they got married, he'd be my son-in-law," Gloria said, sounding more confident. "Which thank God he's not. But meanwhile, he's pulling in close to one hundred thousand dollars a year as an investment consultant, plus whatever he makes on that newsletter he publishes. *Property Market Investors' Guide*. He's a regular whiz kid, is Howie."

"Then why are you so glad he and Rachel aren't married?" I asked.

"Because he's a creep," Gloria answered promptly. "It makes me sick to think that Rachel likes him. But if you want to talk real estate, Howie's your man. I'll call Rachel tonight and try to arrange something for tomorrow. Take me out to dinner tomorrow night, and we'll compare impressions. If you're still in one piece."

I had forgotten all about my face, but now I fingered the damage. By tomorrow night I should be able to chew without even noticing.

"Okay," I agreed.

"Good," said Gloria, sliding back under the sheet. "Now, where were we?"

Chapter 26

It took a lot of will power to get myself out of Gloria's bed and over to the Pinnacle Room at eleven. It felt like tomorrow morning to me, but the place was jammed with people warming up for the weekend. Lyder was down in the dining room, chatting it up with the customers and doing the same dismal imitation of Lombardo's charm I'd seen every night this week. It was interesting to see how far ambition could push a man to make a fool of himself in a field for which he had no talent.

Down in the kitchen, waiters were still scurrying around, carrying dessert dishes and pots of coffee, but all the real cooking was over. Four nights after Lombardo's death the little world he'd created had decided it would be able to continue without him after all. Not that they were exactly a happy-go-lucky bunch. Everyone was vibrating with the edgy knowledge that Lombardo's killer was still at large. All I had to do was say "boo," and the place would have exploded. Would they be relieved, I wondered, to know that Janine had been arrested? Or would that make them all the more nervous, thinking about how they'd been harboring a killer and never even known?

My standing with the cooks hadn't improved any over the last few days. They still avoided me, blamed me, and hated me, and I expected they always would. When I came in, most of them made a big show of turning away. Only Pierre acknowledged my presence, and then only to ask if I was done with the wine inventory he'd given me because he'd lost his copy. Lyder had taken over the restaurant, but Pierre was in charge of the cellar now, and he had a notion to make it even more of a showpiece than Lombardo had done.

"Monsieur Lombardo always consulted with me on his programs, because we know each other for so long a time, but for this ravishing room he had no idea to use it except for himself. For a tribute to his genius now, I think we must open for the wine tastings. Monday I make the big presentation of my idea to Mr. Donohue, the vice-president. We will make this place *spectacular!*" Then the zip went out of his voice, and he started patting the napkin over his arm in an anxious kind of way. "Do you think it is too soon to have such ideas?" he asked. "I do not want to lack respect for the dead."

I gave him my blessings, for whatever they were worth, and the wine list besides. I handed it over gladly. At least I didn't have to hunt for the sneak thief anymore. I wondered how the people here would take it when they found out their genius hero was also a petty thief. Not that they would learn it from me. I had enough to do finding Lombardo's killer without blackening his reputation. Then another possibility came to mind.

"Hey, Pierre," I asked, "you know that little bar upstairs in Mr. Harwell's office, the one behind the wall?"

"The executive wine cellar," he corrected me. "But of course. I stock it myself, for Mr. Harwell's use."

"Anything missing?"

Pierre drew in his breath. "You think there is the connection? Mr. Lyder, he asked me for the key this morning, to do the inventory inspection. Have I made an error, giving it to him?"

"Oh, no," I answered. Pierre had already told me what I needed to know. The little wine cellar was locked. "It was just a thought. You would have noticed long ago if there was anything wrong."

Nodding uncertainly, Pierre turned back to his work.

It was after midnight by the time Lyder shook hands with the last customer and came through for his usual late-night inspection. Ever since I started on this lousy job, he'd been treating me like I might spring up and bite at any time. We circled each other the whole time he was in the kitchen, but all he did was give me a shaky reprimand about coming in late last night.

The time passed slowly after that. I toured the premises. I ate the dinner they had left for me. I watched a cruise ship come out of the mouth of the Hudson and cross paths in the harbor with a garbage scow making its way back up the East River. I called Sam and made a date to take him and Faerbrother up to the roof tomorrow morning, right after the building opened. Sam screeched like the devil at the idea of getting downtown at 7:00 A.M., but I shut him up with a reminder that early morning was when they exercised the horses.

"Maybe your hayseed swami can put the fix on some nag running tomorrow night," I suggested. "A freebie bonus for your good-faith investing."

"Yeah," Sam said. "'Cept by the time I find him, man, it's gonna be *mañana*, and then I gotta turn around and come down on the train with not enough time in the sack to rest these tired bones."

"Forget the rest," I told him. "Stay up all night." Why should I be the only one who felt lousy all the time?

The rest of the night I spent moving from room to room, staring out all the different windows to catch the first sign of dawn. When daybreak finally came, I was facing the wrong direction, looking west from the manager's office. I had gone there searching for the annual report of the Interdine Corporation, but I guess Lombardo wasn't sufficiently interested in the parent company to hold on to its records. I looked back over the restaurant ledgers to see if they had any new information. When I sat down, it was dark, and when I looked up, the lights across the river in Jersey had taken on an eerie glow against the soft gray of early morning. Everything seemed so quiet and peaceful I nearly jumped through the glass when the telephone rang.

It was Gloria, and she sounded disgustingly hearty for six o'clock in the morning.

"Sorry to call so early," she chirped. "I had to catch you before you left work. Howie wants you to meet him at nine this morning. You'd never make it in time if you went all the way home."

"Howie?"

"Howie, the real estate hawk," Gloria said. "World's largest boy wonder. The expert you wanted to consult, remember?"

"Of course," I lied. "Where's his office?"

"Who said anything about an office? Howie thinks they're a needless expense and a drag on your time, answering the telephone and all. He's got an answering service and a beeper for emergencies, but mostly he operates out of the Big Apple Ice Cream Emporium, on the concourse of the World Trade Center. They open at nine in the summer, and Howie likes to be the first customer."

"An ice cream store?" I asked. I couldn't believe it. Gloria acted like it was the normal way to do business.

"You can't miss him," she assured me. "And remember, Howie is *very* big in real estate."

Laughing at some private joke, she said good-bye. I turned off the lights, closed the ledgers, and went back to the kitchen to wait for the morning crew.

At three minutes after seven I was down in the lobby. Hector and Ysidore hadn't made it, but Sam was there. So was Ezra Faerbrother, wearing the same pressed jeans and faded shirt I'd seen him in on Monday and staring at the blank marble wall like the hand of God had etched a message there that only he could read. I'd been hoping Faerbrother had skipped town already, pocketed Sam's advance and cut back to wherever he came from before he could do any more harm, but I should have known he'd stay with his suckers as long as they kept swallowing his line. Never in all my days had I seen a fish so grateful to be hooked as Sam.

The guard at the console was eyeing them suspiciously, but he hadn't quite gotten around to booting them out.

"Trainees," I called out quickly, and hurried them both into the elevator before he could ask any questions. Sam had a few comments about my face, but after that we rode up to the Pinnacle Room in silence. When the doors slid open, I gestured to them to stay quiet, and the three of us practically tiptoed over to the stairs so as not to let the bakers hear us. I didn't want anyone running up from the kitchen, thinking there were prowlers on the premises. We walked the three flights to the roof, Sam tapping up the stairs in his open-weave loafers, Faerbrother following silently in black low-cut sneakers, and me making an awful noise in my heavy oxfords. Nobody stopped us, though, and the exit door was still ajar, just the way I'd left it Thursday morning. I hadn't heard the elevator go up this morning, but it was a relief to see for myself that Lyder wasn't there.

Once I was sure the roof was clear, I opened the door wide and gave Sam and Faerbrother the grand tour. Statue of Liberty to the south, New Jersey docks to the west, World Trade Center to the north, Verrazano Narrows Bridge to the east. Then I checked out the elevator to make sure they could get down without a key.

"Get all the fresh air you like," I told Faerbrother. "If anybody questions you when you leave, say you're roofing inspectors."

"I am grateful to you for your kind assistance," he said, bowing his head in that sitff way he had. I bowed back and left them to their game. There were a few things I wanted to do on the roof myself, and I didn't have much time.

I walked back to the shed that sheltered the stairs and slowly looked around. Something was different from the way it had been two days ago. Not the staircase door—that was just the way I'd left it. Not the elevators or the place where the reception desk would be, still draped in their plastic covers. Not the flat tar roof, spotted around the pool area with pieces of indoor-outdoor carpeting. I went over to where Lyder had been standing, next to the construction crane. No man today, of course. No backpack either. But strapped to the side of the crane was something I hadn't noticed before, a compact winch wound tight with what looked like miles of thin, strong nylon rope. The rope went a few feet up the side of the crane, passed through a small pulley, and ended in a kind of harness designed to pass between the legs and fasten over the hips. On top of the harness buckle was a colored sticker, the kind that kids collect. A picture of Spiderman.

So there it was, the explanation for Lyder's trips to the roof. I'd had my suspicions, of course. Everything pointed to it. The exercise equipment. The break with the mountain climbing club. The urgent need to stay in shape. Powers was expecting it. It had been a feature on the evening news. Everybody knew they were coming, but I still needed to see the evidence before my eyes to believe that a man like Robert Lyder—reasonably stable, reasonably sane, with a company job that was growing more responsible by the minute—was actually planning to dress up like a comic book hero and climb the walls of the Interdine Tower.

What was making him do it? I wondered. Did that fantastic loyalty everyone praised him for extend to going along with the crazy stunts of his exercise buddies? Or was this something that had occurred to him after Lombardo had been killed, a desperate play for fame to make up for the fact that he would never equal Lombardo's charm? Now I knew what Pierre had been talking about that night I'd overheard him in the pantry, trying to assure Lyder that he would attract customers his own way. Now I knew why Lyder was so nervous. Pierre would back him up, he said. Did that mean Harwell didn't know what Lyder was up to, or had he gone upstairs for permission before he began training for his giant publicity stunt?

I looked back at the rig dangling from the crane. How much

209

faster could you climb down a building if you were using a rope and pulley? Not fast enough for Lyder to have killed Lombardo after midnight and been down in the garage twenty minutes later. The only way to make that kind of time was to jump clean over the edge, which was a sure way to smash yourself to pieces, harness or no.

But if Lyder hadn't had time to do it, that didn't mean it hadn't been done. If he had had the right clothes and enough nerve, just about anybody could have made it down using Lyder's equipment. If he had had enough nerve, the clothing wouldn't have mattered either. There was one more suspect, someone so much in the middle of things I was amazed I hadn't given him more than a passing thought before. Blount Harwell. Mr. Interdine himself. Just came up from Valley Forge, he said on Monday night, but wasn't it more likely that he had just come down from the roof? He was in good shape, and he knew the building as well as anyone, including the only place the killer could have hidden.

He also had a lot at stake. Lombardo's restaurants were great for publicity, but they must have looked lousy on the corporate balance sheets. Now that he had this fancy new building, Harwell didn't need the restaurants to give Interdine visibility. But the building must have cost a pretty penny, and Lombardo's contract probably had a lot more years to run. A lot more years to drop hundreds of thousands of dollars into flashy, popular, unprofitable restaurants. Of course, Harwell could just have fired his genius, but from the picture I'd built up of John Lombardo, I bet anything it would have cost Harwell plenty to break Lombardo's contract. Cost him more than money, too, because I'd bet a fired Lombardo would be a nasty Lombardo. Did the stockholders know just how much money their restaurants were losing? Would they move to dump the chairman of the board if they found out the kind of balance sheets he'd been approving? Now *there* was a reason for murder. Keeping Lombardo on was too expensive for Harwell;

firing him might have risked everything he'd worked for. How nice it must have been to imagine Lombardo magically gone, replaced by loyal, reliable, budget-minded Robert Lyder. How simple to make it happen.

The funny thing was, if Harwell had only waited Lombardo would have cut out on his own, just like Janine had predicted. But Janine had also said that Harwell never did understand Lombardo. It was beyond his imagination that a man would break a good contract to run away to Italy with a pretty boy who worked in the kitchen. And now Janine was in jail while Harwell was enjoying a comfortable weekend down in Pennsylvania.

I was wondering if I should call Captain Powers. "I want proof," he had said. "Not just hunches and suspicion. Proof." I didn't have any yet, but Robert Lyder wasn't the only one who could play Spiderman, I told myself. The time had come for me to weave a web of my own. I waved good-bye to Sam and sprinted for the elevator. I had only five minutes to make it to the World Trade Center, and I didn't want to keep Howie the Real Estate Hawk waiting.

Chapter 27

It wasn't hard to pick him out. He was the only person in the place. Before I even got inside, I saw why Gloria joked about the guy being a big man in his field. The denim overalls, the T-shirt, the mop of uncombed curly hair could have belonged to anyone of Howie's age, which I estimated at very early twenties. The body, though, was one of the fattest I had seen outside the circus. There was no question about it. Rachel's roommate was a real porker.

I watched him through the window, observing the way his backside overflowed the little metal chair he was sitting on. He had already bought himself a banana split for breakfast and was busy pushing the little plastic spoon in and out of his mouth with a series of dainty jabs. He ate like a raccoon—furtive, neat, and very fast. A raccoon in overalls, size fifty-seven waist. I pushed open the door to hear what the Fat Boy had to say.

When he saw me come in the door, he waved his spoon in greeting, then gave his dish a quick inspection to make sure he hadn't missed anything before he threw it away.

"You must be Jacoby," he said. "Have some breakfast."

The girl at the counter was eyeing me curiously, but gooey sundaes were not my idea of what to eat first thing in the morning. I ordered a cup of coffee. The place sold nothing but ice cream, coffee, and orange soda. Some heavy market research must have been behind those choices.

I could tell that Howie disapproved of my skimpy selection, but he was nice enough to let it pass. "So," he said, rubbing his chubby mitts together, "I understand you want to know all about investing in Manhattan real estate. Let me start by telling you that you have come to the right man."

And then he launched into a ten-minute monologue. To make money, he said, you have to spend money, and there were very few people around with the capacity to profit from real estate in any significant way. For every actual investor, he told me, there were a thousand people who would never do any more than dream.

"That's very interesting," I said politely.

"Yes, indeed it is," he agreed, missing my great irony. "That's why I'm rich," he added. "To be a serious force in real estate around here, I'd say you need over twenty million. How many people you know have that kind of money lying around?"

"None," I answered. "Unless you're talking about yourself."

"Let us continue," he said, shrugging off the question. "How many people you know have two hundred and seventy dollars?"

"Not too many of those either," I answered. "But I see the difference."

"Not yet you don't. Two hundred and seventy dollars a year, a measly twenty-two dollars and fifty cents per month, gets you a ten-page report on hot properties, fast trends, mortgage rates, juicy repossessions. Plus tips on how to figure out rates of return, the tax benefits of going solar, banks you can trust if you're dealing with someone from Argentina. For two hundred and seventy dollars you can go out for a single night on the town, or you can get a subscription that will come to you every month, the whole year long, helping you plan your finances so if you're smart, you'll never have to think about money again. Even if you don't have the dough to really make these investments, which my average reader doesn't, it's nice to think about. The pleasure, my friend, is in the planning as much as in the having."

"Sounds good."

"Good? It's great! Right now I've got three hundred paid subscribers, which is to say, eighty-one thousand a year—and the rag only costs me a thousand a month to put out, leaving the editor and sole proprietor with a clean sixty-nine thousand a year profit. Plus consulting fees, plus whatever deals I myself come up with. After all, in my business you get to hear about a lot of hot properties that change hands before you ever make it to press."

"Then why would the big investors bother to wait for you?" I asked. "They must have their own sources of information, right?" It was like trying to stick a needle in a whale. He never even noticed the sting.

"True," he conceded happily. "Anybody who's really got the megabucks for real estate investment doesn't need me. The opportunities will find him if he has the cash. He still has to know me, though," he added, leaning back proudly in his chair. If he ever tipped over, he'd probably take the whole World Trade Center with him. "We're a small fraternity," he continued, "and we all know each other."

So maybe he knew something after all. I'd about given up on Howie as a self-important tub of lard, but I decided to stick with him a little longer. "Can I get you a refill?" I asked.

"Don't mind if you do," he answered. "I've been meaning to try the banana raspberry ripple. Double scoop."

I came back with the ice cream and a refill on the java that the management had thrown in gratis.

"Ever hear of a real estate outfit called Eternal Happiness?" I asked.

Howie was holding his dish up to his mouth, but now he stopped eating and peered at me over the rim.

"How'd you hear about that?" he asked. "That's a strictly pri-

vate operation. They run it as a club, so there's no public dis-
closure. I don't even know who actually owns the place." He
looked at me sharply. "You making any money from them?"

"Out of my league," I said. It seemed like a safe observation.
Howie nodded. "I hear you need a cool million just to join the
club. But how'd you learn about them?"

"From a guy I met at work," I said truthfully. "Over at Interdine."

"You work for Interdine?" he asked, looking more interested
than he had by anything yet. He was bouncing around excitedly
on his chair. I felt sorry for the furniture. "What's their secret
for keeping the place afloat? The condos are only half-sold, and
their biggest renter is themselves. They've got no stores to speak
of, no walk-through traffic, not even a hotel, but the most reputable accounting firm in the city just gave them a triple A rating
on the corporate balance sheet. I hear the restaurants are doing
great, but that can't be enough to support the whole operation.
They got a gold mine on the roof or something?"

He looked at me like he thought I might really have the an-
swer. "Maybe they're planning to charge a lot for the health club,"
I offered. I meant it as a serious suggestion, but he roared like
I had made a great joke.

"No wonder Gloria said you needed help," he chortled. I was
glad to see I had made him so happy. Maybe now he would do
the same for me.

"Tell me more about this Eternal Happiness club," I said. "Do
you know where their money comes from? Or what they specialize in? They hire any outside people? I've been by their office,
and it sure doesn't look too impressive to me."

"Very simple," he said, shoveling in another spoonful of banana
raspberry ripple. "The office is a dump because nobody goes
there. The business is all by mail. And the answer to where they
get the money and what they specialize in lies in the same two
words: Hong Kong." He slurped down the remnants of his ice

215

cream, completely satisfied with his answer. Which made one of us.

"What's the big deal with Hong Kong?" I asked.

He looked at me with pity. "Now, if you just subscribed to my newsletter, you'd never ask a dumb question like that."

"Okay, okay. As soon as I win the Trifecta, I'll subscribe. But just for now, if you don't mind..."

He put down his spoon and wiped his fingers with the finicky neatness I had noticed before.

"Hong Kong," he explained patiently, "is a crown colony of Great Britain. In 1898, the Chinese granted the British a ninety-nine-year lease on the territory, and since then the colony has become one of the leading financial centers in the world. The Hang Feng, the Hong Kong stock exchange, is the most important market in that part of the world. It's the banking hub of Asia. And for real estate, it makes New York look like Bulgaria in terms of price and demand. Plus there's no suburbs to go to if the costs per footage get to be too much. Lots and lots of money to be made in Hong Kong.

"As of now, though, all that is changing. By everybody's calculations, the British lease on Hong Kong is due to expire in 1997, which is not so far away that the smart money isn't looking ahead. What they see is that the British Empire has faded and the government of China has, shall we say, changed hands, both of which mean that the lease doesn't have a ghost of a chance of renewal. The mainland government means to take over and get a slice of the financial action, but most people expect they'll just drive the economy into the ground. The real estate market there is falling so fast soon you'll have to look over your shoelaces to see it. Which is where the Eternal Happiness club comes in."

Howie stopped talking long enough to wave at the girl behind the counter, who came trotting over with a large cup of orange soda. He took a long swallow, then went on.

"Let's say you're looking ahead and you get your money out

of Hong Kong now. The next question is, where you gonna put it?" He waited, but I had no answer. "South America and the Middle East are too unstable," he said. "Europe has too many taxes, plus socialism and inflation and not much available land. But the U.S. of A.—now there's a sweet place to sink your profits, and that's just what a lot of them have been doing. In case you haven't noticed, Little Italy is being swallowed up by Chinatown. Some people say that's because of all the new immigration. Some people say the Chinese have too many kids or don't move out to the suburbs like the Italians do. But the real thing is that all these Hong Kong investors are coming in, buying up the properties, naturally expanding the boundaries of the tribe. What you don't realize is that it's not just Little Italy that's getting taken over. It's SoHo, and TriBeCa, and the whole waterfront under the West Side Highway. New Yorkers don't know from waterfront property. They think it's just a strip on the edges where you're too far from the stores and too likely to get mugged. But these guys from Hong Kong find out about the parcels available and see how undervalued they are, and they go nuts. Can't wait to sign the papers. I'm amazed your friends at Interdine had the good sense to buy up their property before one of these Far East combines got to it."

"It's not so surprising," I said. "They've got some sharp guys over at Interdine. Or they used to. You by any chance have a John Lombardo on your mailing list?"

"Can't tell offhand," he answered. "I'll check when I get home and give you a ring. My clientele is mostly confidential, but I'm happy to make an exception for a friend of Rachel's mother."

"Don't bother," I said. "If his name is there, you can cross it off. The man's dead."

Chapter 28

I left Howie sitting there in his ice cream office, licking his spoon and looking surprised. Gloria's boy wonder had come through after all. For one thing I now had a better idea of the kind of money you needed to play with Manhattan real estate, and it was a level of dough I doubted Lombardo had had. That didn't mean he was out of the game, though. If Eternal Happiness was a money funnel for Far East investors, they would need somebody local to sniff out the properties for their clients. John Lombardo, with his nose for undervalued real estate, could have gotten big commissions for tips on areas where the prices were about to take a jump. Enough to pay for a seaside restaurant in Italy. Enough to keep him from caring whether or not the Pinnacle Room was turning a profit.

The brass at Interdine still cared, though, and they were keeping the truth very close to the vest. That was the other thing I'd learned from Howie that morning. He'd thought the restaurants were doing great, which meant everybody did, which meant that it was very much in Harwell's interest to keep the facts quiet any way he could. A few whispers from Lombardo, and Mr. Interdine was in deep trouble. It was all beginning to fit. I'd picked up a lot of new information this morning, but none of it gave me any reason to change my plans.

On the main level of 2 World Trade Center the same banners advertised the same Balinese dancers. Very little had changed in the world from Monday to Saturday. John Lombardo had been killed. Janine DuPage had been arrested. Angel Ruiz had put himself in the hospital. Quentin Jacoby had missed a lot of sleep. But the ladies with the cymbals on their fingers were still dancing every day at noon, and the wait for the observation deck was just as long. Standing in line for my ticket, I suddenly remembered that I had never paid Sam back for the ride on Monday morning. One more debt to add to my tab.

When I finally got upstairs, I made right for one of the telescope machines that ring the edges of the deck and plunked two quarters in the slot. Very fine line to East Rutherford, Faerbrother had said. I swung the telescope around toward New Jersey and saw that he was right. Then I turned back to the south and studied the top of the Interdine Tower.

The first thing I saw was Ezra Faerbrother facing west toward Jersey, arms stretched out like a big scarecrow. The wind off the Hudson was blowing the hair off his forehead, and I could see the wrinkles above his eyebrows when he sent an extra-strong eyeball message across the river. I looked for Sam, to see how he was appreciating the show, and finally spotted him stretched out by the empty swimming pool. His eyes were closed, his mouth was open, and I doubted even Marilyn Monroe could have gotten his attention right then. I inched the eyepiece up a fraction to focus on the edge of the roof over by the crane. Through the telescope it looked like it was just below me. It felt like I could reach out and push the harness like a swing. Then the timer inside the telescope stopped clicking, and a metal plate blocked my view.

I fished out some more money and continued my investigations. What I discovered was that anybody taking pictures from the observation deck Monday night would have had a clear shot of the entire Interdine Tower roof and eighteen stories below, which was plenty far enough to notice a killer climbing down the side of the building. Of course, there wasn't anybody taking pictures from the observation deck Monday night, but Blount Harwell didn't know that. Meanwhile, it was ten-fifteen Saturday morning. Time to call Valley Forge.

I was in luck. Harwell answered the phone himself and agreed to accept the charges.

"Yes?" he said. "What is it? What's happened?"

"I'm sorry to bother you at home," I said, "but I think I have some news on John Lombardo's murder. I'm afraid it involves one of your people, and I didn't want to have to wait until Monday."

"Miss DuPage, you mean?" The worried urgency had all gone out of Harwell's voice. "Captain Powers contacted me yesterday afternoon. Shocking, of course, but also something of a relief. Having it settled, I mean. Poor John." He clucked his tongue sympathetically into the phone. "Well," he continued after a moment, "thank you very much for calling. Contact my secretary on Monday, and we'll see about extending your contract. Very pleased with your work. Very pleased indeed."

"I'm not calling about DuPage," I interrupted. "Something new has come up. It seems there was somebody else at the Pinnacle Room the night Lombardo was killed. Somebody who escaped out over the roof. I won't have the pictures until tomorrow morning, though, and I wanted to show them to you first."

There was a long silence on the line. "What kind of pictures?" Harwell asked at last.

"Photographs of the Interdine Tower, taken from the top of the World Trade Center. A whole series, starting at midnight last Monday night. I have the negatives. Bought them from a shutterbug fellow, happened to be fooling around. He called the security service as soon as he saw what he had. I'll get the prints tomorrow, first thing. Can you come into town to see them?"

"What?" asked Harwell. "Into town? Yes, yes, of course. But have you been to the police with these?"

I put on my best obedient employee voice. "Oh, no, Mr. Harwell. Right now nobody knows about this but you and me. I'd like you to see them first. Then you can tell me what to do."

"Yes," said Harwell slowly, drawing the word out into a long, speculative sigh. "Yes, I suppose that would be best. Can you come to my office?"

"The roof would be better," I answered. "There's some equipment there I'd like to show you."

"That's all right then," he said. He sounded like he was talking to himself, not me. "I'll come up to town tonight. Meet you at eight sharp, tomorrow morning." Then he hung up.

I went to the snack bar and converted a dollar into dimes. First I tried Lyder's apartment, but I wasn't surprised when nobody answered. I expected to find him at the Pinnacle Room, fussing over the menu, like he usually was, but the girl who answered the phone said he wasn't there either. Gone until Monday, she said, and would I care to speak to the floor captain instead? I thought about the floor captain, with his trim blond mustache, and was about to give up. Then I remembered the wine steward. Maybe Pierre knew where Lyder had gone.

There was a long wait while the girl went to look for him. I propped the receiver against my ear and tried to avoid seeing my reflection in the chrome plate of the coin box. The silence was broken every once in a while by the voice of an operator asking for more money. I was just drifting off to dreamland when the connection sprang to life.

"Pierre Morel on the line. May I help you?"

"Quentin Jacoby here. It's very important that I talk to Robert Lyder before tomorrow. Do you know where I can reach him?"

"Before tomorrow I regret I cannot help you. I know only that Monsieur Lyder is away on urgent personal business. Should he call here, is there the message I can give him?"

"Yes," I answered. "Ask him who else knows about the roof. He'll understand. Tell him it's very important that I find out before tomorrow morning. Tell him it's a matter of life and death."

Chapter 29

I got home, took a shower, and surveyed the current condition of my body. I still had a black eye, but my mouth was back to its usual size, and my ribs were already passing from purple into lime green. Howie hadn't even seemed to notice, so maybe I was back to looking normal. Not myself, but normal. I put on a clean pair of pajamas and got into bed. Pleasant as it was to visit Gloria, it was also very nice to be home.

I woke at five. I don't know how long Sam had been pounding on my door before the noise reached me in the bedroom, but he'd had long enough to get good and mad.

"You let me in right now!" he was screaming. "I know you in there! You let me in!"

"Okay!" I yelled back at him. "Keep your shirt on."

When he saw me in my pajamas, Sam got real contrite. "I wake you?" he asked. It wasn't the kind of question you bother to answer.

"What's the matter?" I asked instead. That reminded Sam that he was still outraged.

"The matter is, where's my money? That's what's the matter, baby!"

Sam's money. One thousand dollars. The poor guy still expected me to join in on his crazy scheme. One of the things I'd meant to do this week was a brilliant investigation of a certain con man by the name of Ezra Faerbrother, but somehow it hadn't quite worked out. The moment had come when I was going to have to let a buddy down.

"Sam," I said, "there is something I've got to tell you. I've been thinking a lot about this Faerbrother fellow, and nothing I've thought has changed my opinion that the man's a fraud. I got you up on the Interdine roof, but that's as far as I go by way of cooperation. As far as I'm concerned, you've got as much chance of taking a swim in that empty pool you were napping by as you have of collecting on Sunday. You can throw away your money if you want, but include me out."

"How you know I was sleeping?" Sam demanded.

"I'm psychic," I answered. "Just like Faerbrother. And you can stop smirking because I know what you're about to say, and it won't work. It's true you and Hector and Ysidore did me a couple of favors, but I think you'll agree they didn't come anywhere near a thousand dollars' worth of time. More like a hundred, I'd say. Fifty you already got, and I've got another fifty waiting for you in the bedroom. But that, my friend, is it."

I braced myself for his reaction. Would he spring at my throat, screaming Spanish threats, or wait to call out his friends for a full-scale vendetta? What I wasn't prepared for was when he started to cry.

"Oh, man," he whimpered. "You don't understand. A chance like this, it ain't never gonna come back. Seventy years I been nothing. Now I got the chance to hit it big one time before I die, and you don't believe it's for real." He turned away so I wouldn't see the tears coming down his face. I don't think I have ever felt so low.

"Believe me, Sam," I said awkwardly, "it's for the best this way. It really is." I could hear him sniffling all the way across the living room. "Tell you what," I offered. "Let's go out, do something fun. Get your mind off this nonsense."

Sam had his back to me, but I could see his shoulders straighten hopefully. "Let's go out to the track, baby," he suggested. "You see Mr. Faerbrother again, doing his communication with the horses, I know you're gonna change your mind."

"No, I'm not."

"Just come," he pleaded, turning around. "Can't hurt to come. They got some sweet little trotters out there tonight. Painted Lady in the second race, with Sal Vincent riding, and Cucumber Soup in the fifth. Remember last month, we won big on Cucumber Soup? Please?"

"All right, Sam," I said finally. There was nothing I could do about the Interdine case until tomorrow morning. Besides, my body wouldn't know what to do if it got any real rest. "We'll go out to the track. But don't get any big ideas about the Hampton Stake because I am not giving Faerbrother any money, and that is final. Get it?"

"Sure, baby, sure," Sam answered, smiling in a way that meant he didn't believe me for a minute. "You get out there, smell the sulkies, see the horseflesh on parade, I just *know* you are going to change your mind." He went downstairs to get ready, and I called Gloria to tell her we'd be having dinner in New Jersey.

Going to the track is something about which very few people feel neutral. Thoroughbred racing has a kind of classiness about it, images of mint juleps at the Kentucky Derby and the Queen of England watching the nags at Ascot, but harness racing is different. Nobody has ever put on airs about watching grown men drive around in little bikes pulled by no-name horses whose sires are descended from the best milk wagons. Harness racing you either love or hate, and that's that.

Some people get hooked right away, in love with the lights, the noise, and the sweet smell of easy money. I've seen real sourpusses break out laughing from just watching the action in the grandstand, which usually resembles what the future will look like if the robots ever get religion. If you can tear yourself

225

away from the betting windows and get up to the rail, it's also a very pretty sport, the buggies shining with paint and chrome, the drivers all dressed up in their racing silks, and the big horses flying by so fast you think any second they're going to take off and sail over the river to Manhattan. Most people come to gamble, but there is a certain minority that simply admires the show.

I've also known a lot of people who hate the track. If they want to look at horses, they tell you, they can go to Central Park, and as for paying five dollars' admission to mingle with a lot of bums and dummies looking for a quick profit that almost surely is not gonna come... well, there's no need to repeat what such people say about that. The interesting thing is that there's no way of predicting in advance which type a particular person is going to be. It's even money until you get inside, and I guess it's curiosity that keeps me bringing out new potential converts. That and the fact that I happen to like the races myself, and it's more fun if you don't go alone.

I could see right away that Gloria belonged to the second group.

"Where did all these people come from?" she asked, pulling at the throat of her blouse like she wished it were some kind of protective armor. It had taken us a long time to get there, up from her apartment to the Port Authority Bus Terminal on the West Side and then across the Hudson River to the Meadowlands, and she hadn't had much to say along the way. "I mean, I know Mars," she added, "but what section?"

"Look, Gloria," I said brusquely, "if you can't tell the difference between Mars and East Rutherford, New Jersey, you need to go back to the travel business for a refresher course."

"Oh, is that it?" she said brightly. "New Jersey. We didn't get too many calls for cruises there, but now that you mention it, I've heard of the place."

I looked around, but it didn't seem like a very extraordinary crowd to me. There were maybe more guys in nylon shirts than is strictly the fashion and more ladies with their hair teased up into big beehives or tortured into curls and pompadours in front and falling flat down to their waist in back, but Gloria had hardly led such a sheltered life that she didn't know there were lots of people who don't dress out of the pages of the *New York Times'* report on style. Anyway, the majority were just regular types— lots of people in T-shirts and blue jeans, old ladies who had brought along their lawn chairs, young guys with big bellies they must have gotten drinking beer for breakfast. Gloria was still staring out like we were on some Martian landscape, though, so I asked her what was so strange.

"I don't know exactly," she answered. "They're all so intense. I guess that's it. All these pefectly normal-looking people, clutching their programs and looking over at the tote boards like that's all there is in the world. I mean, I know there are lots of gamblers, and these places exist for betting. I subcontract guards to the Off-Track Betting offices, so I know the scale we're talking about. But somehow, I thought. . ." Her voice trailed off, like she wasn't sure what she thought or was afraid to say so. But Gloria isn't the timid type when it comes to having opinions. "I thought when you came out here, it was supposed to be fun," she said stubbornly.

I had to laugh. "It *is* supposed to be fun," I answered.

"Then why does everybody look so grim?" she countered. "Here they are in a pretty park on a Saturday night, where it costs less to get in than the price of a sleazy movie on Forty-second Street, and I haven't seen a single person smiling since we arrived."

I guess nobody ever explained to Gloria that gambling is a business that takes a lot of concentration.

"Ever been to Las Vegas?" I asked.

"Of course. Discount rates. I used to be a travel agent, remember?"

"What did you do there?"

227

"Do? I went to the shows. Sat by the swimming pool. Wandered through the gambling halls. Nothing special."

"Win anything?"

"Sure. I put five cents into a slot machine and won a dime."

"And then lost it again a second later, right?"

"Wrong, buddy." She smiled proudly. "I know how to play the odds. I quit when I was ahead."

This was going to be harder than I thought. I decided to forget the whole thing. "Just take it from me, Gloria. Most people aren't as smart as you. It's quitting when you're behind that gives you that grim expression."

If Gloria didn't like the races, she was going to positively hate Sam Fuentes, especially after she remembered that he was the kingpin of her expensive team of private investigators. It was only six-thirty and I wasn't planning to meet Sam until eight, which gave me ninety minutes to soften her up to the fact that we would be having a chaperon for the rest of our date. Food, I decided, would definitely help.

This particular track has a fancy restaurant with a closed-circuit television set built into the ceiling above every table, so people can follow the races while they eat. It also has a medium-level dining room where you can get a quick meal and still be served at a table, and then there are a lot of refreshment stands for the folks who like something to munch while they're standing in line at the betting windows. Being a man of moderation in all things, I went for the middle-level dinery, which I upgraded by ordering the shrimp cocktail appetizer.

As soon as we sat down, Gloria started in on the questions. "Did Howie tell you what you wanted?" she asked. "Or did he just stick you for a free tub of butter pecan? That's his favorite," she added, wrinkling her nose.

"Howie was very helpful," I said. "Don't be so hard on the guy. Maybe it's glandular."

"Right. His glands weigh two hundred pounds each. What

does Rachel see in him? What if they get married? They probably wouldn't even fit down the same aisle. But what about the real estate? Did he have the information you wanted?"

"I'm not sure," I said slowly. While we ate, I told her about the Eternal Happiness club, the drop in Hong Kong real estate values, and how Interdine seemed to be losing money on both its new building and its restaurants. I also told her about the rig I had discovered on the roof, what I thought Lyder had been doing up there, and who else might have been making use of the equipment.

Gloria stared at me, then swallowed the last of her chicken.

"What are we doing out here?" she demanded. "Let's get back to the city and call the police about Harwell!" She started gathering up her purse, then stopped when she noticed I wasn't moving. "What *are* we doing here anyway?" she asked. So then I had to explain about Sam.

"We'll get Harwell," I assured her. "He's going to be at the Interdine Tower tomorrow, and he doesn't suspect a thing. Until then there's no harm in spending an hour or two with Sam Fuentes."

Gloria looked at me like I was out of my mind. "No harm?" she repeated incredulously. "Quentin, what are—" Then she stopped and counted silently to ten. I could tell because she moved her lips. "All right," she said at last. "I'm going along with you as an act of trust. But I want you to know it goes against my nature."

By the time we met up with Sam at the top of the grandstand, Gloria had decided to go beyond patience and into charm.

"How do you do, Mr. Fuentes?" she said, sticking out her hand like the Queen of England. "Won't you introduce me to your friends?"

Like I should have expected, Sam had brought along Hector and Ysidore and also Ezra Faerbrother. So everybody shook hands like we were at some kind of tea party, and then, before I knew what was gong on, Sam and his pals had Gloria in a huddle, explaining to her all about Faerbrother's special talent. Gloria always liked to brag a lot about how she could take care of herself. I sat back and let her do it.

Sam was doing most of the talking, with lots of hand gestures and a little gem of a pantomime of the famous time the swami got that horse to run backwards. Hector was pointing out details in a preview program for tomorrow's races and passing around a lot of Polaroid photographs that doubtless showed some miracle or other. Ysidore was mostly there for nodding, which he did very well without ever seeming to get tired. I tuned out for a while to watch the second race, which Painted Lady won by about four inches, but when I looked again, they were still at it.

Faerbrother, meanwhile, was standing five rows up, at the very top of the grandstand. His body was absolutely rigid, and every once in a while he would lean forward from the ankles, like his feet were nailed to the bench, and peer down in the direction of the paddocks. Since it was dark by now and Sam had assured me his eyeball communication with the ponies worked during daylight hours only, I assumed he was practicing. Whatever it was, I didn't interrupt.

I couldn't help thinking, though, that the man was a very interesting phenomenon. It didn't really matter if he could communicate with horses or not. What was important was that he made people believe he could. Watching him up at the top of the grandstand, so solemn and formal and concentrating so hard, I almost began to believe it myself. If he had been like the ordinary characters who hang around the track, tired-eyed hucksters in cheap shoes who talk too much and always want to slip you a hot tip for every race, Sam never would have fallen for his line.

But looking at this guy, you felt like he might really be able to pull if off. Like he had some kind of special genius that you should just respect without even trying to explain it. In a funny way he reminded me of John Lombardo. Very different fields, of course, but the same talent for inspiring trust. I wondered how well the guy functioned when he wasn't giving harness horses the hairy eyeball. Was he taking care of all the finances himself, or did he have some kind of manager who watched out for the business details while he brought in the suckers? Mr. Big, sitting back silent and anonymous, skimming off most of the profits while Faerbrother put on the show. That was another way he reminded me of Lombardo. Whatever else Faerbrother's hustle was about, he wasn't in it only for the money. I believed he meant the part about bringing other people pleasure.

So there I was thinking all this while watching Faerbrother with one eye and Sam and Gloria with the other and meanwhile keeping my antennae open for what happened to China Doll in the fifth, when all the little pieces got jolted in my head and fell into another pattern. What if Lombardo had been working for Interdine when he gave advice to the Eternal Happiness investors? What if Blount Harwell was the Mr. Big to John Lombardo, the power behind the prophet?

Finally I had an explanation that made sense. Gloria had told me right off that Interdine was moving into real estate. That was the first thing Lombardo had mentioned to her. That and the fact that she was talking to a genius. Howie had told me that Interdine had a great credit rating, though he hadn't realized it was real estate commissions, rentals, and consultants' fees that were putting the company in the black. Harwell himself had said that Lombardo made a lot of money for the business, and I knew from looking at the books that it wasn't from peddling pork chops. If Interdine was behind the Eternal Happiness operation, keeping it secret so as not to inspire a lot of competition, that was also a better explanation of what Lyder was doing in Chinatown and why Harwell hadn't been surprised to hear he was down there. Probably sent him there himself, to see if the new manager could cover that end of Lombardo's job, too.

231

There was only one problem with this explanation. From what Angel had said, Lombardo had meant to keep on working for Eternal Happiness after he left the Pinnacle Room. But if Eternal Happiness meant as much to Interdine's profits as I suspected, Blount Harwell had lost more than anybody when Lombardo died. And I had made a terrible mistake.

Gloria and Sam were still talking, conferring over a racing form with glances at one of Hector's Polaroid pictures. The lady was right. It was crazy to stay here and watch grown men drive around in circles while just across the river there was a murderer at large. I didn't like to leave her there, but I didn't have a choice. I charged down the stairs and broke into their little circle.

"Something's come up," I said briefly. "I've got to get down to the Pinnacle Room right away."

Gloria looked at me blankly. Her mind was fixed on the winner's circle for the Hampton Stake, and she was having trouble bringing the focus back to me.

"Have you seen these pictures?" she demanded. "This man is truly amazing! When you told me about him, I thought the whole thing was a big joke, but now I do believe there's something solid here!"

"Gloria, I have to go. Sam and Hector will take you home. I'm sorry."

"Stop apologizing all the time," she said automatically. "And listen—Sam says Mr. Faerbrother is going to make an exception for him, talk to the horse without them raising the full five thousand dollars. Tomorrow you take that hundred dollars I gave you and put it on Sir Edmund Hillary for me, okay? Mr. Faerbrother's sure he's going to win."

A twenty-to-one long shot, like I might have expected.

"Sure, sure," I said. "Whatever you want."

"To win," she added. "Don't forget. Sam says you never miss the Hampton Stake."

I nodded and scrambled down the stairs and out into the parking lot. Usually there was a bus back into town after the fifth, for folks who couldn't stand to lose any more money. I'd been there all night and hadn't staked a penny on a single pacer, but I had a sinking sense I'd feel right at home with all the other losers, riding back in silence while we all thought over just where our calculations had gone wrong.

Chapter 30

There's no way you can rush a bus. I was drumming my fingers
on the seat in front of me all the way, but it was still after ten
by the time I got up to the Pinnacle Room. Then it turned out
not to matter. Pierre had left hours ago. Right after he talked to
me, in fact. Got a phone call from Mr. Harwell and rushed out
without saying where he was going or when he'd be back either.
I learned that when I waylaid Tom, the floor captain, as he was
searching the kitchen for an extra one of those standing ice buck-
ets.

"It's completely crazy here," he complained. "We've already
lost half our supervisory staff, with no replacements, and then
on Saturday night the manager decides to take a vacation and
the wine steward trots right after him. You think I'm going to
get any credit for picking up the slack? Don't make me laugh."

I hadn't come there to hold Tom's hand while he cried about
how overworked he was. "Did Mr. Lyder call in at all today?" I
asked. "Did he leave word about where he could be reached?"

"Don't make me laugh," he said again. Not that he seemed to
be in any danger. I asked a few more people, but none of them
had heard from Lyder either. I had no choice but to wait for
morning after all. If the killer would let me.

After the restaurant staff had left, I toured the premises just like usual, being extra-cautious when I went around corners just in case someone was lying in wait. At one in the morning I called Gloria, but there wasn't any answer. She couldn't still be at the track. I hoped Sam had gotten her on the right bus and not landed her in downtown Hoboken. From two to three in the morning I checked through the manager's office to be sure I had gotten everything right. At three-thirty I was in the kitchen to greet the cleaning crew. At four I went back to studying the restaurant accounts. And at six-thirty I heard the elevator make its way to the roof.

I'd been waiting for it all night. Now that the time had come, my palms were wet and the inside of my mouth tasted like old cardboard. What if my latest theory was wrong, like so many of my other ideas had been? What if Lyder was the killer after all? Instead of saving his life, I'd be putting my own neck on the line, and with no help in sight for over an hour. Why hadn't I called the police?

Even while I was thinking, I was creeping up the fire stairs, retracing the path I'd gone with Sam yesterday morning. It was much too late to send for reinforcements now. I inched open the door at the top of the stairs. And there in front of me was the strangest-looking person I had ever seen.

He was dressed in a tight blue stretch suit, with red boots and gloves and a red hood covering his head and shoulders. He'd been hunched over the crane when I came, but as soon as he heard the door slam closed, he spun around. Over the chest of the suit was a big red medallion with a pattern of black webbing printed on it. It was Spiderman, all right, just like he looks in the funny papers.

"Wait!" I shouted. "Don't do it!"

"Jacoby!" Lyder yelled in surprise. "What the hell are you doing here?" He bolted back to the crane and started fumbling with his ropes and pulleys.

235

I ran after him. He was struggling into the harness, but I still had a chance of reaching him in time.

"You can't go," I panted, skidding to a stop a few feet from the edge of the roof. "You'll get yourself killed."

"Sure I can," he said, fastening the buckles across his hips. "One chance I've got to make a name for myself, you're not going to hold me up. Only person in danger here is you. Come any closer, and I promise you'll regret it."

I was bigger, but he was younger. I had to take the chance. I reached out to pull him back from the edge of the roof. Lyder stumbled against the crane and clutched my neck to keep himself from falling. And then suddenly, very fast and very hard, somebody rammed me from behind.

The shock of the blow jerked me forward and broke Lyder's hold around my neck. I felt his hands grab my shoulders as I fell on the hot tar of the unfinished roof. And then he let go.

The harness should have held him, given him a chance to grab the rope and climb down the side of the building, like he'd been planning all along. He'd been practicing all week, telling himself how he'd be a hero when he finished his climb, sometime early Sunday afternoon. The police had been warned, and patrols had been stationed at all the likely buildings to stop Lyder and his buddies before they even got off the ground. Nobody had thought about how spiders always start at the top, though. Lyder and his pals would have pulled off the trick of the week. And for a day or two, at least, he would have gotten his wish. He would have been famous.

But the harness didn't hold. He never finished fastening it on, and when he fell over the edge, there was nothing stronger than a cobweb keeping Lyder from his fall.

Anyway, he got his name in the papers. All the networks had their camera vans out, circling the tall buildings so they would be ready with the videotape the second any of the climbers appeared. Already a news chopper was sinking down onto the Interdine landing pad. I crawled to the side of the roof and peered over the edge, but all I could see was a small red and blue splotch out in the middle of the street. One of the little ants down below was running toward a van that bristled with antennas. A patrol car was on the scene, doors gaping open, and I knew they'd be on the radio for an ambulance. Not that it would do any good. I crawled back from the edge, sat up, and turned around.

Standing in front of me was Pierre. He was still wearing his black suit from the day before. Above the black satin vest his face was a chalky greenish white.

"Robert?" he managed to pant out. "Were you...? Did he...?" He stood before me, full of more questions than he could get out, and then all of a sudden he folded up like a wooden puppet and collapsed onto the ground.

"Excuse me," he gasped. "The shock."

I nodded and gave him time to catch his breath. I needed some myself. Pierre found his voice first.

"So now we will never know," he said sadly. "Never know why this good man feels he must do this stupidity. He confides in me, Robert, about his wish to descend from the sky like a hero. He confides in me long ago. But he fears Monsieur Lombardo will be very mad, you know? There is always the tension between them. But to kill him, so he can pursue his silly little exercise! To try to kill you. And now we will never know."

I thought about how Lyder had grabbed me at the end and how close I had come to being a crimson outline on the pavement myself. Pierre was a small man, a good four inches shorter than I was and thin to boot, but he hadn't hesitated to jump in when it looked like Lyder might pull me over the edge. What had he meant by that final threat? Would he really have tried to hurt me? Pierre was right. We would never know. I looked back over

237

his shoulder, past the empty swimming pool and over to the open door of the fire stairs. The sound of sirens drifted up from the street, their urgency lost over the distance. I wondered how long it would be until anybody joined us.

"Robert Lyder didn't kill John Lombardo," I said, carefully getting to my feet. "You had me fooled for a while, acting all concerned and sympathetic and meanwhile doing everything you could to make me think it was Lyder. You were working on him, too, weren't you? Making him feel bad about all the things he didn't know, offering help that was really criticism, pushing and pushing until finally he would quit and you'd be able to take over his job. And all the while the poor sap confided in you. Told you all his plans and worries. Told you how he was coming up here this morning. That was a real godsend, wasn't it? No wonder you were urging him to stick with his plans the other night—it wasn't a silly little exercise then, was it? You were saving that line for Harwell, to use at the meeting you already set up for Monday morning.

"Then you got nervous," I continued. "After I called yesterday, you realized I was on to something. You had to make sure I didn't talk to Lyder. Even if you couldn't reach him yesterday, you always knew you could find him here this morning. Not that it wasn't tricky. You really had to watch your timing, to make it seem like you were saving me while you made sure that Lyder went over the edge for good. Then there would be no way he could defend himself against your accusations. But one thing all those years of hovering over tables has taught you is timing, isn't it? You're a regular expert at hanging around unnoticed, until just the right instant to dart in and do your thing. Tell me, though—if we had been turned the other way, would you have saved Lyder and pinned Lombardo's murder on me?"

"But this is madness," Pierre whispered.

"No, it's not," I said loudly. I was getting back my wind, and

I wanted the world to hear. "It's not madness at all. You told me to think about who would profit from Lombardo's death, so that's what I've been doing. All the other suspects were losers. The only one with anything to gain was you. How long is it that you've been supplementing your salary with some creative wholesaling from the company liquor supplies? Years probably. Lombardo knew all about what you were doing, with your private directory of wine merchants who would sell—or buy—the great vintages any time, no questions asked. But Lombardo liked you. Enough to take you with him from restaurant to restaurant. Enough to tell you about his plans for the future. Enough to cover for the drain on his budget. Hell, he was lifting things himself, so why should he care? But never wine, Angel told me. He never stole anything from the cellar. So who took the Bordeaux that was missing Monday? Angel didn't have it, and neither did Janine DuPage, because the police would have found it long ago if she did. If Lombardo didn't take it, it had to have been somebody else with the keys to the wine cellar. And that left you. Everybody else made the mistake of thinking the thefts were all part of one big package. You were counting on that, weren't you?"

Pierre just sat there, staring and silent, so I went on.

"As long as Lombardo was running things," I said, "you were safe. As long as he was keeping track of the accounts and bringing in the real profits somewhere else, he figured it was nobody's business if you lifted a case of booze now and then. 'The staff has to eat, too,' he told Lyder.

"But then he told you he was going to leave the Pinnacle Room, get out of doing restaurants for Interdine. That must have scared you plenty, even before I appeared on Monday. Maybe Lombardo had no intention of turning you in, but it was a risk you couldn't afford to take, was it? You've worked hard to get where you are. You've got a family. You've got ambition. Killing Lombardo protected your hide and gave you a chance to rise in the company, too. You were going to make the wine tasters' dinner something spectacular, didn't you say?"

Pierre ignored the question. "How do you imagine I did all this?" he asked quietly.

"Easy," I answered. "Just like a magician. You did it with mirrors. You hung around after work on Monday, hiding someplace in the restaurant. After everyone else had left, Lombardo went to the wine cellar for the makings of a nightcap, just like you knew he did every night. You followed him in with one of the brass skewers from the vase outside the door, and that was the end of John Lombardo. Then you arranged things to make it look like an interrupted theft and made a noise loud enough to draw me from the kitchen. When you heard me in the hall upstairs, you dashed through the pantry, into the kitchen, up the dumbwaiter to the executive dining room, and into the secret little wine cellar there.

"That was a great idea. With the doors closed, the police never even realized there was a room there. Just an unbroken wall of mirrors. I never would have known about it, either, except that the door was open when Mr. Harwell called me up to his office the next night. So you waited in the executive dining room until they were done searching the offices and there was a lot of traffic up and down the elevators, which gave you your chance to get to the roof. You knew all about the ropes and the harness because Lyder had to confide his big plan to someone. He probably even showed you how they worked. All the while the police were rushing through the building, searching the floors, you were inching your way down the outside, a small dark figure against a dark building in the middle of the night. It must have been a scary trip, but you've never lacked for nerve, have you? Stealing the wine all those years. Waiting patiently to skewer Lombardo. You must have just gotten down when I saw you the next morning, but you were ready with a story right away. Came as soon as you heard the news, you said. Rushed in all horrified, coming to save the restaurant. Except there was no news yet. Not that early in the morning."

All the while I was talking, Pierre had sat quiet and calm. Much too calm. Now he started patting his arm, his nervous little waiter's gesture. Only this time what he was doing was pulling something from his sleeve. A very familiar-looking brass skewer.

"I am very sorry I must do this," he said. "But there is no other way. The police officers will be coming soon, to find where poor Robert had come from. They will discover that their Spider-man has stabbed you and left you dead on the roof, just as he had stabbed John Lombardo before. I am small, but I am very strong. It will be as I say. And then they will find me up here, arriving too late to stop the tragedy. I will be in a condition of shock, I think."

"You will be in the slammer, I think," interrupted Captain Powers, while Thorson grabbed Pierre from behind. The two of them had been inching forward all the time we were talking, while Blount Harwell stayed behind, just outside the elevator's plastic shroud. Harwell hadn't trusted me any more than I'd trusted him. He'd brought a police escort for our secret appointment, and he'd arrived early, too, bless his suspicious heart. Powers walked over to me.

"Good work, Jacoby," he said.

"Glad to be of help," I gasped. Pierre had been waving that pointy metal stick at my guts for a good minute before Powers butted in. I thought for a while the captain had been waiting for him to skewer me, too, just to cement the case.

After they had taken Pierre away, I went down to the station house with Powers to go over it all once more with a stenographer taking notes.

"What a waste," he said at the end. I didn't know if he meant Pierre Morel, or Robert Lyder, or John Lombardo. At that point I didn't really care.

While they were typing up my statement, I sat in Powers's

office, staring out the window. The captain left me alone while he went over some papers on his desk. It was nice and quiet in there, and the bulk and weight of the old oak furniture were a kind of comfort to me just then. I kept on thinking of Bob Lyder and what it must have been like in those seconds before he hit the ground. Had his heart stopped from fear right away? Had his whole life flashed before him, like they say it always does? Or had he spent his last seconds going over all the things he'd left undone? I hoped he'd spent the time in a kind of blissful freedom, floating in space, unconcerned and irresponsible at last. I hoped his last words weren't "What else?"

Then it was time to sign my statement and for all the awkward business about promising not to leave town in case they needed me for the trial. At the end Powers shook my hand. "If you were still on the force," he observed, "I'd have you up for a medal."

"Yeah," I agreed. "Don't worry about it." I took a last count of the geraniums across the way and headed out for the Brooklyn Bridge station and the long train ride home. At that point I would have traded all the medals in the world for a shower and a few hours' sleep. I guess the gods were listening because that's what I got.

I went to sleep Sunday morning and didn't wake up again until Monday was a few hours under way. I probably would have missed that, too, if it hadn't been for the telephone ringing in my ear. It was Sam Fuentes, backed up by a lot of happy shouting and what sounded like several different rumba bands, each with its own music.

"Hey, baby," Sam was shouting. "I win! You lose! How you like that, *amigo?* I win! I win!"

"I'd like it better if I knew what you were talking about," I said. Not that I expected him to hear me over the din in the background.

"Today the sidewalks are turned into gold," Sam chortled. "Twenty to one! Twenty thousand beautiful dollars, baby. You are missing one hell of a party, and that is for sure. La la la, la la la, la, la la la," he yelled into the phone, more or less in time with the beat of the loudest band. Then I remembered. Sunday. The Hampton Stake. Sir Edmund Hillary.

"So your long shot came in," I said.

"Of course, he come in! I tol' you. Mr. Faerbrother, he tell that horse what to do. When he talks to a horse, man, that horse, he *listen*."

"And where's Faerbrother now?" I asked. I tried to imagine that lanky redneck at Sam's fiesta, dancing with one of the little nieces that Sam seemed to have so many of.

"Back to Kentucky," Sam answered, suddenly solemn. "We divide up the money, just like he promised, and then he asked Hector to take him to the bus station. Says parties and strong drink interfere with his concentration, you know?" Sam indulged in a few seconds of silence, out of respect for the trainer's purity and sacrifice. Then he launched into a long series of directions. Finally I figured he was telling me how to get to the party.

"Thanks, Sam, but I don't think so."

"Aw, baby," Sam coaxed. "Don't feel bad, just 'cause you lost your chance. Free champagne for losers, too. Today I am king. *El rey del Bronx,* right?"

"Of course, Sam," I agreed. "It's just that right now I've got another date. You ever get Gloria home last night?"

"Last night?" To Sam, anything before this afternoon was another world. "Sure, I get her home. First we stop at a bar, so I can finish teaching her about the handicapping. But don't you wanna come celebrate, hear all about the race?"

"Later, Sam. Later." He had invested $1,000 in a miracle and landed in the winner's circle, and I knew perfectly well I'd be hearing about it for some time to come.

"Okay, baby," he screeched. The music had gotten louder, which I hadn't thought was possible. "I drink double for you. I win, man! I win!"

243

I hung up while he was still shouting into the phone. I don't think he even noticed, and I was sure he wouldn't take it the wrong way when he did catch on that I was gone.

I hadn't been kidding about having to go see Gloria. She'd promised me a dinner if I stayed on the job for a week, and we had already agreed that this was my night to collect. I wondered what she was going to say when I told her I had been too tired to make it to the track to place her bet. I would have to make it up to her somehow, that I knew.

I grinned at the possibilities and started to get dressed.